# HIDING FROM THE ENEMY

Thorn and Stig slid quietly back into the long grass. The sentry on Thorn's side called in a low, anxious voice. He spoke in the Temujai tongue, so they couldn't understand the exact words. But the intonation indicated it was a question and the meaning was all too obvious: *Where are you?*

Hal was right, Thorn thought. They weren't going to risk the Sha'shan's anger by raising the alarm until they were sure there was a problem.

A short time passed and the sentry called again, a little louder this time but still voicing a question, not sounding the alarm. This time, the sentry on Stig's side of the wagon replied, also in a low voice. A short conversation followed. Thorn, with his head just above the grass, saw the two men start to walk toward the position where the missing sentry should be. He slowly lowered himself back into hiding and said in a low voice:

"They're coming."

## BROTHERBAND CHRONICLES
Book 1: *The Outcasts*
Book 2: *The Invaders*
Book 3: *The Hunters*
Book 4: *Slaves of Socorro*
Book 5: *Scorpion Mountain*
Book 6: *The Ghostfaces*
Book 7: *The Caldera*
Book 8: *Return of the Temujai*

## THE RANGER'S APPRENTICE EPIC
Book 1: *The Ruins of Gorlan*
Book 2: *The Burning Bridge*
Book 3: *The Icebound Land*
Book 4: *The Battle for Skandia*
Book 5: *The Sorcerer of the North*
Book 6: *The Siege of Macindaw*
Book 7: *Erak's Ransom*
Book 8: *The Kings of Clonmel*
Book 9: *Halt's Peril*
Book 10: *The Emperor of Nihon-Ja*
Book 11: *The Lost Stories*

## THE ROYAL RANGER SERIES
Book 1: *The Royal Ranger: A New Beginning*
(previously published as *Ranger's Apprentice Book 12*)
Book 2: *The Royal Ranger: The Red Fox Clan*
Book 3: *The Royal Ranger: Duel at Araluen*
Book 4: *The Royal Ranger: The Missing Prince*

## RANGER'S APPRENTICE: THE EARLY YEARS
Book 1: *The Tournament at Gorlan*
Book 2: *The Battle of Hackham Heath*

# BROTHERBAND
## CHRONICLES

## BOOK 8:
## RETURN OF THE TEMUJAI

## JOHN FLANAGAN

PUFFIN BOOKS

PUFFIN BOOKS
An imprint of Penguin Random House LLC, New York

First published in the United States of America by Philomel Books,
an imprint of Penguin Random House LLC, 2019.
Published by Puffin Books, an imprint of Penguin Random House LLC, 2020.

Philomel Books is a registered trademark of Penguin Random House LLC.
Visit us online at penguinrandomhouse.com

THE LIBRARY OF CONGRESS HAS CATALOGED THE PHILOMEL BOOKS EDITION AS FOLLOWS:
Names: Flanagan, John (John Anthony), author.
Title: Return of the Temujai / John Flanagan.
Description: U.S. Edition. | New York : Philomel Books, [2019] |
Series: Brotherband chronicles ; book 8 | "Companion to the bestselling Ranger's Apprentice." |
Audience: Ages 10 up. | Audience: Grades 4–6. |
Summary: "The Herons are home in Skandia, but the usually peaceful country is in danger.
The Temujai—ruthless warriors from the Eastern Steppes—have never given up on their
ambition to claim Skandia for their own . . . and now they're on the move. Hal and his crew
will have to brave the treacherous icy river and rapids to stop them, no matter the cost"
—Provided by publisher.
Identifiers: LCCN 2019034201 | ISBN 9781524741440 (hardcover) |
ISBN 9781524741457 (ebook)
Subjects: CYAC: Apprentices—Fiction. | Adventure and adventurers—Fiction. |
Sailing—Fiction. | Fantasy.
Classification: LCC PZ7.F598284 Ret 2019 | DDC [Fic]—dc23
LC record available at https://lccn.loc.gov/2019034201

Puffin Books ISBN 9781524741464

Printed in the United States of America

1 3 5 7 9 10 8 6 4 2

U.S. edition edited by Kelsey Murphy.
Text set in Centaur MT Std.

# A Few Sailing Terms Explained

**B**ecause this book involves sailing ships, I thought it might be useful to explain a few of the nautical terms found in the story.

Be reassured that I haven't gone overboard (to keep up the nautical allusion) with technical details in the book, and even if you're not familiar with sailing, I'm sure you'll understand what's going on. But a certain amount of sailing terminology is necessary for the story to feel realistic.

So, here we go, in no particular order:

**Bow:** The front of the ship, also called the prow.

**Stern:** The rear of the ship.

**Port and starboard:** The left and the right side of the ship, as you're facing the bow. In fact, I'm probably incorrect in using the term *port*. The early term for port was *larboard*, but I thought we'd all get confused if I used that.

*Starboard* is a corruption of "steering board" (or steering side). The steering oar was always placed on the right-hand side of the ship at the stern.

Consequently, when a ship came into port, it would moor with the left side against the jetty, to avoid damage to the steering oar. One theory says the word derived from the ship's being in port— left side to the jetty. I suspect, however, that it might have come from the fact that the entry port, by which crew and passengers boarded, was also always on the left side.

How do you remember which side is which? Easy. *Port* and *left* both have four letters.

**Forward:** Toward the bow.

**Aft:** Toward the stern.

**Fore-and-aft rig:** A sail plan in which the sail is in line with the hull of the ship.

**Hull:** The body of the ship.

**Keel:** The spine of the ship.

**Stem:** The upright timber piece at the bow, joining the two sides together.

**Forefoot:** The lowest point of the bow, where the keel and the stem of the ship meet.

**Steering oar:** The blade used to control the ship's direction, mounted on the starboard side of the ship, at the stern.

**Tiller:** The handle for the steering oar.

**Sea anchor:** A method of slowing a ship's downwind drift, often by use of a canvas **drogue**—a long, conical tube of canvas closed at one end and held open at the other—or two spars lashed together in a cross. The sea anchor is streamed from the bow and the resultant drag slows the ship's movement through the water.

**Yardarm, or yard:** A spar (wooden pole) that is hoisted up the mast, carrying the sail.

**Masthead:** The top of the mast.

**Bulwark:** The part of the ship's side above the deck.

**Scuppers:** Drain holes in the bulwarks set at deck level to allow water that comes on board to drain away.

**Belaying pins:** Wooden pins used to fasten rope.

**Oarlock, or rowlock:** Pegs set on either side of an oar to keep it in place while rowing.

**Thwart:** A seat.

**Telltale:** A pennant that indicates the wind's direction.

**Tacking:** To tack is to change direction from one side to the other, passing through the eye of the wind.

If the wind is from the north and you want to sail northeast, you would perform one tack so that you are heading northeast, and you would continue to sail on that tack for as long as you need.

However, if the wind is from the north and you want to sail due north, you would have to do so in a series of short tacks, going back and forth on a zigzag course, crossing through the wind each time, and slowly making ground to the north. This is a process known as **beating** into the wind.

**Wearing:** When a ship tacks, it turns *into* the wind to change direction. When it wears, it turns *away* from the wind, traveling in a much larger arc, with the wind in the sail, driving the ship around throughout the maneuver. Wearing was a safer way of changing direction for wolfships than beating into the wind.

**Reach, or reaching:** When the wind is from the side of the ship, the ship is sailing on a reach, or reaching.

**Running:** When the wind is from the stern, the ship is running. (So would you if the wind was strong enough at your back.)

**Reef:** To gather in part of the sail and bundle it against the yardarm to reduce the sail area. This is done in high winds to protect the sail and the mast.

**Trim:** To adjust the sail to the most efficient angle.

**Halyard:** A rope used to haul the yard up the mast. (Haul-yard, get it?)

**Stay:** A heavy rope that supports the mast. The **backstay** and the **forestay** are heavy ropes running from the top of the mast to the stern and the bow (it's pretty obvious which is which).

**Sheets and shrouds:** Many people think these are sails, which is a logical assumption. But in fact, they're ropes. Shrouds are thick ropes that run from the top of the mast to the side of the ship, supporting the mast. Sheets are the ropes used to control, or trim, the sail—to haul it in and out according to the wind strength and direction. In an emergency, the order might be given to "let fly the sheets!" The sheets would be released, letting the sail loose and bringing the ship to a halt. (If *you* were to let fly the sheets, you'd probably fall out of bed.)

**Hawser:** Heavy rope used to moor a ship.

**Way:** The motion of the ship. If a ship is under way, it is moving according to its course. If it is making leeway, the ship is moving downwind so it loses ground or goes off course.

**Lee:** The downwind side of a ship, opposite to the direction of the wind.

**Lee shore:** A shoreline downwind of the ship, with the wind blowing the ship toward the shore—a dangerous situation for a sailing ship.

**Back water:** To row a reverse stroke.

So, now that you know all you need to know about sailing terms, welcome aboard the world of the Brotherband Chronicles!

*John Flanagan*

# PART ONE

# FORT RAGNAK

The closer they came to the border fort, the narrower the valley became. The steep, almost sheer walls towered high above them, blotting out the sun although it was only a few hours before noon. The floor of the valley was in shadow, the sun only reaching it for a couple of hours each day, which probably accounted for the snow that still lay thick and deep on the ground, even though spring was only a few weeks away.

In spite of the snow, the small party was making better time now that they had reached the top of the steep climb that led to the pass, and they were moving on level ground again.

There were two carts, each with a single pair of wheels and pulled by a small, sturdy horse. They were stacked neatly with sawn lumber, and as they were past the steep uphill climb, most of the

Heron brotherband rode on them, finding space among the stacks of planks and beams that filled the cart trays.

Hal and Stig rode two saddle horses, leading the way for the carts. It was a newly acquired skill for the two Heron leaders. Stig had decided that they should learn to ride.

"After all," he'd told his skirl, "we always find ourselves in places where they *expect* us to ride. We might as well know how to do it. It'll save us a lot of walking."

Hal had agreed and Stig had searched around and procured two horses, rescuing them from a life where they would be destined to pull carts, and instead turning them into saddle mounts. They were stolid little creatures, quiet and unimaginative, nothing like a fierce, thundering battlehorse or a speedy, slender-limbed Arridan from the deserts to the south. But they carried the two riders uncomplainingly—even Barney, the one tasked with bearing Stig's large frame. If need arose, both horses could be coaxed into a slow canter or, in extreme situations, a clumsy gallop.

Once Stig had found them, Hal hired one of the Araluen archers, who was familiar with horses, to teach them the rudimentary points of riding. After suffering the inevitable tumbles, bruises and minor injuries, both of them emerged as reasonably capable riders. They were, after all, fit and agile young men, with a good sense of balance and the rhythm necessary to match their movements to the horses' gait.

With one exception.

"I don't like trotting," Hal stated. "I always seem to be going down when the horse is coming up. It's an unnatural way to travel and it's painful."

His Araluen teacher, who could sit to a trot instinctively and so had no idea how to teach someone else to do so, took the easy way out.

"Why bother?" he had told the young skirl. "If you're in a hurry, canter or gallop. If you're not, just walk."

That seemed reasonable to Hal, so he simply ignored the concept of trotting from then on. Occasionally, when he saw Stig managing to sit smoothly as Barney trotted beneath him, he felt a pang of jealousy. He was tempted to ask Stig how he managed it but refused to admit his own deficiency.

"I choose not to trot," he would say, his jaw set stubbornly, whenever the subject came up.

Thorn, on the other hand, chose not to ride at all, even though Stig had offered to find a horse for him.

"I don't trust horses," Thorn said, glaring suspiciously at the two stocky little mounts his friends rode. "Even the small ones outweigh me by several hundred kilos. They have big teeth and hooves as hard as clubs. And they're shifty."

"Shifty?" said Hal, stroking Jake's silky soft nose affectionately. "They're perfectly trustworthy."

"Maybe to you," Thorn replied darkly. "But not to me. Those big teeth could take off a few fingers—and I've only got one hand."

And in fact, Barney and Jake seemed to sense his unease around them and his antipathy toward them, and they reacted in kind. If Thorn walked too close behind Barney, the horse would often lash out, trying to kick him. And, several times, Jake had whipped his head around and given Thorn a painful nip on the shoulder. But with the cunning of their kind, the horses didn't do so *every* time he came within range, allowing him to be lulled into a false sense of security, whereupon they would kick or bite once more, without warning.

Even now, as the old sea wolf trudged determinedly beside them through the snow, Jake was tending to sidle closer to him, measuring the distance between his teeth and the shabby, patched sheepskin vest that covered Thorn's shoulder—Jake's favorite point for biting. Knowing what his horse was planning, Hal twitched the reins against his neck and pressed his right knee into the horse's side, urging him away from Thorn.

Thorn noticed the movement, and Jake's indignant toss of his head as his plans were thwarted.

"See?" he said. "I told you those beasts there cannot be trusted."

Stig, sensing that Thorn might be about to launch into another discourse on the evils of the equine species, hurried to redirect the conversation.

"So, what's got Erak up in a lather?" he asked Hal. "Is it something serious or is he just getting clucky in his old age?"

Hal grinned. "Try saying that 'old age' thing around him. He'll likely brain you with that big silver-headed walking stick he carries." He paused, then answered the question. "No. He's had word that the Temujai have been nosing around the border."

"They're always doing that," Stig said dismissively.

But Hal shook his head. "They've been doing it a lot more than usual," he said. "That's why he wants Lydia to scout around across the border while we check out the fort itself."

With their ship laid up for repairs and maintenance during the winter months, the Herons found themselves with time on their hands. Erak, the Oberjarl of the Skandians, had summoned Hal to his lodge in the center of Hallasholm. The young warrior was one of Erak's most trusted skirls. Hal led an elite group of fighters in his crew, but Erak knew that Hal was more than just brave in battle. He was smart, which a lot of wolfship captains weren't. Hal could observe a situation with a keen and intelligent eye, and that was what Erak wanted in this case.

"Take a look at the border fort," he instructed the younger man. "See if it's secure against attack. And see if there's any way you can make it more secure."

Fort Ragnak defended Serpent Pass, a narrow pass at the junction of the Skandian, Teutlandt and Temujai borders. The pass was the only practical way to travel down from the mountains and access Skandia's flat coastal strip. Hal moved to the large map on the wall of Erak's lodge and studied the pass and the fort. The walls of the pass were steep, he knew, and the fort was positioned where they came close together, closing a gap of only twenty meters.

"You have archers here?" he asked.

Erak nodded. "Fifteen of them. I rotate them in and out every three weeks, along with the rest of the garrison—thirty troops. It's too cold and miserable up there to leave them on site for much longer—although in winter it's sometimes hard to get men there to relieve them."

Since the Temujai attempt to invade years previously, Skandia received a detachment of one hundred archers each year from their ally, the Kingdom of Araluen. The archers tended to redress the imbalance between Skandia's own warriors, who were armed with axes, spears and swords, and the mounted Temujai archers. It meant that the Skandians could fight fire with fire, particularly when they were ensconced in a secure position, like the border fort.

"I was thinking," Hal said slowly, "maybe we could set up a couple of manglers on the sides of the cliffs—here and here." He pointed to the cliff walls behind the fort and either side of the fort. "That'd give the Temujai riders a nasty shock if they attacked."

"Manglers?" Erak said. "You mean like that giant crossbow you carry on the bow of your ship?"

Hal nodded. "We could build shooting platforms halfway up the walls. Then we could sweep the approaches to the fort before the Temujai got in range."

"It's a good idea," Erak said, reflecting that this was why he had chosen Hal for the task. The young man had an ability to come up with new and unexpected ideas like this, and Erak could see how two of those massive crossbows could make a powerful addition to the fort's defenses.

"I'll get onto it straightaway," Hal said, stepping back from the map. "I'll build them here, then break them down for transport, and reassemble them once we have the platforms ready. I'll need to take lumber to build those as well."

Erak shrugged. "Plenty of trees up there."

But Hal shook his head. "It'll take us time to cut and saw them into posts and planks. Better if we take whatever we need. We should be able to get a couple of horse-drawn carts up through the pass. And we don't want to give the Temujai too much notice that we're strengthening the defenses. If they are planning an attack, they might decide to go early."

"That's true. Do it that way. And while I think of it, you might get that girl of yours to scout across the border and see if the Temujai have any troops gathering there."

They both knew that Lydia, the only female member of the Heron brotherband, was an expert scout. She could cross the border and infiltrate Temujai land without being seen or heard by the enemy. Hal had no qualms about agreeing to the suggestion.

"She'd rather do that than help build the platforms," he said, and left the lodge to start gathering tools and equipment.

"So, what do you think?" Stig asked. "Are the Temujai really getting ready to invade again?"

The Temujai were a warlike, nomadic race from beyond the mountains east of Skandia. They were committed to a path of conquest and domination and had long cast jealous, hostile eyes toward the wealthy countries of the west—Gallica, Teutlandt and even Araluen. But before they could spread their influence so far, they would need to conquer Skandia and gain control of its ships. Some years previously, they had launched an all-out attack on the Skandians, breaking through the mountain pass and down onto the narrow coastal plain around Hallasholm. The Skandians, with the help of a small Araluen force of hastily trained archers, had repelled them. In more recent times, the Temujai had turned their attention elsewhere, conquering and plundering the lands to the east. But they constantly returned to the Skandian border, the site of their only defeat, testing the strength of the defenses at Serpent Pass, the scene of their previous incursion.

They were a cruel and pitiless enemy, small, hardy warriors who were skilled riders and expert archers, shooting from horseback with their short, curved bows. Their army was highly mobile and their generals were skillful and cunning. All in all, they were a formidable enemy.

The presence of the Temujai, and their longstanding threat to the welfare of Skandia and its people, was a fact of life to Hal and his companions. Hal's generation had grown up all too aware of the Temujai and their aggressive stance toward Skandia. It was something to be guarded against and prepared for. They knew that the threat could not be ignored. The Temujai, if they sensed any slackening of the Skandians' readiness or will to fight, would sweep down from the high country like a malevolent flood. But Hal and his fellow Skandians were well aware of their own ability and battle skills. So long as Serpent Pass was kept secure and Fort Ragnak maintained and garrisoned strongly, the Temujai were a problem that could be dealt with. Constant vigilance was the answer to the threat they posed. Danger would come if the Skandian nation ever slackened that vigilance, or if the Temujai happened to find an alternative, and undefended, route down from the high country to the coastal plains.

So far, neither had happened. From time to time, the Temujai probed the defenses at Fort Ragnak. When they did, they found the garrison there ready and more than capable of repelling them.

Thorn had fought the Temujai many years before when they had penetrated down to the coastal strip.

"They want access to the sea," he replied to Stig's question. "They always have. And they want our ships. Their plan is to dominate our part of the world."

"Charming people," Hal commented.

Thorn shrugged. "War and conquest is what they're good at," he said. "It's their reason for being. Their leaders know that if they're not conquering new territories, they'll begin fighting among themselves and the confederation of tribes will eventually be broken up. They're like a shark that has to keep moving to stay alive. They have to keep moving, fighting and conquering."

"Do they seriously think we'll just let them walk in and use our ships?" Hal asked.

Thorn shook his head. "I'd say they assume that if they invade us and conquer us, we'll do as we're told." He paused and smiled. "Of course, first they have to invade us and conquer us."

"And before they can do that, they have to break through the border up here. Which is a tough nut to crack," Stig said.

"And which we plan to make a whole lot tougher," Hal agreed.

The three of them fell silent for a few seconds as they considered the task ahead and its importance to the well-being of Skandia and the other nations around them.

Thorn raised his hook in a warning gesture to Jake, who had once again begun sidling closer to him.

"Just try it, you shaggy barrel," he said. "I've eaten horsemeat before. Next time, I might just bite back."

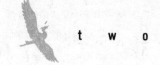

esper eased his hip into a more comfortable position on the pile of sawn planks. Riding on the cart was a not-unpleasant way to travel. The horse's rhythmic motion and the fact that the cart traveled on two wheels set on either end of a single axle imparted a gentle fore-and-aft rocking motion to their progress—not unlike being on board a ship.

But of course, on the cart, there was no need to constantly re-trim sails or raise or lower the yardarms as the ship tacked.

"Do Thorn again," he said now to Stefan, who was leaning comfortably against the side of the wooden cart.

Stefan was an expert mimic. In the past, the Herons had made use of this talent several times to mislead or confuse enemies. Once Stefan heard a voice, or even a sound, he could reproduce it almost at will. He had been amusing his companions for the past half hour doing impersonations of people like Erak, Thorn and Hal. No matter how many times Jesper heard him do this, he was still amazed at the accuracy of his shipmate's impressions. With his eyes shut, he could barely tell the impersonation from the real thing.

"If anybody else says 'Let's get 'em,' I'll brain him with my club," growled Stefan in a near-perfect copy of their battlemaster's voice.

Jesper laughed out loud and applauded. "That's perfect!" he said. "Just like him!"

Edvin, who was riding on the cart with them, laughed as well. "You've got him exactly," he said.

Stefan grinned ruefully. "Orlog knows, I've heard the old windbag often enough."

Jesper motioned for him to repeat the impersonation. "Do him again! Make him throw his weight around and boss us the way he does." He leaned back and closed his eyes to hear the impersonation, smiling as he did so. It was a fine way to pass the time, he thought to himself.

"We'll be stopping soon," said Thorn's voice in his ears. "Time for you to get off your lazy backside and gather some firewood."

Jesper, eyes still closed, laughed out loud. "Perfect!" he said. "Just like him. Old windbag indeed! He never gives me a moment's rest."

Next moment, he felt the impact of a hard, callused hand as it cuffed the back of his head. He jerked forward and opened his eyes, to find himself staring at close range at Thorn's bearded, frowning face. Opposite him, Edvin and Stefan were shaking their heads in warning. Too late.

Thorn had heard the laughter from the cart and had parted company with Hal and Stig, dropping back in the small convoy to see what was going on. Stefan, who was facing backward, hadn't seen him approaching until Thorn was almost upon them. Jesper, of course, had his eyes shut to enjoy the impersonation more fully.

"Oh, hello, Thorn," he said, trying for a tone of cheerful innocence. "We were just talking about you."

"So I heard," Thorn told him. He looked at Stefan, frowning. "You know, that sounds nothing like me."

"No, of course not," Stefan replied dutifully.

Unfortunately, Jesper chose the same moment to blurt out, "It does! It's just like you!" Then he froze as Thorn's eyes bored into his. There was a long and rather unpleasant silence.

Thorn turned to the third rider on the cart to adjudicate. "What do you say, Edvin? Has Stefan got *the old windbag* right?"

"Um . . . er . . ." Edvin hesitated, not knowing what the right answer might be. He glanced quickly back and forth between his two companions but there was no help there.

"Um . . . no, not really, Thorn. No . . . ," he said uncertainly. "Nothing like you," he added with more conviction, avoiding the accusing eyes of Stefan and Jesper.

"But you do agree I'm an old windbag?" Thorn said.

Edvin jumped as if he were stung. "No! Of course not! I never said that!"

"You never disputed it either," Thorn continued, and Edvin had no answer to give him. Thorn glared at the three of them, then shook his head slowly.

"When we get to the border, you three are going to get all the dirty jobs while we build the platforms," he told them. Then he strode off, leaving them whispering accusations back and forth.

"Why didn't you warn me he was here?" Jesper asked bitterly.

"I only saw him at the last minute." Stefan shot an angry look at Edvin. "You must have seen him coming. You were facing that way."

But Edvin held up a ball of black wool, knitting needles and a half-finished Heron watch cap.

"I wasn't looking," he protested. "I was working on this watch cap."

"You and your blasted knitting!" Stefan told him. "Maybe you should find something more useful to be doing while we're on the cart."

"It's *your* cap," Edvin said coldly. Derogatory comments about his knitting always annoyed him. "Remember? Kloof chewed your old one and you asked me to make you a new one."

"Oh . . . ," said Stefan, more than a little nonplussed. He really couldn't complain about Edvin's knitting when he was doing Stefan a favor. Edvin never charged his shipmates for the caps he made them. "Well, in that case, never mind."

Thorn, striding away from them to check on the occupants of the second cart, smiled to himself as he overheard their sotto voce disagreement. He saw Lydia watching him as he approached the cart, her head tilted to one side in an unspoken question.

"Got to keep them on their toes," he said cheerfully.

She smiled. "I take it Stefan is impersonating you again?"

Thorn nodded. "Not that it sounds anything like me at all." He waited for her to agree, but she continued to smile at him, saying nothing. "Well, it doesn't!" he insisted with some heat.

Lydia nodded, the smile replaced by a look that was so sincere he simply knew it couldn't be genuine. "Of course it doesn't," she agreed.

He decided there was no future pursuing the matter and looked around the cart, where Ingvar, Ulf and Wulf were sprawled. Kloof lay on her side, her shaggy head resting on Lydia's knee. The dog's tail thumped the floorboards of the cart once in greeting to Thorn. There was more room in this cart, as it only carried the disassembled components of the two manglers.

"Everything all right here?" he asked, deciding it was safest to change the subject.

Lydia nodded and the others grunted assent. "It's a little too comfortable," she said. She had an austere nature and she tended to distrust any situation that was too relaxing. "I'd like to get out and stretch my legs for a while."

Thorn made an inviting gesture. "Well, go right ahead."

But she patted Kloof's big head. "I don't want to wake up the dog. She looks so content."

Kloof, feeling the touch on her head, arched her back and stretched all four legs out luxuriously, groaning with pleasure as she did so.

Thorn nodded understanding. "I can see why you wouldn't want to disturb her." He glanced up at the sun, which was now visible above the narrow cleft of the pass. "We'll be stopping for the noon meal anyway in about half an hour," he said. "Might as well leave her undisturbed until then."

He turned and strode back toward the head of the small column. As he passed the first cart, he recomposed his features into a dark scowl and glared warningly at the occupants.

Not that they were doing anything wrong, but as he had told Lydia, it always paid to keep them on their toes.

Jesper and Stefan watched him as he passed, waiting till they judged he was out of earshot.

"I always feel like he knows what I'm thinking," Jesper said softly.

"I do," Thorn called back over his shoulder. Then he lengthened his pace to overtake Stig and Hal where they walked their horses in the lead.

Several minutes passed, then Jesper, who could rarely keep still for any length of time, nudged Stefan with his elbow.

"Do some more," he said.

But Stefan shook his head. "Are you mad? He'll hear me. He's got ears like a hawk."

"Does a hawk have ears?" Edvin asked, mildly curious.

Stefan pursed his lips in annoyance. "Well then, he's got ears in the back of his head!" he amended, and the other two looked at him, puzzled, until he realized how ridiculous that statement was. "You know what I mean!"

Jesper decided to change the subject. "You don't have to do him again. Or anybody for that matter. Do some animals."

Stefan considered the request. "Like what?"

"Remember when we were competing for the Andomal? You did a bear."

Stefan smiled at the memory. "That's right. And Ingvar charged around shaking the bushes so that people thought there really was a bear."

"Do that!" Jesper urged.

Stefan thought for a moment, hunched his head down on his neck and cupped his hands around his mouth. After a few seconds, he produced a very realistic impression of a very angry bear growling a warning.

The result was startling. The little cart horse, plodding along half awake, suddenly heard the sound of a bear growling, seemingly right behind him. He shied and reared up, breaking the traces and capsizing the cart, sending people and lumber spilling out into the snow. The driver, equally startled, managed to jump clear. Jesper, Stefan and Edvin covered their heads with their arms as beams and planks rained down around them, breaking the ties that secured them and spilling out into the snow in all directions.

"You idiot!" Edvin said, shoving aside a pile of sawn planks that had landed on top of him and rising to his feet. Startled and more than a little contrite, Stefan picked himself up, rubbing a bruise on his forehead where one of the heavier beams had landed.

A few seconds later, Edvin's accusation was echoed by Thorn, who had turned back to survey the scene when he heard the panicked horse whinnying and the crash and clatter of the overturned cart. "Idiot indeed!" he said. He gestured at the overturned cart and the scattered lumber.

"You three can pick this lot up and restack it in the cart," he said. "In the meantime, we'll be having lunch."

"But I had nothing to do with it!" Edvin protested. He quailed as Thorn turned a belligerent eye on him.

"Then you can cook the lunch," Thorn ordered.

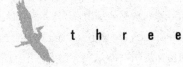

hey camped that night in the pass and reached the border fort midmorning the next day.

The walls of the pass narrowed even further as they approached the fort, until they were barely twenty meters apart. The fort was constructed across this narrowest point. The rock walls either side were almost sheer—difficult for a man to climb and impossible for a horse.

Fort Ragnak was a simple structure. Two wooden walls, four meters high, were built across the pass, twenty-five meters apart. They consisted of massive logs, driven into the ground, and formed two of the walls of the fort. Each one had a heavily reinforced timber gate. The other two walls were formed by the rock faces of the pass itself.

A raised walkway ran around the interior. From this vantage

point, the garrison could hold off attackers trying to scale the walls or breach the gate with a battering ram. A ditch had been dug on the northeastern side, a few meters out, to further discourage such activity. To bring a ram into action against the gate, the ditch would have to be filled in first, exposing the would-be attackers to the archers manning the log walls.

The gate leading back to Skandian territory was a similar structure. But it was not set directly opposite the northeast gate, as might logically be expected.

In the event that the first gate was breached, attackers would find themselves facing a blank wall. The second gate was set at the eastern end of the wall and was built so that it blended in with the rest of the structure. This asymmetric design was only a minor point, but it would momentarily confuse attackers, and as they searched for the way out, they would be trapped in a killing ground inside the fort, with no cover from the spears, arrows and rocks that would rain down on them from the walkways.

Beneath the walkway and backed up against the western rock wall, single-story buildings provided sleeping, eating and living quarters for the men assigned to the fort. They were well sealed against the wind and heated by open fireplaces. Erak had decreed that if men were to be posted here, high in the mountains in the snow and wind, they should be kept as comfortable as possible.

On the opposite wall, there were more buildings. These were stables and storage rooms and workrooms for the smith and armorer.

These interior details weren't immediately apparent to the approaching Herons—although Hal was aware of them, having been briefed by Erak—but one major feature of the fort was.

An angled roof, covered in timber shingles, projected above the northeast wall, reaching back to cover the interior space of the walkway and the ground below. This had been added to the original structure after the last major Temujai incursion into Skandian territory. At that time, the walls and walkway had been uncovered, other than by canvas screens to keep off the worst of the weather. The deficiency in this design had been exposed when Temujai archers dismounted and clawed their way up the stone walls farther up the valley, then began to pour a storm of arrows down onto the exposed garrison. The Skandians lost most of their men that way, and the reduced numbers who were left were not sufficient to hold off a determined Temujai assault on the wall. The riders from the east had broken through, slaughtered the remainder of the garrison, and poured across the border in their hundreds. The angled timber roof was designed to stop a similar attack.

The gate opened as the little cavalcade drew near. Hal could see faces high above them peering over the log walls, studying them curiously. He guessed that, in addition to the cold and bleak weather, the isolation in this post would be one of the major hardships. Boredom would be a big problem, particularly as it would tend to blunt the edge of the garrison's alertness. Life here would be a monotonous sequence of one day following another, with no difference other than changes in the weather conditions. But then, when the men guarding the border least expected it, the Temujai would mount a sudden raid to test their vigilance and the boredom would be replaced by an adrenaline rush of fear and alarm.

As Hal had been observing the fort, his horse had taken the opportunity to stop, lowering his head and pawing at the snow in the hope of finding a scrap of green to tear up and chew. Seeing Jake stop, Barney had done the same. Hal nudged Jake with his heels and set him moving again, leading the way through the open gate, feeling the eyes on his small party as he came to a halt in the center of the cleared ground inside the fort. He glanced around and saw a tall, gray-haired man descending a ladder from the southern walkway. Hal recognized him as a fellow skirl and brotherband leader called Leks Longshanks. He held up a hand in greeting.

"Leks!" he called. "Good to see you."

Leks hurried across to shake hands. "And you," he replied, then he looked at the two carts and the people sprawled comfortably on them. "I see you've brought your brotherband with you. Are you here to relieve us?"

This last was said with a puzzled frown. The normal strength of a brotherband was thirty men. Leks knew the Herons, having a much smaller ship, numbered only ten, which wasn't enough to garrison the border crossing.

Hal shook his head. "No. You'll have to wait for your normal relief. That'll be . . . in eight days, won't it?"

Leks nodded. "That's right. Villi Whitebeard and the *Wolfpaw*'s brotherband are due to relieve us. So, what are you doing here?"

Hal dismounted. Beside him, Stig did the same. The young skirl stretched and moved his legs to relieve the stiffness of several hours' riding.

"Erak wanted us to check out the defenses here." He gestured to the two carts, now parked in the fort's courtyard. "We've brought you some new weapons, as well."

Leks smiled. "They'll be welcome." He nodded a greeting now to Hal's companions. "Stig, Thorn, welcome to Fort Ragnak," he said, using the official name for the fort. It had been named for Erak's immediate predecessor, who had led the Skandians against the Temujai during that previous invasion and lost his life in a berserker attack on the riders from the east, saving the life of the Araluen princess, who had been helping with the defense of Hallasholm. Paradoxically, Ragnak had planned to execute the girl once the battle was done.

"Lovely spot you have here." Thorn grinned, taking in the bleak rock walls, with patches of snow still evident in pockets and crevices.

Leks followed the look. "Best thing about it is we'll be leaving soon," he said. Then he shrugged. "Actually, it's not all bad. The beds are soft, the rooms are warm and the food is very good."

"That's nice to know," Stig said cheerfully. The tall first mate could put up with a lot of inconvenience if he were kept well-fed.

Leks regarded him speculatively. "If you're going to be here for a few days, I'm glad we'll be leaving soon," he said. "I'm not sure the food will last."

"We've brought supplies with us," Hal interposed. "Erak knows Stig's reputation for eating."

Stig smiled, not the slightest bit offended by these references to his prodigious appetite. "Speaking of which, when's lunch?" he asked.

Leks raised his eyebrows. "Lunch? It's barely past the eleventh hour!"

Stig shook his head. "Somewhere in the world, it's well past lunchtime," he told the garrison commander.

Leks relented. "Very well. Get your horses and carts into the barn there and unload your gear. I'll get you settled into your rooms and then—"

"Lunch," said Stig, before the other man could finish his sentence.

Leks sighed. "As you say. Lunch," he agreed.

The meal was excellent, as Leks had predicted it would be. Among the other comforts provided in the fort, Erak ensured there was a constant stream of good chefs and first-rate provisions for them to work with. Edvin was particularly appreciative as he pushed his chair back and rested his hands on his slightly distended stomach.

"It always tastes better when someone else does the cooking," he said, to no one in particular. Edvin was an excellent chef himself and was in charge of providing meals for the *Heron*'s crew when they were at sea or traveling overland—as they were at the moment. Having someone else to do the job for him was a welcome change.

Stig grinned at him. "I always have someone else do the cooking," he said. He was demolishing his third large helping of a savory mutton-and-potato stew that the cook had provided for them, tearing off a chunk of crusty fresh bread to mop up the remaining gravy.

"And that's a full-time job," Edvin replied, looking forward to the ensuing days at Fort Ragnak when he wouldn't have to provide food for the seemingly insatiable first mate.

Hal glanced around the table, making sure that the crew had finished their meal. It was time to get them to work, he knew. If he allowed them to sit here relaxing, half of them would fall asleep and the other half would sink into a semi-waking torpor.

"Jesper, Stefan, start getting the timber for the two platforms sorted out," he ordered briskly.

For a moment, Jesper looked ready to demur. But then he saw the grim look in his skirl's eyes, and the watchful expression on Thorn's face, ready for any argument. He sighed and pushed back his bench from the table. "Come on, Stefan," he said, in a long-suffering tone. "Seems we get to do all the work while the others relax."

The two of them donned their sheepskin jackets, gloves and watch caps—Stefan's new cap had been completed by Edvin—and shoved open the door to the courtyard. The wind swirled into the room as they did so, causing the fire to flare up momentarily. Then they shut the door behind them and trudged across to the storage rooms, where the precut timber was piled inside, out of the weather.

Back in the communal eating room, Hal caught Leks's eye. "We might as well take a look and see where we can site the two platforms," he said, and the tall man nodded agreement. Over the meal, Hal had explained his idea to build shooting platforms for the two manglers.

Leks had greeted the idea enthusiastically. "Anything to catch those damn Temujai on the hop," he said. He rose now and, gesturing for Hal to follow him, led the way to the door.

Hal paused and turned back to Thorn. "You coming, Thorn?"

The old sea wolf, who had claimed a seat at the end of the table near the roaring fire, shook his head and smiled beatifically.

"I'm sure you and Hal can manage without me," he said. "I'll make sure the fire doesn't go out. That's an important job."

L et's take a look up the valley first," Hal suggested. Leks led the way to a flight of stairs running up to the north-east walkway. When they reached the top, Hal leaned his elbows on the sharpened tops of the pine logs, which formed a natural set of crenellations to partially conceal the defenders, and studied the land below him.

The rock-walled valley they were in continued for thirty or forty meters, then gradually began to widen—although the steep walls remained as forbidding as ever. As more level ground became available, the ubiquitous pine trees had taken hold, fringing the open area of the path and even gaining footholds on the steep rock sides of the pass. The dark green branches were covered in thick layers of snow.

Hal indicated them. "Has it been snowing lately?"

Leks shrugged. "It snows a lot, even at this time of year," he said. "We're pretty high up. The last fall was two nights ago."

"I guess that makes it hard to see if the Temujai are on the move," Hal said. The flat ground in the center of the pass was kept clear, with the trees concentrated on the sides, close to the walls. But in a blizzard, he guessed, enemy troops could approach without being seen.

"Yes. Anytime there's a heavy fall, we stand to, just in case. Sometimes those wily devils will have a crack at us."

"Have you had any serious attempts to break through?" Hal asked.

The garrison commander shook his head. "No. It's more in the nature of nuisance raids—aimed to keep us guessing and to ruin our sleep. We can't see around that bend in the valley about two hundred meters out." He indicated a point where the widening valley made a sharp turn past an elbow in the rock wall. "They could be massing on the other side and we'd never know—unless the wind was from the north."

Hal frowned at the last statement. "Why would that make a difference?"

"Noise. When there's a few hundred of their horses gathered together, they can't keep them perfectly still. The jingling of harness and the stamping of hooves carries on the wind and gives us some warning."

"Well, Erak suggested that Lydia might go out and take a look around," he said. "See if the Temujai are out there in any numbers."

"Lydia? The girl who's with you?" Leks said, surprised. "Is that safe? There could be a couple of hundred Temujai in that valley for all we know. What if they see her?"

"She's pretty good at not being seen," said a voice behind them. "Or heard."

Startled, Leks whirled around to find Lydia standing a few meters away. She had followed them out of the dining room and, seeing them mounting the stairs to the rampart, decided to join them. But, as usual, she moved silently so that Leks had no idea she was within earshot.

Hal grinned at the commander now. "I think she'll be all right."

Lydia leaned over the parapet, examining the exterior of the log wall. "How do I get out?" she asked. "Do you have any kind of wicket gate?"

A wicket gate was a small gate set into the main gate, allowing access for one or two people at a time.

Leks shook his head. "It'd weaken the main structure," he said. "And we never open the big gate unless we're sure there are no enemies in the vicinity. We'll put over a rope ladder for you, if that's all right?"

Somehow, he knew it would be. The girl had an athletic build and she moved easily.

Lydia pursed her lips. "That'll be fine," she said, then turned to Hal. "It's a bit late in the day now. I'll go out tomorrow before dawn."

"Sounds like a good idea," Hal said. In the uncertain predawn light, she'd be able to leave the fort and reach the cover of the trees without being seen. Then she'd have a full day to scout the surrounding countryside. "In the meantime," he said to Leks, "let's find somewhere to build those platforms."

They turned back toward the stairway. Lydia remained leaning on the parapet.

"Coming with us, Lydia?" Hal asked.

She shook her head. "That's your line of work. I'll stay here and study the lay of the land."

They descended the stairs and made their way across the courtyard. There was a small wicket gate set into the south wall, where the need for security wasn't as pressing. Leks led the way through— the gate wasn't wide enough for two people abreast—and they strode briskly down the pass, peering at the walls. Fifteen meters away from the fort, Leks stopped and pointed up at the rock wall to the east.

"I thought there," he said. "See that small ledge, above the sapling growing out of the rock? It'll give you a start on building. You can anchor your platform there and support the outer edge with timber props."

Hal narrowed his eyes, studying the spot. "Yes. That should do nicely," he said. The ledge was a meter and a half wide, enough to provide solid support for the platform. "What about the other side?"

Leks led the way farther down the pass, then stopped again, pointing to the western wall.

"Up there. It's higher than the other one, but it'll give you a good field of view up the pass beyond the fort."

This ledge wasn't as wide as the first one, but it would offer enough support for the platform. As Leks said, it was a little higher, being some ten meters above ground level. But that meant it would have a clear view over the fort walls and up the pass into Temujai territory.

Hal glanced at the sky. The sun had already crossed over from its highest point and the lower reaches of the valley were in shadow.

"Still a few hours of daylight left," he said. "I'll get to work marking out the positions for the props."

Returning to the fort, he loaded his tools and a portable workbench into the bed of one of the carts, along with several coils of rope. Then he ordered Ulf and Wulf to tail onto the shafts and wheel the cart down the valley.

"What are we? Horses?" Ulf complained good-humoredly. In truth, the lightly laden cart wasn't difficult to tow.

Hal grinned at him. "No. Horses are smart."

Wulf snorted disdainfully. "I'm smarter than a horse," he claimed.

His brother couldn't resist replying. "So how come you're out here, pulling a cart in the wind and the cold, while the horses are tucked up in a nice warm stable?"

Wulf missed the obvious rejoinder, that his brother was out here with him and so wasn't as smart as a horse either. He often missed the obvious, Hal noted.

"I still say I'm smarter than a horse!" Wulf said.

Ulf eyed him sideways. "I knew a horse once that could count to eighteen."

Wulf's reply was immediate. "I can count to eighteen!"

"Yes. But he did it with his hooves," Ulf replied triumphantly.

Wulf frowned, not sure how to take that comment. Hal was a

little mystified by it himself, but Ulf seemed inordinately pleased with himself and Hal guessed that in the ongoing, nonsensical world of conversation between the twins, Ulf had just scored a winning point.

"Need some help?" Stig said, jogging up to join them. He'd seen the party leaving the fort and thought Hal might be able to use a hand as he marked out the structure for the platforms.

Hal smiled appreciatively. Things would go faster with another pair of hands to measure and mark out the footings—particularly as they would be doing the work ten to fifteen meters above the ground. "Some sensible conversation would be good," the skirl said.

Stig, glancing at the twins, with Wulf's lips moving silently as he searched for a suitably scathing reply to Ulf's last comment, grinned. "I know what you mean."

They set up at the site of the first ledge. Hal donned a leather toolbelt with a hammer thrust through one loop and a hand pickax through another. A pouch at the front of the belt held a supply of iron pins. Stig slung a coil of rope around his shoulders and the two friends scrambled up the rock face, finding hand- and foot-holds easily. They had grown up near the mountains and had spent their boyhood scrambling up and down seemingly sheer rock faces. There were always support points to be found, as long as you knew what you were looking for.

And as long as you maintained three points of contact with the rock while you climbed.

As they ascended, Hal hammered a succession of iron pins into cracks and crevices in the rock wall. Stig then tied the rope securely around them, providing a permanent web of support for the climbers in case they should slip. The ledge itself was wide and level. Stig sat with his feet dangling over the edge, watching as Hal measured and marked out points on the rock where the timber platform would be anchored. The rock was hard enough to provide stable support, but not so hard that Hal couldn't cut and shape and mark it with the pickax.

Once he had marked out the plan on the ledge itself, where the inner side of the platform would be secured, Hal clambered down the web of ropes they had created and found points where the supporting struts could be anchored to the rock wall. Again he marked the spots with his pickax, deftly cutting steps into the rock where the diagonal props would sit.

"That'll do it for today," he said. "Let's get back to the fort."

They scrambled back down the rock face, to where Ulf and Wulf were waiting by the cart. As they approached, they saw Wulf tapping his right foot on the ground while he kept count.

". . . fifteen, sixteen, seventeen, eighteen!" he said, finishing on a triumphant note. "See? Anything a horse can do, I can do just as well."

"Maybe," Ulf replied. "But he wasn't using his fingers to count."

And, once again, Wulf had no reply.

F our hours after midnight, a small party assembled on the walkway at the western end of the north-facing wall.

The stars were still bright in the cold night sky, and as yet, there was no sign of the coming dawn. Lydia examined the rope ladder rolled up on the planks of the walkway. She unrolled it a few meters. The ladder's sides were stout rope. The steps were pieces of hardwood, shaped flat to provide better footing, and at every third step there were hardwood battens designed to hold the ladder out from the wall, making it easier to get a grip on the rope sides—and easier for a climber to fit his or her feet onto the rungs.

"That's fine," she said, glancing up to meet Leks's gaze.

The gray-haired man gestured to the top of the wall. "Do you want it over the edge now?"

But Lydia shook her head. She turned to Hal. "Is that brazier ready?" she asked, and Hal nodded. At her request, he had arranged for an iron brazier full of firewood and kindling to be placed at the far end of the wall. "All right," Lydia continued, "get it lit up. But don't be in too much of a hurry to get the tinder burning."

The burning brazier was planned as a distraction, to draw the gaze of any possible observers hidden among the trees while Lydia went over the wall. The longer Hal took to kindle the blaze, the more often he would strike sparks from his flint. The resulting half dozen or so brilliant flashes of light would be highly visible in the predawn darkness and would effectively draw the attention of any potential observer.

As he turned to make his way across the walkway, he heard Lydia instructing the two members of the garrison who stood by the rope ladder.

"Lower it slowly," she said. "Don't just toss it over so it rattles and clatters all the way down."

The men nodded, lifting the heavy bundle of rope and wood onto the top of the parapet. Lydia held up a hand and watched as Hal reached the brazier at the far end of the walkway. A brilliant flash of light momentarily lit up his crouching form as he struck his saxe blade against the flint in his hand. Another flash followed almost immediately.

"Let it go," Lydia said quietly, letting her hand drop. The two men began unwinding the rope ladder, allowing it to drop quietly down the face of the wall. When it touched the ground below, they fastened the two end loops at the top of the rope over the pointed logs. Lydia swung easily over the wall, staying flat so that she didn't present a silhouette. She reached with one foot for the first rung of the ladder, found it and began to climb quickly down.

More brilliant flashes lit up the night at the far end of the wall. Then there was an orange glow as the tinder caught, followed by a soft *whoosh* of flame as Hal thrust the burning tinder into the oil-soaked kindling in the brazier. The light wood caught immediately, and yellow flames rose eagerly into the night.

That should keep people watching, Lydia thought as her right foot touched the snow-covered ground. She stepped clear of the ladder, reaching back to jerk the right-hand rope three times. Slowly, quietly, the ladder began to rise up the wall in response to the prearranged signal.

Lydia was wearing a gray woolen cloak with a hood. The previous evening, she had smeared the garment with ash and soot from the fireplace, creating random patterns on the material that would break up her shape. She pulled the hood up to conceal her face, then wrapped the cloak around her and stepped away from the fort, hugging the stone wall of the ravine.

She made no sound as she proceeded up the valley. Behind her, the brazier sent up a cheerful yellow light and several of the sentries on the wall gathered round it appreciatively. Her heart beat a little faster, fueled by the adrenaline that came with stepping into enemy territory. There was an unavoidable tendency to feel alone and exposed when you left the shelter and protection of the fort, she thought, and the support and assistance of your friends. She didn't mind being alone. In some ways, she preferred it. But the sense of possible danger, the awareness that every shadow, every tree, could conceal an enemy lying in wait, was always with her at times like this.

Probably a good thing, she thought. It'll keep me on my toes.

And she was right in thinking so. Every nerve, every sense, was attuned to its highest possible level. She could *feel* the surrounding ground as much as she could see it or hear it. She was aware of it, of every aspect of it, the sight, the smell, the sounds. It was a total impression of the land around her.

The trees were becoming thicker, and she slid into the shadows beneath them, staying to the side of the ravine. The open ground stretched away in the center but now the level walls moved farther apart and she was three trees in from the edge of the cleared ground. Her view of the sky was obscured now, and the shadows under the heavily branched pines were deep. Her stained gray cloak did its job well, creating an amorphous, unidentifiable mass that slipped ghostlike between the trunks.

To her left, she heard a sudden slither, followed by a soft thump. She was between two trees, and her nerves shrieked at her to move quickly into the shelter of the nearest one.

But she didn't. She froze in place, senses jangling so that she thought anyone nearby must hear them.

But of course they didn't. Long experience told her that the safest move in this situation was *not* to move, but to stay dead still, assessing the terrain around her, feeling with all of her heightened senses to determine what had caused that sound.

Then she heard it again, but this time from in front of her and much farther away. Her nerves jumped again, but this time she recognized the sound. It was snow sliding off an overloaded branch and falling to the ground below: *slither—thump*. She waited several seconds, poised with one foot in front of her, then she continued to move forward, gliding into the shelter of the tree she had been heading for. She paused there, letting her nerves calm, and became conscious that a light predawn breeze had begun to blow up the valley from the fort toward her.

The leaves around her moved gently, and she listened for a few moments as the breeze soughed gently through the pine needles. As ever, she was struck by the way the wind moving through pine needles sounded like distant surf on a beach. In among the other sounds, she heard a suggestion of voices talking quietly—too quietly for her to understand what was being said. Again, she tensed, then relaxed as she realized that, with the wind blowing from the fort to her, it was carrying the muted conversation of the men on the wall, grouped around the warmth of the brazier.

She nodded to herself with satisfaction. The noise of the wind and the voices and the moving branches would effectively mask any sound she might make—although there would be precious little of that.

She stepped out, moving deeper into the cover of the trees.

Hal and Leks waited on the walkway for some thirty minutes after Lydia had gone.

Leks spent the time peering into the dim shadows up the valley. He had seen Lydia moving for the first ten or twenty meters, sliding along the rock walls, semi-concealed by the smudged cloak that blended with the uncertain light. Then he had been distracted by a low-flying night bird and had looked away. When he looked back, he could see no sign of her.

He said as much to Hal. The young skirl smiled in response. He was familiar with Lydia's stalking skills.

"And you won't see her again," he told the older man. "Once you take your eyes off her, she's gone. She's been doing this all her life," he added, by way of explanation.

"So why are you still here?" Leks asked.

"I'm listening. If she strikes trouble, we'll hear it. But by now, I'd say she's in the clear. I think I'll go back to bed."

Suddenly, in the predawn chill, the thought of his warm blankets in the barracks room, close by the glowing fireplace, was a very attractive one. He moved toward the top of the stairs.

"Coming?" he asked.

But Leks, who lacked Hal's confidence in Lydia's skills, shook his head. "I'll stay here," he said. "And listen."

Hal shrugged, understanding the man's anxiety. "Suit yourself," he said. "See you at breakfast."

After breakfast—a substantial meal of sausage, fried potato and toasted flatbread washed down with hot, fragrant coffee—Hal took Stig and the twins down the valley to the site of the second shooting platform. As before, he clambered up the valley wall and quickly marked out the plan for the platform, cutting steps into the rock where the support beams would rest.

When he was finished, he eyed his handiwork with satisfaction.

"You can take over now," he told Stig. "Put the crew to work building the platforms. I'll start assembling one of the manglers. I want to show Damien how they work."

Damien was the commander of the fifteen Araluen archers

assigned to garrison duty in the fort. They had met him the previous night and discussed Hal's plan to install two of the massive crossbows to augment the fort's defenses. Damien would be providing the marksmen to man the weapons, and he was eager to see them at work.

Hal and Stig returned to the fort, leaving the twins relaxing beneath the site of the eastern platform. Stig pulled the empty cart back with them. They had unloaded the tools and some of the timber for the platforms. Now he summoned the rest of the crew and put them to work loading the rest of the materials onto the cart. Hal went to where the two disassembled manglers lay, wrapped in canvas. He untied the thongs that held the cover of one in place and called to Ingvar.

"Ingvar, you stay with me. I'll need you to help me demonstrate the mangler."

The huge young man nodded. On board ship, he worked with Hal, who sat behind the sights of the Mangler. Ingvar would traverse the giant weapon, using a long pole to swing it left or right as Hal directed. These manglers would be set on tripods, and the shooter would stand behind it and do his own traversing. But Ingvar's mighty strength would be useful for cocking and loading the big crossbow.

Quickly, Hal began assembling the components, checking as he fitted them together that there were no faults in the wood, no cracks or splits that might suddenly—and catastrophically—give way when the limbs were under tension.

When he had the body, the limbs and the trigger mechanism assembled, he stood the weapon on end, butt to the ground, and took the heavy cord, looped at either end. He slipped one loop over the notched end of the right-hand limb and gestured for Ingvar to bend the arms of the bow down so that he could position the cord over the other limb. Normally, it might take two or even three men to do this. But Ingvar, with a loud grunt, flexed the bow down so that his skirl could slip the loop over the second limb.

Hal regarded him with admiration. "I'm glad you're around," he said. "Don't know how I'd manage that on my own."

Ingvar smiled quietly. "I'm sure you'd invent a machine to do it for you," he said, his faith in Hal's ingenuity all too obvious.

Hal shrugged. "Maybe. But it's a lot easier when you do it," he said.

Once the body of the mangler was ready, Hal hefted it over his shoulder and headed for the stairs leading to the ramparts. Ingvar followed, carrying the folded tripod and a canvas sheaf of darts.

Damien, the commander of the Araluen archers, met them at the top of the stairs. Eight of his men were with him. The others were currently on guard duty, relaxing in the ready room in a small tower at the eastern end of the ramparts. Four of Leks's men were stationed on the ramparts themselves, keeping watch up the valley for any sign of an attack.

The archers gathered curiously around the big weapon as Hal set it down, leaning it against the timber parapet. They studied it with professional interest.

"It's big, isn't it?" Damien said, and Hal nodded as Ingvar

unfolded the legs of the tripod and set it up beside the wall. The skirl unwrapped the canvas sheaf and took out one of the heavy wooden darts. He passed it to Damien.

"I imagine this would make quite a mess if it hit someone," the commander said, turning the heavy projectile back and forth in his hand, studying the stiff leather flights and the metal warhead. He handed it on to the other archers.

"They usually don't stop at one," Hal told him, stepping aside as Ingvar lifted the mangler onto the tripod, setting it in place and making sure it was firmly attached. He traversed it back and forth a few times, then elevated it up and down, making sure the movement was smooth. When this was done, he tightened the screws on both adjustments so that the weapon was held more firmly, while still free to move.

"I've set out the targets you asked for," Damien told him, indicating the three man-sized wooden targets that one of his men had placed out in the center of the valley.

"Good," said Hal, judging the range to the three with narrowed eyes. "About fifty, one hundred and two hundred paces, right?"

"Near enough," Damien told him. He turned as the fort commander appeared at the top of the stairs and came toward them. "Morning, commander. Come to see the show?"

Leks nodded, looking at the mangler with interest. "Never seen one close up before," he said to Hal. "You carry one on your ship, don't you?"

"That's right. We're usually outnumbered when we face an enemy, so it tends to even the odds a little," Hal told him.

Damien made a small moue of interest. "Never heard of a ship carrying a weapon before."

"Neither had a lot of the people we've fought," Hal said. He glanced at Ingvar. "All right, Ingvar, load it up."

The archers watched as the massive young man seized the two cocking handles and heaved them back and up, catching the thick cord and drawing it back to click into place behind the retaining latch.

"It might take two of you to do that," Hal told them, and they nodded among themselves, impressed by the young giant's power. Hal stepped up behind the weapon now, but stayed slightly to one side so he could demonstrate to Damien and his men. He flicked up the rear leaf sight and pointed to it.

"Unlike your longbows, where you have to estimate elevation and direction, the mangler is fitted with these sights, which make things a lot easier." Highly skilled archers like these, he knew, would have little trouble adapting to the system he had devised. Araluen archers were among the best in the world, used to estimating distance and elevation by eye. The sights would make the task much easier.

"Let's have a dart, please, Ingvar," he said quietly. He waited as his companion placed one of the heavy darts into the slot on top of the crossbow, sliding it back until the shallow notch in its rear end was nestled against the thick cord of the bowstring. Hal studied the nearest target for a few seconds.

"Maybe a touch over fifty paces?" he said.

Damien nodded, suppressing a smile. He had instructed his man not to bother being too accurate in his measurements. He was interested to see how good this young Skandian leader might be.

"You got sloppy there, Willis," he said to the man who had placed the target.

Willis grinned. "Sorry, chief," he said, without any note of apology in his voice.

Hal looked from one to the other for a few seconds. He knew what had gone on here. Whenever you tried to show warriors a new weapon or technique, they always wanted you to mess it up. It was standard behavior.

So be it, he thought. He stepped closer to the mangler, leaned down and put his shoulder to the butt. Then, without seeming to take too much care over it, he traversed the weapon until the blade foresight was aligned with the target, twisted the elevating wheel until the V of the backsight was sitting slightly above the top of the target, with the blade foresight centered in the V, and almost casually squeezed the trigger lever.

*SLAM!*

The surrounding archers flinched with the sudden shock of the release. The bolt streaked away from the ramparts and smashed into the target where it narrowed to form a rough approximation of a head. The wood shattered under the massive impact and the target cartwheeled end over end in the snow, coming to rest nearly three meters from where it had begun.

"Orlog's toenails!" Damien muttered. It was a local curse and one he had grown fond of during his time here in the north. "That thing is dangerous!"

"Just a little," Hal agreed, and nodded to Ingvar to reload. This time, he took aim at the second-farthest target. He estimated this one to be slightly less than the stipulated hundred paces, so he set the sights at the base of the man-shaped figure. Again, there was the massive *SLAM!* of the release, and another bolt streaked away.

This one hit the middle of the target, showering splinters in all directions, splitting the target in two and causing the two halves to fold up on themselves.

The third shot, at the most distant target, was off center, catching the side of the timber shape. More splinters flew and the target spun away crazily under the impact, with a large hole torn in its edge.

Hal stood back from the weapon and looked at the archers. After the first shot, they had remained silent. But he could see they were impressed by the power and accuracy of the big crossbow.

"Care to try it?" he asked quietly, and the group were galvanized into activity, with all of them clamoring to try this devastating new weapon.

Damien silenced the eruption almost instantly. "I'll go first," he announced. He looked sidelong at Hal with a grin and added, "No point in being the commander if you can't pull rank, is there?"

Hal gestured for the archer to take his position behind the weapon as Ingvar reloaded it for him. He watched as Damien lined the sights up on the target at fifty paces. He could see there was no need to tell him what to do. But he did offer one piece of advice.

"Don't snatch at the trigger. Squeeze it," he said.

Damien, head bowed over the sights, eyes intent on the target, nodded. His shot smashed into the target, which was lying cocked up on its side where it had fallen.

He stepped back, gesturing for one of his men to take his place, and met Hal's eyes.

"Amazing," he said. "That'll shake up those riders if they come poking around here again."

"I've got something else to show you," Hal said. "But we'll wait until your men have taken a few shots."

All of his men wanted to try the new weapon, but Damien shook his head. He had selected three men to train with the manglers and they would be the ones who shot it. The others grumbled but gave way relatively cheerfully when their leader told them: "If you all practice with it, we'll run out of darts." They had to admit the sense of that.

Once the three selected archers had each shot three darts, Hal reached into the canvas wrap and produced another dart. This one had a bulbous clay head instead of the sharpened metal warhead. On closer inspection, Damien could see a small thread protruding from it.

"This is something new," Hal told the assembled men. "We don't use it on our ship. It'd be too dangerous. But for a static setting like this, it should be fine. It's designed to cause panic among your attackers—particularly their horses."

He indicated the clay head. "This is a reservoir that holds a mixture of oil and pitch," he said. "You can see the fuse here." He indicated the threadlike piece that could be seen underneath the warhead.

"The idea is, you line up the shot, light this fuse and let fly. When the warhead hits the ground or a rock or a rider's shield, it shatters and spills out the sticky oil and pitch. The burning fuse ignites it and there's a sudden burst of flame." He paused. "And I have it on good authority that horses won't like that."

Several of the archers murmured agreement. Damien smiled wolfishly. "Not sure I'd like it myself," he said. "Let's see it in action."

Gently, Hal removed the cork stopper from the top of the warhead and made sure that the reservoir was full of the combustible oil and pitch—and that the fuse was firmly seated in it.

"It weighs a little more than the standard iron warhead," he explained. "So, you need to aim higher. But it doesn't have to be as accurate, as the flames spread over a wide area once the head shatters."

He waited while Ingvar cocked the mangler and set the new dart in the shallow trough on top, turning the projectile so that the fuse stood clear above it. Hal surveyed the valley below them and pointed to a rock outcrop on the northwest wall of the valley.

"I think that black rock will do nicely," he said. He crouched behind the mangler and lined it up, aiming slightly above the target to allow for the heavier warhead and the extra wind resistance of the bulbous clay reservoir. Ingvar took a burning brand from the brazier that had been lit early that morning. The fire had been kept alive to provide warmth for the sentries on the walkway. Before he could light the fuse, however, Hal held up a hand to stop him.

"Just a moment, Ingvar," he said, then turned to the expectant semicircle of faces watching him. "One thing I should mention," he told them. "We've been testing these for a while throughout the winter. We've found that they work, on average, three out of five times. The other times, the fuse doesn't ignite the oil and pitch— or it's extinguished in the rush of air. So, don't be too surprised if nothing happens."

He nodded to Ingvar, and the big youth stepped in and applied the burning brand to the fuse. He waited for a second or two until he could see it hissing and spitting as it burned.

"It's afire," Ingvar said.

Hal made a final adjustment to his aim and squeezed the trigger lever.

*SLAM!*

The mangler rocked back on its tripod as the arms sprang forward. The fire bolt streaked away, leaving a faint gray trail of smoke behind it. Then it smashed into the rocks.

There was a shattering sound as the clay head exploded, spilling its contents out. Then, after a second, the oil and pitch caught with a loud *WHOOF* and a tongue of flame leapt into the air, surrounded by coils of black, acrid smoke.

Again, the assembled archers voiced their appreciation at the effectiveness of this new weapon.

"Who thought of this?" one of them said.

Hal said nothing, but Ingvar elbowed him proudly, very nearly sending him off the catwalk. "He did," Ingvar told them. "He's full of good ideas."

Hal made a self-deprecating gesture as they gathered around him, congratulating him. They were all experienced warriors, and they respected anyone who could come up with a more efficient way of waging war against their enemies.

"Imagine one of those going off among a tight-packed group of riders," Damien said. "Their horses wouldn't stop bolting until they were halfway back to the steppes."

One of the younger archers stepped forward and studied the

mangler more closely, running his hands over the smooth timber and metal.

"I could almost wish they'd have a crack at us," he said, "just to see this scare the pants off them."

The older soldiers among them shook their heads at the enthusiastic youngster.

"Be careful, Simon," said one. "You might get what you wish for."

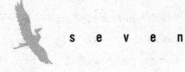

L ydia continued to ghost her way through the trees as the valley widened and flattened. She stayed inside the tree line, but close to the open ground.

From time to time, she saw evidence that the eastern riders had passed this way. Usually it was in the form of piles of horse dung in the snow. She emerged from the trees when she saw one of these and, crouching down, poked it with a twig. The dung was half frozen, and quite dry on the inside. Obviously, it had been here for several days.

As she broke it up with the twig, the rank smell of the manure assailed her nostrils and she sniffed, rising to her feet and casting a look around.

There was no sign of the horse that had deposited it, or its rider, although that didn't surprise her. The rider would hardly wait around for several days. As she proceeded, moving back to the concealment of the edge of the trees, she saw increasing numbers of dark piles. Several had been dusted over with light snowfall. Most of the piles were several days old, at least, although she saw two that were still moist. In addition to the manure, the snow was disturbed by hoofprints. She studied them closely. They were left by small, unshod horses.

She regarded the tracks curiously. She had never encountered the Temujai before, but Thorn had instructed her about them.

"Don't take any chances," he had said. "They're fierce warriors and expert shots with the bow. They were born on horseback—and the day after they were born, they had a bow placed in their hands."

"Are they as good as the Araluen archers?" she'd asked.

Thorn had pursed his lips, considering his answer. "Not as good as a Ranger like Gilan," he told her. "But they're pretty much on a par with the other Araluens. Each squadron of horsemen has a highly trained sharpshooter assigned to it. He's selected for his above-average skill and accuracy. His task in battle is to look for enemy commanders and shoot them."

Lydia had wrinkled her nose. "Charming."

Thorn reached out his left hand and seized her wrist firmly. "Don't take any chances with them," he said. "They could be the most dangerous enemies you'll ever encounter."

She noted the serious tenor of his voice and nodded. "Are they good trackers?"

Again he considered his answer. "Not as good as you," he said. "But they're capable. So—"

"Don't take any chances with them," she finished for him.

He drew breath to speak, but she patted his forearm reassuringly. "Thanks, Thorn. I've got the picture," she told him.

He studied her for a few seconds, saw that she wasn't joking and gave her a satisfied nod. "Keep it in mind," he said gruffly. He was very fond of the young woman whom they had rescued from a sinking skiff some years before. The Heron brotherband had come to rely on her tracking and scouting ability, and her uncanny accuracy with the big darts she threw from her atlatl.

Now, crouching in the snow in the middle of the cleared ground of the valley, Lydia tensed as a slight sound came to her ears.

It was a metallic sound—a light jingle, carrying to her from the north even though the slight wind was out of the south. That meant that whoever was making the noise must be close, and she was exposed in the open. She ran toward the cover of the trees, casting an anxious glance up the valley to see the source of the noise.

It took her a few seconds to identify the sound: It was the metallic jingle of a horse's harness—either the bit or stirrup buckles. The dim shadow of the trees closed around her before she saw any sign of a rider approaching from the north. She ran to the second row of trees and dropped to her belly, sliding in the snow to the cover of the thick trunk.

And waited, her heart in her mouth.

For a few more seconds, she saw nothing. Then a movement caught her eye at the edge of a blind corner forty meters away. A dark horse sidled into sight, staying close to the outer row of trees, on the opposite side of the valley to where she lay concealed. The rider was swathed in fur and leather. The tip of a recurve bow was visible above his right shoulder, and a heavy-laden quiver of arrows rode at his right hip.

She lay still, unmoving, barely daring to draw breath, as he rode closer. His eyes, under the conical fur hat he wore, darted back and forth, constantly moving and appraising as he studied the valley and the tree line on both sides. His gaze passed over her and she felt convinced that he must have seen her. Yet she lay still as a rock, even though her nerves were screaming for her to leap to her feet and run.

You know that's the worst thing you could do, she told herself. Why do you always feel like doing it?

She guessed it was a natural instinct for flight, overlaid and countermanded by her years of training. It was the same natural instinct that made a grouse, or other small game bird, break from cover—usually with fatal results.

The jingling harness was louder now, and she could make out the soft thud of his horse's hooves on the snow and the creaking of leather as the saddle moved slightly under the rider's weight. Her hood was up, shading her face. She was able to watch him without making any movement to lift her head.

She felt a sudden surge of panic as a thought occurred to her. What if he saw her footprints in the snow?

She was tempted to look for them, to see how obvious they might be. There would be slight scuff marks on the snow's surface that she had made when she moved out to study the horse dung, and larger, deeper tracks left behind when she ran back to the shelter of the pines. She'd never miss such a clear sign as that, she thought.

But to look for the marks, she'd have to lower her head, and she knew any movement could give her away. She remained still, her eyes deep inside the cowl, fastened on the solitary rider as he moved down the valley.

But he wasn't looking for tracks. He was alert to the possibility that there might be enemies concealed in the trees either side of the valley. If he were planning an ambush, that was where he would choose to be. He continued on, head constantly moving, eyes constantly searching.

Finally, he was far enough past her for her to be able to move without fear of being seen. She squirmed around the bole of the pine tree, staying low to the ground and positioning herself so that the tree was between her and the rider. The soft clumping of the horse's hooves was almost inaudible now. The thinner sound of the jingling harness still carried to her. Then the rider passed around a bend in the valley and disappeared from her sight.

She sat up, leaning back against the tree trunk to think, brushing excess powder snow from her jerkin and knees.

"So, where are you off to?" she asked herself. The answer came quickly enough. Keeping an eye on proceedings at the fort.

She cast her gaze back up the valley, to the north. "And where have you come from?" she asked, barely speaking above a whisper.

Once again, the answer was self-evident. There must be a Temujai camp somewhere close by, where the commanders could dispatch observers like the one she had just seen to keep watch on the fort and its defenders.

Which raised a further question: *Why* keep watch on the fort?

One possible answer was that the Temujai leaders were planning a raid, or even a full-scale attack, on the border crossing. Of course, the rider might have been detached out of sheer curiosity. But somehow, from what she had been told about the Temujai, she doubted it. There'd be a more serious motive.

Next question: Were they planning a raid or a full-scale attack?

And that depended on the size of the Temujai force gathered in the vicinity. If there were fewer than a hundred, odds were that they would be planning a raid—to see if they could catch the garrison unawares or with their guard down. There were forty-five men in the garrison, all trained warriors and skilled archers. And the fort was well built and well sited—all but impregnable to bows and swords and lances. An attacking force, without the advantage of surprise, would need siege engines and scaling towers to make an impression.

Or an overwhelming number of men.

The question hung in the air. Raid or full-scale attack?

She checked once more, making sure the rider was well out of sight by now, then glanced along the valley to the north.

"Well," she said, "that's where you came from. I guess that's where I'll find the answer."

The east-side platform was finished before its western counterpart. The ledge was wider on the east side, as Hal had noticed, and there was less need for supporting structure underneath it.

He assembled the second mangler. The first was still on the ramparts, where Damien's selected shooters and their assistants were practicing with it—getting the hang of cocking and loading the big weapon as well as improving their accuracy and judgment of range. The loud *SLAM* of the weapon releasing had echoed around the narrow valley at intervals through the afternoon. Hal was relieved that the shooters spent a lot of their time practicing the loading and aiming drills as well as simply shooting. He'd brought a large number of bolts, knowing that the men would need a lot of practice to achieve the high level of accuracy that he wanted, but the supply wasn't infinite. Ammunition economy was important. It would be no use having the two manglers in place if they had nothing to shoot with, and there would be a need for more practice when the weapons were sited on the shooting platforms. Once that happened, the shooters would have to reassess their ranges and elevations. The manglers would be shooting from a high position on the wall and the bolts would travel farther as a result.

He and Ingvar carried the weapon and its tripod down the valley, setting it below the completed platform. Hal scrambled up the rock face to the platform. Ulf and Wulf, who had been working on this site with Edvin and Stefan, made room for him as he scrambled onto the rough wooden planks. They watched anxiously as he paced back and forth, testing the platform's solidity by occasionally stamping heavily and at other times jumping half a meter in the air to come down with both feet. After a few minutes, he nodded in satisfaction and they heaved a discreet sigh of relief. With Hal, you never knew how good your workmanship was until he had tested it.

"Good work," he said briefly, and the three exchanged grins. Then he whistled to Ingvar and let a coiled rope down, so that the big youth could attach the mangler and its tripod.

"Haul it up," he told the twins, and the ungainly bundle soared up the cliff face. As it was coming, Damien scrambled up the rope web that had been installed and surveyed the shooting position. He frowned and jerked a thumb up the valley toward the ground beyond the fort.

"You're still in range here, you know," he said. "And those horsemen are excellent shots."

Hal nodded. "The platform will have a solid timber wall facing them," he said. "And there's a timber shield that attaches to the front of the crossbow itself, protecting the shooter."

"That's as well, then," Damien replied. He watched with interest as Ingvar, who had now joined them, busied himself setting the tripod's legs into the sockets provided for them. Then he mounted the big weapon on the tripod and moved it experimentally back and forth to make sure it was properly set. Stefan clambered down the cliff and began assembling bundles of ammunition, tying them in groups of ten, then attaching them to the rope so that Ulf and Wulf could haul them up and stack them ready.

"Your boys know their job," Damien said.

Hal smiled at them. "They're a good crew," he admitted. The four workers overheard him and smiled to themselves. They enjoyed it when their skirl appreciated them.

"Damien!" They were interrupted by a shout from the valley floor. One of Damien's crew was peering up at them. When he saw he had their attention, he beckoned them down.

"You'd better come see this. Bring Hal with you."

• • • • •

They followed him at double time back to the fort and up onto the northeast rampart. The shooting practice had ceased, and the men were peering up the valley, some of them shading their eyes with their hands.

"There," said the man who had hailed them, thrusting out one arm to point.

About two hundred and twenty meters away, close in by the trees just before the valley angled to the right, a solitary horseman on a dark horse was sitting watching them.

"How long has he been there?" Damien asked.

One of the archers shrugged. "Could have been a while. We only just noticed him. Soon as we did, we stopped shooting the big bow."

Hal nodded approval. "No sense in showing him what it's capable of."

Another of the archers, one of the younger men, pushed forward eagerly. "Why don't we have a crack at him?" he said, indicating the mangler on its tripod. "I reckon I've got the ranging pretty well worked out."

Hal regarded him coldly. "As I said, no sense in showing him what the mangler can do," he said. "If you miss—and you probably will—that's all you'll achieve."

The younger man opened his mouth to protest, then thought about what the *Heron's* skirl had said and realized he was right. He stepped back, chastened.

"Where do you think he came from?" Damien asked.

Hal gestured toward the north. "Somewhere up the valley. My guess is they have a camp up there."

A concerned look crossed Damien's face. "Do you think he might have run into your scout?"

Hal was about to answer, but Ingvar, who had accompanied them, got in first.

"If he had, he'd be dead," he said flatly.

Gradually, the steep walls of the pass became lower and flatter, until eventually they were nothing more than rolling, tree-covered hills, stretching out to either side. The flat central plain remained clear, although now it was three to four hundred meters wide. No trees grew on this section, but there was coarse grass, which showed through the melting snow in tufts and patches of dark gray-green.

Lydia studied the ground as she moved northward, traveling at a steady lope. She saw numerous signs that horses had been this way—sometimes singly or in pairs, sometimes in larger groups. It became apparent that there must be a significant force of Temujai in the vicinity, and she edged closer to the fringe of the trees. It wouldn't do to be surprised in the open, she told herself.

She had barely had the thought when she heard the muted thudding of hooves on the snow-covered ground.

This wasn't a single rider, she could tell, but a party of horsemen. There was a shallow depression in the ground in front of her and she dropped flat in its cover, lying prone and gathering the cloak around her. As before, she kept the hood up and well forward, concealing the pale shape of her face.

The thudding grew louder, and a few seconds later, a group of horsemen burst into view over the next rise, riding in two files. She held her breath as they cantered diagonally across the clear ground. Fortunately, their present path would take them well away from her. Now, superimposed over the thudding of hooves, she could hear the jingle of multiple harness fittings and the grunting of the horses. The men remained silent.

Abruptly, at a hand signal from the man leading the left-hand file, the horsemen swept in a wide arc to the right, circling until they were headed back the way they had come. The sound of their hooves and harnesses gradually faded, and they disappeared back over the slight rise.

Cautiously, Lydia rose to her feet and followed them, moving closer to the sheltering trees.

"Must have been just a drill," she muttered to herself. She often spoke aloud when she was on her own. She had done so since she was a child. The sound of her own voice could be strangely comforting.

As she neared the low ridge, she dropped to all fours and scurried forward through the snow. There was always the chance that the riders had stopped once they crested the ridge, and she didn't want to take a chance on blundering into them. Slowly, she raised her eyes and peered beyond the ridge. The open ground sloped away from her and then took a sharp dogleg right, around the trees. There was no sign of the horsemen, but now she could sense something else.

A smell. A mixture of odors—horseflesh, sweat, dung and campfire smoke. The latter was harsh and acrid, and she wrinkled her nose. She recalled that Thorn had told her the eastern riders used dried horse and cattle dung to fuel their fires. The smell was sharper and harsher than woodsmoke, and it carried farther on the cold mountain air. Also, it wasn't an odor you'd expect to encounter. Woodsmoke was natural to the area. It might be caused by a lightning strike or a carelessly doused cooking fire at a small campsite. But the smoke from a dozen or more of these fires would be an unmistakable message that there were strangers in the area. She raised an eyebrow.

"They'll need to change that if they don't want us to know they're here," she said softly.

She rose to her knees and checked the land in all directions, listening as much as looking. There was no sound of horses or men moving, no low mutter of voices—although with disciplined troops like the Temujai she thought that might be unlikely. So far as she could ascertain, the way was clear. She rose from her knees and, staying in a crouch, ran smoothly to the trees on the far side. From there, she'd have a better view around the dogleg in the trail.

Her senses were stretched to near-breaking point, waiting for the slightest hint that someone was near or that she had been spotted. But there was no shout, no pounding of pursuing hooves.

Gratefully, she slid into the shadow of the trees and moved north, toward the dogleg, standing more erect now that she wasn't exposed and in the open.

She left a margin of three trees between herself and the open ground. The dappled light beneath the pines would conceal her movements effectively—if a watcher did suddenly appear.

The smell of that smoke was becoming stronger, and now she could hear the soft sounds of horses whinnying and pawing at the ground to find forage under the thin layer of snow. She must be coming up on the enemy horse lines, she realized.

Then, abruptly, she reached the corner and the enemy camp was laid out before her.

As she'd surmised, the horse lines, where the riders' horses and remounts were enclosed in a rope paddock, were closest to her.

She gasped at the vast number of horses in the rope enclosure. Moving closer, she could see that it was subdivided into four smaller areas. That made sense, she thought. It'd be hard to maintain the integrity of the enclosure over one large area. But there must have been at least five hundred horses milling around inside the ropes, pawing at the ground for grass, bumping each other and occasionally showing their teeth or even kicking as another horse infringed on what was deemed to be personal space.

Studying them further, she came to the conclusion that there were more than the initial five hundred she had estimated. There must be six or seven hundred animals milling about.

She smiled mirthlessly when she recalled an old joke of Thorn's when he had been discussing how to determine the numbers of a cavalry force. "Easy," he'd said. "Count the legs and divide by four."

Of course, with this constantly moving mass of horseflesh, it was virtually impossible to get an exact count. But even six hundred horses meant six hundred cavalrymen, and that was a seriously large force.

Then she revised her estimate. Each rider would travel with a string of two or even three horses, she realized. So that meant there were maybe two hundred men in the party—which was still a force to be reckoned with.

She edged forward so she could see more of the camp beyond the horse lines. The smoke of a score of fires—that acrid smoke she had been smelling for some time now—rose from a huddle of untidy-looking brown tents. They were rounded in shape, like large beehives, and seemed to be covered in a thick material— maybe felt, she thought. The material was placed over a framework to hold its shape and lashed in place with crisscrossing lengths of rope.

It was this lashing that gave the tents their untidy appearance. The felt was thick and shapeless and it bulged out unevenly between the strands of rope. She curled her lips dismissively at the sloppy appearance. Life on the *Heron* had accustomed her to a sense of order. Sails would be neatly folded and lashed down. Ropes would be coiled and hung on wooden pegs. Spars and oars were stowed in racks along the length of the ship, above the deck. Everything had a place, and the deck was kept clear and uncluttered, insofar as that was possible.

Then, as she had done about the horses, she revised her

opinion. The thick felt that covered the tents would be necessary to keep the interiors warm in the freezing winds of the high steppes where the Temujai roamed. Canvas or linen wouldn't suffice. And the bulky nature of the material dictated the lashing and the resultant apparent untidiness. Those same freezing winds would carry away any covering that wasn't firmly tied down.

The Temujai tents might look sloppy, she thought, but they would be effective. She also recalled that Thorn had told her these people were nomads. The tents weren't meant for temporary accommodation, as Skandians might view them. They were their permanent homes.

And while troops might endure the discomfort of a cold, drafty canvas tent while on campaign, it was a different matter altogether when they were in a permanent dwelling.

Men were moving around among the tents, and she watched them keenly. They were unarmed and seemed at ease. However, she could make out a line of pickets surrounding the entire camp, spaced fifty meters apart, each man armed with a stubby recurve bow and a quiver of arrows. They were all facing outward and were constantly on the alert. Discipline in the Temujai ranks was tight, she thought. But that was only to be expected.

She heard hoofbeats behind her, on the far side of the cleared ground, and she froze in place. She waited as a rider slowly rode past her position and turned into the camp. She thought he was the man she had seen earlier that day, heading toward the pass. He had a similar red patch on his left sleeve.

One of the men in the sentry cordon hailed him and he answered with a casual wave. Obviously, he was recognized, as he was allowed to proceed into the camp. He bypassed the horse lines and rode to a central tent, slightly larger than those surrounding it. He dismounted and went inside.

"Reporting in," muttered Lydia under her breath. "But what exactly are you reporting?"

She realized she'd spent enough time simply watching. She'd have to report back to Hal herself before long, and she'd better have something concrete to tell him. Best way to estimate the size of the Temujai force, she decided, would be to count their tents. That was easier than counting men or horses, who constantly moved around and came and went.

She began to count the strange, hump-shaped, little felt hives. They weren't pitched in any particular order or in regular rows, which would have made it easier. And her view to the far edge of the camp was restricted—by distance and the drifting smoke. She counted as high as fifty-eight and estimated that there might be a dozen more that she couldn't see clearly.

"Let's make it seventy," she told herself. "Now it's time I wasn't here."

"Seventy tents?" Hal asked.

She shrugged, not wanting to be pinned down to a definite number.

"Maybe seventy-five. Maybe fewer," she replied. "And I'd say there were five hundred horses in those paddocks." Leks gave a start of alarm at the number but she hurried on. "That doesn't mean five hundred riders."

Thorn nodded, agreeing with her. "The Temujai are always on

the move. Each rider will have a string of horses with him. Maybe two—three for the ones who can afford that many."

"How many men do you think would fit in those tents?" Hal asked.

She considered the question before answering. She had been a long way from the tents but she had seen men enter them several times. Sometimes two, but on occasion as many as three.

"Three, at a maximum," she said. "There was a command tent in the center that was larger. I saw the horseman go inside and he didn't need to crouch to get in. The others were lower."

"So, let's say three to a tent, and seventy-five tents," Leks said, a note of inquiry in his voice.

She nodded. That was a close-enough estimate.

"That's two hundred and . . ." He hesitated. Mental calculations weren't his strong point.

"Two hundred and twenty-five men," Thorn said promptly, and they all turned to look at him, more than a little surprised. He saw the looks and reacted indignantly. "What are you staring at? You don't think I can figure? I lost my hand, you know, not my brain."

Hal made a pacifying gesture. "Sorry, Thorn. It's not a skill we might have expected of you."

"We're more used to seeing you bashing enemies, not counting them," Stig put in, a wide grin on his face. Thorn sniffed, a little mollified by their apologies. In truth, he was always quite pleased to be able to catch them on the hop.

"So, let's round it up," said Leks, relieved that his own hesitation in calculating the figure had gone more or less unremarked.

"Assume there were some tents Lydia couldn't see." He glanced at her for confirmation and she nodded. "That's maybe two hundred and forty, two hundred and fifty men."

"And that tallies with the number of horses you saw," Hal said.

Thorn cleared his throat and they looked at him again. "The Temujai organize their squadrons in sixties."

Leks interrupted him. "Actually, they call them *Ulans*."

Thorn shrugged. "Whatever. So, two hundred and forty might be close to the mark."

The others pondered this figure for some seconds.

"That's more than a nuisance raid," Hal said.

"Not a full-scale invasion, however," Stig said.

"Maybe not. But it's a pretty serious attack," Leks told them. "It's been a long time since the Temujai have attacked in force like that. Maybe they think it's time they really tested our defenses. If they overrun us, they open the way for more troops to join in and launch a serious attack on Skandia."

"And if they don't," Stig said grimly, "they stand to lose a lot of men."

Leks shook his head. "That's never bothered a Tem'uj general," he said. "They have a lot of men to lose."

Hal rapped his knuckles on the table to get their attention. "The point is," he said, "I think we can expect an attack any day now. They may try to catch us before we have the manglers properly installed. That spy got a pretty good look at what they can do." He looked at Stig. "Get the men to work tonight finishing those platforms and installing the two manglers. We may need them tomorrow morning."

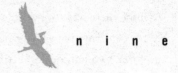

he little garrison stood to before dawn the following morning. But there was no sign of the Temujai.

They came on the second day and they came in strength. Once again, the Skandians and their Araluen allies were standing ready before the sun rose. As the first streaks of light began to paint the sky to the east, they heard the enemy approaching.

It was a rolling sound, like muted thunder: the sound of hundreds of unshod hooves on the hard-packed ground.

They rode in their *Ulans*, in two columns. There were three of them in all, each comprising sixty riders.

"Nearly two hundred of them," Damien commented to Thorn. With Hal and Stig manning the two giant crossbows, the one-handed sea wolf was in command of the Herons on the walkway. "Not as many as we thought."

"Always good to overestimate the enemy," Thorn replied. "That way, you're never disappointed. But there are a few extra."

As the last of the three *Ulans* swept round the curve in the valley, they saw a smaller group of fifteen to twenty Temujai riding on three wagons. The wagons themselves were loaded with what looked like lengths of timber.

"Scaling ladders," Damien said. All garrison commanders were thoroughly briefed on Temujai attacking tactics.

Thorn raised an eyebrow. "No sign of a battering ram?" he queried.

Damien shook his head. "Their horses are light cavalry ponies, not draft animals. They can't drag heavy siege machinery into place and the riders think such manual work is beneath them. They'll try to come over the walls. But first, they'll soften us up a little."

The three *Ulans* had changed formation. Each was now assembled in two ranks, thirty men across. They formed up in the narrow valley in a slightly staggered formation, with each squadron overlapping the one in front so that they stretched from one side to the other.

The fourth group galloped their carts up to the rear of the assembled *Ulans* and brought them to a halt. Damien turned to Lydia, who was a few meters away, watching with interest.

"Keep an eye out for the sharpshooters," he told her. "They wear a red insignia on their shoulder. Usually, they hang back behind the rear ranks."

She nodded, her eyes narrowed to slits as she sought the expert archers whose task it was to shoot down the enemy commanders. So far, she could see no sign. They heard a shouted order and saw a ripple of movement from the squadron on their far left as sixty arrows were drawn from quivers and laid on the bowstrings. Then another shout saw the bows rise. The defenders could hear the creaking sound as the strings were drawn back. There was no command to shoot. Each archer released in his own time as he found his aim. But that tended to coincide with the timing of his comrades. The men on the ramparts heard the slithering *twang* of multiple bow releases.

"Down!" shouted Leks, and the defenders crouched behind the pine log wall. A few seconds later, there was a rattle as some arrows slammed into the logs, and a chorus of whistling hisses as others passed over the top of the wall, angling down to bury themselves in the courtyard.

"Anyone hit?" called Leks. There was no answering cry.

Thorn grinned to himself. He always enjoyed a battle. "Call out if you've been killed," he ordered, and there was a chorus of laughter from the men crouched along the walkway.

In the valley, a second *Ulan* nocked and drew arrows, releasing in another extended volley. There were more rattling crashes against the pine logs, more hissing projectiles passing overhead. Then, almost immediately, the third *Ulan* released and more arrows flew.

"They're not hitting anyone," Thorn observed.

Leks nodded grimly. "Maybe not. But they're keeping us pinned down. Look." He peered through the gap between two of the pointed logs. Thorn followed his line of sight and saw that the three wagons were moving forward, passing between the left-hand *Ulan* and the sheer stone wall of the canyon. As he watched, Leks's hand gripped his shoulder and pulled him down, just as the first

Temujai squadron shot again. An arrow whipped through the small gap where Thorn's head had been a few seconds earlier.

"Don't stay up too long," the commander cautioned him.

Thorn smiled gratefully. "They're quite good, aren't they?" he said, taking note of Leks's instruction to keep his observations short.

"They do tend to hit what they aim at," the gray-haired commander told him.

Farther along the rampart, Damien was shouting instructions. He could hear the rumble and rattle of the carts and knew they'd be in position before too long—unless he did something about it.

"Bring up the shields!" he ordered, and his archers complied. There were a dozen two-meter-high timber shields ready on the walkway behind them. The Araluen troops seized hold of them and erected them along a section of the rampart, projecting above the pine logs and leaving a small gap between each shield.

"Third squadron!" Damien ordered. "Take a look."

The first squadron was just drawing back its arrows for another volley as a dozen archers peered quickly over the rampart between the shields, noting the position of the third *Ulan* and committing it to memory. They heard the multiple *slither-slap* as the first *Ulan* released. By the time their volley arrived, slamming into logs and timber shields, the archers were safely below the rampart once more.

More hissing and rattling. A chance arrow found its way through the narrow gap between the shields and sent one of the archers flying, crying out in pain as he hit the timber floor of the walkway.

"Replacement!" Damien yelled, and one of the men in reserve

stepped forward to take the wounded man's place, unslinging his massive war bow as he did and crouching down in cover.

Another volley hissed and rattled around the defenders. Then Damien shouted his orders.

"Right-hand side. At the third squadron. Shoot!"

*Shoot* was the command for the archers to release in their own time, as they found a target. *Right-hand side* told them which side of the shields they should emerge from. Damien would vary that with each shot to keep the Temujai guessing. Now, as his men rose from their crouched positions, drawing back the yard-long arrows until the feathers touched their cheeks, he joined them in one of the gaps, drawing back his own bow, sighting and releasing almost immediately.

There was an extended *slither-thump* sound as a dozen archers all released within two seconds of one another.

Damien remained standing to watch the result, although he stayed back a meter or so from the gap between the shields. The Temujai formation had just raised their own bows when the volley arrived, hissing down out of the sky like a dozen venomous snakes.

Eight of the arrows struck home, and eight riders in the front rank were pitched from their saddles by the impact. Some lay still as they hit the ground. Others tried to crawl away through the legs of the riders in the rank behind them. The suddenly riderless horses were panicked and they reared and kicked, buffeting their neighbors, who turned on them in bad temper, snapping at them with their big yellow teeth and spinning to kick out with their hind legs.

As a result, the Temujai volley was disrupted, and most of the arrows went wide. Even worse, the disciplined formation was broken up as the horses plunged and reared and tried to avoid one another. Their riders sawed angrily at the reins, trying to bring the beasts under control again. While this was happening, Damien directed a second volley at the disorganized riders.

This time, six more men were hit, and confusion among the ranks became widespread. The *Ulan* lost all semblance of discipline. Their commander, sensing that he would never restore order while they were under such an accurate barrage, shouted a command and the troop wheeled to their right, forming into two files once more—although without their previous precision. They galloped away from the battle to reform, leaving ten of their number on the ground. The other fallen riders hobbled and limped after their companions.

At that moment, the first of the ladders slammed against the log walls of the fort and the yelling men below began to scramble up them. They had taken advantage of the ongoing duel between the Temujai and Araluen archers to move into position at the base of the walls, scrambling through the protective ditch with their ladders. Now, as they started to swarm up, the first *Ulan* galloped forward to the ditch and dismounted, drawing their curved sabers as they ran to join their comrades on the ladders.

The Temujai had practiced this maneuver repeatedly over the previous week. The remaining two *Ulans* maintained a withering barrage on the tops of the walls, keeping the defenders crouched below the tops of the logs and allowing their comrades to climb the ladders. They were expert shots, and most of their arrows went over the top of the wall. A few fell short and struck their own men, plucking them from the ladders and sending them screaming to the ground below.

But to a Temujai commander, that was regrettable but inevitable. War was war, after all.

As the first of the dismounted riders swung themselves over the log wall, the arrow storm was lifted and the defenders were able to fight back. But the delay had been too long and the first half dozen Temujai swarmed over the wall, hacking and stabbing around them. They came from two ladders placed close together and they rapidly joined ranks to form a wedge, driving into the defenders.

"Let's get 'em!"

The traditional battle cry of the Heron brotherband rang out over the struggling men, and Thorn led a counter-wedge of steel into the attackers.

Even though three of their most fearsome warriors—Hal, Stig and Ingvar—were absent, stationed at the two shooting platforms, they were still an irresistible force. Thorn's mighty club smashed down on the leader of the Temujai wedge. The man's knees buckled and he fell, to be trampled underfoot by Thorn, then Ulf and Wulf as they followed his lead. The massive club swung in a horizontal arc and sent another of the slightly built riders flying. Jesper, Stefan and Edvin followed in the wake of the twins and the bellowing one-armed sea wolf who led them as they drove the Temujai troops back to the rampart. The Temujai were small men, slightly built. The Skandians were heavy and muscular. They shoved the enemy troops bodily back over the wall.

Elsewhere, Leks and his men had held the attackers at bay,

pushing the ladders sideways with long pikes, causing the men climbing them to crash to the ground.

Damien and his archers, at the eastern end of the rampart, away from the scaling ladders, engaged the two remaining *Ulans* in a deadly archery duel.

On the western shooting platform, Hal had so far not taken any part in the battle. He saw how Damien's tactics had disrupted one of the *Ulans*. Now, as the attackers were bundled back over the ramparts, he sensed that the deadly storm of arrows directed at Damien's men would recommence.

"Let's stir them up," he told Ingvar. The mangler was already loaded, and he swung it toward the second *Ulan*. He crouched over the sights, sheltering behind the solid pinewood shield that was fitted to the front of the mangler. Behind him, Ingvar stooped in the cover of the rampart around the platform.

Hal let out a piercing whistle to attract Stig's attention. His first mate was manning the mangler on the east side of the valley. He was on his own. He was strong enough to cock the mangler himself, and Hal hadn't wanted to weaken the defenders on the wall any more than necessary. As he caught Stig's attention, he gestured toward the two drawn-up *Ulans* as they shot volley after volley at the wall. Hal indicated that he would take the group on the left. Stig waved assent and bent over his own sights.

Hal's mangler was at a slight angle to the ranks of horsemen. That was all to the good, he thought. The bolt would plow through them, taking down two or even three of them.

*SLAM!*

"Reload!" he called to Ingvar, not waiting to watch the bolt's flight. Then he saw a sudden commotion in the front rank of the *Ulan* as a rider was plucked bodily from his saddle by the huge dart. Almost instantaneously, the rider behind him to the left reared up in his stirrups as the projectile hit him, smashing through his light leather armor.

The two horses, highly strung creatures, reared wildly, lashing out with their front hooves as their riders were so violently displaced. That set their neighbors rearing and bucking as well. As they were panicking, Hal let fly with another bolt, aiming farther down the front rank.

Meanwhile, Stig's first shot slammed into the right-hand *Ulan*, causing more panic and confusion among its ranks.

"Give me a fire bolt," Hal said as Ingvar heaved the twin cocking handles back. The big warrior had been about to load with a normal bolt. He stooped now and took one of the fire bolts from the bin beside him. He already had a handful of tinder smoldering in a brass bowl at the rear of the platform. He dipped a wax taper into it, blew on the burning coals until a flame licked up on the taper, then looked at Hal, receiving a nod to tell him that he was ready.

He placed the taper against the fuse and waited until he saw it spitting and smoking.

"She's burning," he said. Hal aligned the mangler on his target, raising the point of aim to compensate for the extra weight of the clay warhead, and released.

*SLAM!*

In the uncertain early morning light, they couldn't see the smoke trail behind the bolt. But they could see the projectile curving out and up, then angling down. It plunged into the middle of the disrupted troop of horsemen. There was a short pause, then . . .

*WHOOF!*

A tongue of red flame, accompanied by a pillar of black smoke, erupted from the middle of the *Ulan*.

It was too much for the demoralized riders and their horses. Confused and on the verge of panic, they broke, spinning in all directions, fighting to get clear of the ranks around them and escape back up the valley. At first, it was a trickle of men, then the trickle became a flood as the entire *Ulan* retreated. They collided with their comrades from the decimated third squadron, who had only just managed to recover some semblance of order. Both squadrons now turned tail and ran. Their companions, seeing them deserting, spun in place and galloped after them.

At least two score of their number remained on the field of battle, unmoving.

hey've gone, you say?" Erak asked, and Hal nodded.

"Lydia went out scouting the following day," he said. "Their camp was deserted and they'd gone. She tracked them for a few kilometers. They were heading northeast."

"Back where they came from," Erak mused. He rubbed his beard thoughtfully. "But for how long?"

"I don't think they'll try another attack at Fort Ragnak in a hurry," Hal said. "They lost too many men and they didn't come close to breaking through."

"You said they got over the wall," Erak reminded him.

Hal shrugged. "A few of them. And Thorn and the boys threw them back almost immediately. The Temujai are simply not equipped to attack a fortified position like that. They don't have the equipment or the tactics for it. They prefer to fight in open country, using their speed and maneuverability and their bows. Arrows aren't a lot of use against a log wall."

They were sitting by the fire in Erak's private chamber. The booty and plunder that he'd amassed over years of raiding was festooned around the room. Most prominent was the crystal chandelier he had "acquired" in Gallica years ago. The ceiling of the Great Hall was too low to accommodate it properly, so it was draped down the wall and across a table, where its myriad twinkling facets caught the firelight.

It was a week since the battle at Serpent Pass. After Lydia's reconnaissance had revealed that the Temujai had departed, Hal and the Heron brotherband had made their way back down from the mountains to Hallasholm, where he reported to Erak.

"The two manglers came as a big shock to them," Hal continued. "The fire bolts were particularly effective."

"But they'll be prepared for them next time," Erak said.

Hal frowned. "You keep assuming they'll try again."

Erak took a long pull at the tankard of ale on the table in front of him. Out of deference to Hal, he had served the young skirl coffee. But Erak was an old-time sea wolf, and ale was his drink of choice.

"They'll try again," he said. "They have to. Skandia is blocking their way. They plan to conquer the western world, and we're the key to their success. They need to reach the sea and they need to get control of our ships. Then they can move on Gallica, Teutlandt, Araluen and the rest."

"Why is it so important to them?" Hal asked. "They've

conquered thousands of square kilometers of country in the east. Isn't that enough?"

Erak shook his head. "With an aggressive, warlike nation like the Temujai, it's never enough. They need to keep conquering new territories. Maybe it's a religious thing, I don't know. But I do know that they'll keep probing, looking for a way to break through to the sea. And that means coming through us."

"But even if they did fight their way into Skandia, we'd never hand over our ships to them. And if they captured the ships, they'd need us to sail them."

"They don't realize that. They're used to having conquered nations submit to them and do what they're told. And if they don't get our ships, there's always the Sonderland fleet."

The Sonderland ships were big, cumbersome, slab-sided vessels—unlike the swift, agile Skandian wolfships. But they were probably better suited to transporting large numbers of mounted warriors across the sea.

"And the Sonderlanders would have no qualms about helping them," Hal mused. Like all Skandians, he had a low opinion of their western neighbors—an opinion that had been proved correct over many years.

"Exactly. So, the fact remains that they'll keep trying to break through to our coastal plain," Erak said.

Hal shrugged. "They can try all they like at Serpent Pass," he said. "It'll simply cost them more and more men."

Erak was quiet for a few seconds. Then he changed the subject. "You say the Araluens did well in the fight?" he asked.

Hal nodded emphatically. "They were invaluable," he said.

"They're every bit as accurate as the Temujai, and their bows hit a little bit harder. It's strange. The Temujai rely on the bow as their principal weapon, and they seem accustomed to cutting down enemy troops with showers of arrows. But they don't know how to cope when they're handed back some of their own medicine. Thorn says they've rarely faced archers before."

"I imagine it's not easy when you're used to standing off a couple of hundred paces, shooting your enemy to pieces, if someone does the same thing back to you. It's good to know that. The treaty with the Araluens is due for renewal next year. I'd been wondering if it's worth it."

"It's worth it," Hal assured him. "Just the knowledge that the border is defended by archers will hold them at bay."

Erak drained the last of his ale and turned to the door, about to call for a refill. Then he changed his mind. His life these days was a mostly sedentary one, and he'd begun to soften around the waistline. He didn't mind being bulky, so long as the bulk was muscle. But he was getting to an age where the muscle was being replaced by fat.

"So, the question remains, where will they try next?" he said softly, almost to himself.

Hal frowned at the thought. "Where else is there?" he asked. "Serpent Pass is the only viable route into Skandia, isn't it? At least if they're looking to move large numbers of troops."

Erak rose and moved to the map of Skandia and its neighbors on the wall. He studied it for several seconds, then replied with an apparent non sequitur.

"Is the *Heron* ready for sea?"

During the winter months, Hal and his crew, like most of the Skandian brotherbands, had kept themselves occupied refitting and repairing their ship. They had been interrupted by the expedition to Fort Ragnak, but the work was mostly completed.

"A day's work will see her ready. There's some rigging that needs replacing," Hal said. "Do you have something in mind?"

He couldn't resist a certain thrill of anticipation. The Oberjarl had fallen into the habit of calling on the Heron brotherband when he had a special mission to be carried out. It made for an interesting life for Hal and his crew.

Erak didn't reply immediately. He tapped a point on the coastline some leagues to the west of Hallasholm.

"Ice River," he said finally.

Hal rose and moved to stand beside him at the map. He knew where Ice River was, of course. It was a large river that flowed down from the mountains through a valley before making its way to the sea. Few wolfships had ever ventured far up the river. As the name implied, it was iced over for at least half the year, and there were several steep, white-water rapids that were deemed to be unnavigable.

"I've been thinking," Erak said, "where else could the Temujai try to break through and make it to the sea? It struck me that Ice River might be such a place."

"Hard to say," Hal replied. "I've never seen it—beyond the entry to the sea. I've sailed past a few times, but that's all."

"Precisely," Erak answered. "We know very little about it because nobody has ever explored it. But if I look at it on a map, it looks as if it could be a viable route down from the mountains. The river has carved out a valley and it's possible you could get men and horses down here."

He traced his finger down the narrow bank at the western side of the river.

"Looking at it on a map and actually making your way down are two different matters, of course," Hal said. "Particularly if you're trying to move an army down there. These three steep sections are probably impassable."

He indicated three sections on the map where the banks narrowed and the mapmaker's notations indicated that the river ran steeply down the mountain face.

"Still, I'm thinking that if I were the Temujai leader and I looked at this map, I might see this as a possible way to break through to the coast." Hal looked skeptical, but Erak continued. "And the Temujai have a history of getting through places that other people have thought to be impassable."

He traced his finger up the river valley to the mountain plateau high above it, where the map indicated unknown land.

"Nobody's ever explored up here," he said. "But that's where the Temujai hold sway."

"You want us to go up there?" Hal said, a slightly incredulous note in his voice. "We can't sail up a mountain."

"You'd need to make a portage at each of these three points," Erak said, indicating the steepest sections of the valley. "Each one is less than a kilometer long and there's a track off to the side where you could drag the ship." A portage meant hauling the ship out of the water and dragging it bodily overland. It was backbreaking work, and Skandians loathed it with a passion.

"The rest of the way you should be able to row, once the ice has cleared."

He glanced at the young skirl. The stubborn set of Hal's jaw told Erak all he needed to know about Hal's opinion of the plan. He continued, in a more placatory tone. "The thing is, Hal, we *need* to know if it's a possible route down from the mountains. We've always assumed that it's impassable. But these days, we can't afford that assumption. If the Temujai are cut off from Serpent Pass, I have to know if there's another way they can come down from the mountains. This river valley may well be a dagger aimed at Skandia's heart.

"And personally, I'd like to know where the river goes after it reaches the top of the plateau. I'd like to know what the countryside is like up there. Is it tree-covered? Or do the grass plains extend this far west and south? If that's the case, the Sha'shan would find it a lot easier to assemble his army up there."

"The Sha'shan?" Hal asked. The term wasn't a familiar one.

Erak explained. "The Temujai ruler. *Shan* means leader, so *Sha'shan* means leader of leaders, or ultimate leader."

Erak shifted uncomfortably. Usually, when he had a mission for Hal and his men, it was based on something more definite than a vague feeling of unease. And it was usually a little more exciting than an order to haul their ship bodily up a mountain.

"I'm sorry to load you up with this one, Hal," he said. "But I need a pair of eyes I can depend on. And I'd like Thorn's opinion of the terrain in the Ice River Valley. I really need to know if we should defend against a possible attack there."

Thorn was an experienced warrior. His opinion of whether or

not the Temujai could bring troops down the Ice River Valley would be a valuable one. Thorn didn't look at a problem and say "too hard." He looked at ways a problem could be overcome.

Hal was silent, staring at the map, trying to see in his mind's eye the rough, overgrown terrain that was indicated by the bland markings and notations.

"Can you get your hilfmann to make me a copy of this chart?" he asked.

Erak heaved a silent sigh of relief. It hadn't been likely that Hal would refuse the mission. But it had always been a possibility. Erak saw now that he was studying the first of the portage points.

"That's another reason I'm asking you to do this," he said. "Your ship is the smallest in the fleet, so it'll be easier to handle getting it through the tight spots on the portages."

Hal nodded, imagining the difficulty in hauling a fifteen-meter wolfship through the twists and turns in a mountain track. With the *Heron* it would be difficult. With a full-sized wolfship, nigh on impossible.

"I'd better warn the lads," he said. "They'll be delighted to hear how easy it will be."

Erak let him have the last word. He thought he owed him that.

# PART TWO

# ICE RIVER

It was good to be at sea again.

There was a fresh wind blowing offshore and *Heron* bowled along at an impressive speed, rising and falling as she swooped over the waves like a gull. Occasionally, an out-of-phase wave would smash into her bow as she was still swooping down over the previous wave's back. She'd smash into the new wall of water before she could soar over it, and silver spray would shower over the deck.

As ever, Hal was exulting in the sheer feeling of the ship as she sped along the coast. To him, she was more than an inanimate mass of wood and canvas. She was a living thing. He could feel the life in the rhythmic movement of the deck beneath his feet, the slight vibrations through the tiller as the sea pressed against it, trying to resist his controlling hand. He could almost believe that she spoke to him. The fin keel had a slight vibration where it passed through the watertight seal in the keel box. It set up a low-pitched hum that reverberated through the hull, using the hollow wooden structure as a sounding box. He knew it was a fault somewhere in the structure of the keel box, but to him it was a happy mistake. He laughed out loud.

"This is better than riding a horse," Stig said, standing a meter away from him and leaning back against the sternpost.

"Better than walking too," Thorn put in, from his position a little for'ard of the steering platform.

Hal grinned happily at his two friends. "We may as well enjoy it for now," he said. "We'll be rowing before too long."

"*We?*" Thorn repeated, raising one eyebrow derisively. Hal, as the skirl, wouldn't have to take part in the rowing, although his friends knew that he often did, handing the tiller over to Edvin to give one of the other rowers a spell. On this trip, however, as they were heading into unfamiliar territory, he would probably stay at the tiller himself, ready to respond to any surprises that they might encounter.

A wave burst over the bow, and silver spray glittered in the sun as it showered down over the ship. Kloof barked and snapped at the flying water, her massive jaws snapping together like a bear trap as she tried to catch the elusive salt spray. She was beside Hal, and her heavy tail thumped his leg as she swept it back and forth. It was too ponderous an action to be described as mere wagging.

"Settle down, girl," Hal told her. She slammed her tail into his leg several more times. Obviously, she was affected by the holiday atmosphere that had gripped them all. Hal glanced at the sky. It was bright blue, with white clouds scudding high overhead. For the moment, the weather was fine, but inland, over the mountains, he could see dark clouds gathering. They could well be in for a late snowfall, he thought, even though winter was behind them.

"There's the river!" Jesper called from his perch on the bowpost lookout. Hal leaned out and craned down to see over the starboard bow. The green coastline was only a few kilometers off the starboard side as they ran parallel to it. Looking ahead about a kilometer, he could see a white line of breaking waves in close to the land. That would be the river mouth. There would undoubtedly be a bar of some kind there, formed by sand carried downriver and out to sea, where it piled up in an obstacle. That would be where the waves were breaking, he thought. They'd need to reconnoiter before they tried to go inland, making sure they could find a safe way around or over the bar.

"Breakers!" Jesper called, confirming Hal's judgment. Hal called back an acknowledgment and eased the tiller over, angling the ship in toward the coast. Ulf and Wulf adjusted the sail accordingly.

They skimmed in toward the land. Once they were a few hundred meters from the breaking waves, Hal ordered the crew to bring the sail down and switch to oars. For the moment, they used four oars only, with Ulf, Wulf, Stefan and Ingvar manning them.

"Bring her in easily," Hal ordered them. "I want to see how deep the water is over the sandbar." He gestured to Stig to take the tiller. "I'm going for'ard," he said.

The oarsmen brought the ship in parallel to the breakers, about forty meters out. They crept along the line of the breaking waves, and Hal stepped up onto the for'ard bulwark, holding on to a stay and peering over the side at the green water covering the bar. The tide was halfway in, and there was plenty of water over the sand— at least for a small ship like the *Heron*. He moved back to the steering platform and took the tiller once more.

"Plenty of water," he told Stig. "At least two meters below us." He nodded to Thorn. "Bring up the fin keel, Thorn," he said. The bladelike fin jutted down a meter below the keel. Once it was raised, the *Heron* needed little more than a meter of water. "We'll ride a wave in just to make sure," he told the others, and took the ship out in a long arc to approach the sandbar at right angles. "Thorn, Stig, on the oars, please."

The two extra oarsmen scrambled down to the rowing benches, sliding their long white-oak oars out through the oarlocks.

"Easy all," Hal ordered, and the rowers rested on their oars, the ship rising and falling gently as the waves passed under her keel. Hal glanced around, making sure everything was ready. Lydia crouched with Kloof on the port side of the ship. She smiled at him as she caught his eye. Edvin moved aft to stand beside Hal. He knew that when they caught a wave over the sandbar, the ship would need to keep its stern down. Jesper left his post on the lookout and moved aft as well.

"Give way," Hal ordered, and the rowers bent to their oars, heaving the little ship forward. Stig called the stroke, setting a rapid pace. Hal felt the tiller come alive in his hands as the water rushed past it. He straightened the ship's course so that they were heading directly toward the sandbar, swooping and sliding once more as the waves passed under the ship. When they were twenty meters from the bar, he glanced over his shoulder and saw a wave building behind them.

"Now pull!" he called, and the rowers heaved on the oars with renewed energy. The little ship shot ahead. Her stern came up as the wave gathered beneath it.

"Pull!" shouted Hal, and as the rowers redoubled their efforts, the ship rode up onto the wave and accelerated, her bow wave slicing high on either side as she knifed down into the water ahead of her, stern high and bow down.

"Belay rowing!" Hal yelled, as he saw they were well and truly gripped by the wave. "Everyone aft!"

The crew were ready for the order. They slid their oars inboard and scrambled aft, huddling together in the stern section of the rowing well. The sudden change in weight pushed the stern down and the bow up.

Jesper let out a whoop of exhilaration as the ship planed forward, passing over the lighter green water that covered the sandbar and slowly losing speed as the wave died away and she slid into the deeper water behind the bar. Hal felt a grin spreading over his own face. Sometimes this life could be a lot of fun, he thought. He glanced around and saw Lydia. The girl was pale-faced and gripping tightly to a cleat set in the deck. Her knuckles were white, and he realized, with some surprise, that she had been nervous as they rode the wave across the bar. He shrugged. Lydia was relatively new to ships and the sea, whereas he and the rest of the Herons had spent their lives afloat since they were toddlers.

She caught his eye and shook her head. He grinned at her.

"We weren't in any danger," he told her.

Lydia let go a deep breath that she had been holding. "So you say," she replied. But she was prepared to believe him. Nervous she might have been, but she trusted Hal's seamanship and skill implicitly. She knew there were things that might bring her heart to her mouth—like that sudden headlong rush down the face of the wave—but as long as Hal was at the tiller and in control, she had faith that things would turn out all right.

"Oars," Hal said briefly, and the six rowers scrambled for'ard again, taking their positions in the rowing well and waiting while Stig called the stroke. Then they all pulled at once and the *Heron* gathered way again, heading for the small beach at the western side of the river.

The river was about eighty meters wide here, with a low, flat bank on the western side and steep hills rising on the eastern side, behind a narrow section of flat land no more than three meters wide.

"Oars in," Hal called as they closed on the beach and steered the little ship in on an angle, running her prow up to grate on the coarse sand.

"We'll have a meal and coffee," he told Edvin. "Then we'll head inland. Stig, take Ulf and Wulf and make sure we're alone."

His tall first mate nodded and gestured to the twins to get their weapons and follow him.

"I'll go with you," Lydia said, slinging her quiver of darts over one shoulder. Stig nodded agreement. Lydia had keen eyes, and she was an expert tracker. Even if there was no current danger, she'd be able to tell if strangers had been on the beach or among the trees in the past few days. The area seemed deserted, but it was wise to make sure.

The four of them headed off into the trees that fringed the beach, staying several meters apart so as not to make a bunched-up target. Edvin busied himself lighting a fire. The rest of the crew stood ready, their weapons close to hand, until Stig and the others returned.

"All clear," Stig reported. "Lydia says there's been nobody here in the past week."

"All right, everyone. Let's relax for an hour. We've got plenty of rowing ahead of us."

An hour later, rested and refreshed, they shoved off from the beach and began to row inland.

The river current was strong and Hal had all six oars run out. The crew worked steadily at the oars, with the spare rowers spelling two of the oarsmen every hour.

Lydia moved to stand beside Hal at the tiller, and Kloof flumped down on the deck with a great exhalation of breath, her nose resting on her two forepaws, her eyes constantly moving as she watched Hal, making sure he didn't suddenly disappear.

The river had narrowed, which served to increase the current. It was now barely fifty meters wide—not wide enough to make it worthwhile raising sail and tacking into the wind.

"What's the point," Jesper asked of no one in particular, but making sure that everyone could hear him, "of having a skirl who's a brilliant inventor if he can't figure out a way to sail directly into the wind?"

Ulf was mystified by the comment. He was, at times, a little slow on the uptake. "How would you sail directly into the wind?" he asked.

Jesper shrugged. "Don't ask me. I'm not a brilliant inventor."

Hal chose to ignore the comment. He was studying the river. There were large floes of melting ice rushing downstream with the current. Occasionally, when he couldn't avoid them, they rumbled loudly against the hull as they brushed past. They were soft and mushy and offered no risk to the ship, but he kept clear of them as far as possible.

"The ice must be melting farther upriver," he told Lydia. "In winter, the river is frozen over."

She leaned over the rail to watch a large mass of slushy ice drifting past them. "Could you bring troops down the frozen river?" she asked.

Hal considered the question, then shook his head. "The ice never gets that thick this far down. It seems solid on the surface, but the water is still flowing under it—it's not solid enough to support large numbers of horses and men."

A few soft flakes of snow drifted down around them, melting instantly when they touched their jackets or faces. He looked up. The black clouds that he had observed earlier had moved closer to the coast. He pulled his collar up, shivering as several snowflakes found their way down his collar and instantly melted into freezing water.

He checked the sandglass beside the steering platform. The last few grains were running out, and he turned it over.

"Change rowers," he ordered. Ulf and Wulf, who were due for relief, handed over their oars to Stig and Ingvar. Instantly, as the two new rowers took up the stroke, Hal felt the ship speed up. She also began to veer slightly to port. Ingvar was on the starboard side.

"Ease up a little, Ingvar," he cautioned. Sometimes the massive young man didn't realize his own prodigious strength. Even with Thorn on the bench opposite him, he could still cause the bow to veer. Ingvar grunted and reduced the length of his stroke. The ship ran true again, and Hal could relax the countermanding pressure on the tiller.

Lydia smiled fondly at the big warrior. "I sometimes think he could row this ship by himself," she said.

Hal nodded. "I'm sure he could."

Ulf and Wulf lay back on the deck, their backs propped comfortably against the folded port-side sail. They had an hour before they were due to relieve another pair on the oars. Most crew members would have been content to use the time to rest and relax. But the twins found it hard to sit quietly for any length of time—particularly if they were sitting together. Neither of them could ever resist goading the other.

Ulf leaned back his head and let some of the snowflakes drop onto his tongue. They melted instantly. Then he held out his hand and caught two. Against the touch of his warm skin, they quickly turned to water. He studied the two small separate pools of water on his palm as they coalesced into one.

"I've heard that no two snowflakes are identical," he said finally.

Wulf caught two flakes on his own palm, watching as they melted. "These two are," he said.

Ulf gave him a pained look. "Well, they are *now*," he said. "But they're not snowflakes anymore. They're little puddles— like rain."

"They looked the same when they were snowflakes," Wulf said. He caught several more, holding them out for inspection before they too melted almost immediately to water. "Like these two."

"But they're not snowflakes anymore either," Ulf said.

Wulf shrugged. "They were," he said. "And when they were, they looked the same. Identical even."

Ulf shook his head. "No. They didn't," he said, with the firm conviction of someone who knows he's right.

"You didn't see them. I did," Wulf told him. "And I tell you, they were identical."

"But if you were able to look at them very closely—"

"Which I was," Wulf interrupted.

"You would have seen that they were not the same," Ulf continued, not allowing his brother's protest to divert him. There was silence for a few moments, then Wulf decided to challenge from a different direction.

"Where did you hear this?" he asked, and when his brother didn't reply immediately, he continued. "You said, 'I heard that no two snowflakes are the same.' Where did you hear that?"

"From a famous philosopher," Ulf replied.

Wulf inclined his head to look at him more closely. He wasn't aware that his brother knew any famous philosophers, let alone spent his time talking to them.

"And his name was?" he asked, letting the question hang in the silence that followed.

Finally, Ulf replied. "Actually, it was my mam who told me."

"If that's the same woman who's my mam," Wulf said, "she's no famous philosopher. She's a great cook and an expert seamstress. But not a famous philosopher."

"I didn't say she was. She heard it from a famous philosopher. And she told me."

"And who was this famous philosopher? What was his name?"

"Aha!" Ulf crowed. "You're showing your male prejudice there. Who said the philosopher was a man?" He smiled, happy to have caught his brother out.

Under his breath, Wulf cursed himself for falling for the old trick. But he refused to be diverted. "Well then, what is *her* name?" he asked.

"It was Old Gert," Ulf said triumphantly.

Old Gert was an elderly widow who lived in a ramshackle hut just above the high-water mark on the western fringe of Hallasholm. She collected driftwood and odds and ends that were washed up with the tide. Young children used to follow after her and tease her until Erak banned the practice. She was a kindly old soul, and it offended Erak to see the children behaving so badly. Still they persisted until the day when he caught three of them at it, and slinging them under his massive arms and carrying them, shrieking, back up the beach, he set them to cleaning out Hallasholm's numerous cesspits. After that, the teasing stopped.

"Gert-by-Sea?" Wulf asked, using the title by which she was most often known.

Ulf nodded emphatically. "That's the one."

"When were you at Gert's home by the sea?"

"I wasn't. I said she told Mam. Mam had taken her a batch of hot honey cakes for her afternoon snack and she told her about the snowflakes. Then Mam told me."

"She never mentioned it to me," Wulf said.

Ulf smiled, delighted that Wulf had walked into another verbal trap. "That's because she loves me more than you."

This nonsense, diverting as it might be for the twins, could have gone on and on, but Stig interrupted, his voice cutting over the twins'.

"Stefan!" he called.

Stefan half turned, without breaking the rhythm of his stroke. "What is it, Stig?"

"You were doing impersonations the other day. I've got a new one for you."

Stefan looked at Thorn. The one-armed sea wolf was hauling on his oar, using his left hand and his wooden hook clamped around the butt end. He raised one eyebrow in warning.

"I'm not sure about that, Stig," Stefan said warily. "What do you want me to impersonate?"

"Can you do the sound of two idiots babbling?" Stig asked. Thorn turned away to hide a grin.

Stefan frowned. "What does that sound like?"

Stig jerked his head at the twins. "Like those two."

They continued rowing through the rest of the afternoon, thankfully without the accompaniment of Ulf and Wulf discussing snowflakes and philosophers. The twins had learned, through bitter experience, how far they could push their shipmates' patience with these discussions, and Stig's request to Stefan served as a warning that the limit had been reached.

The snow continued to fall, and as the sun dropped behind the mountains to the west, Hal began to search for a landing place.

He found one when they reached the first of the portages—where the river flowed rapidly down a steep chute. The force of the water, contained by a narrower section of banks, hurled ice floes down the slope. The eastern bank continued to be steep and difficult. The western bank was wider, but the slope was just as steep. Studying the terrain, Hal could see a narrow track winding off to the left, between the trees.

He brought the ship in to the bank, grounding the stem in the fine gravel.

"Stig. Lydia," he said, and gestured to the path leading off among the trees. Stig and Lydia dropped lightly to the ground beside the bow and headed off into the trees to reconnoiter. The rest of the crew remained on board, and they remained alert. As ever, their hands never strayed far from their weapons. This was unfamiliar territory, and the trees could conceal any number of enemies.

Or none.

Fifteen minutes later, the two scouts returned. Stig gave Hal a reassuring wave.

"All clear," he said.

Hal relaxed. "All right, everyone, we'll camp here. Edvin, get a fire going. Jesper and Stefan, you can collect wood for him. We'll post sentries tonight, and tomorrow we'll get started on the portage."

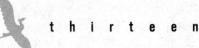

he following morning, Hal surveyed the track they would use for the portage.

It ran up the hill, twenty meters inland from the riverbank, where the slope was slightly easier. It was narrow and it twisted and turned as it made its way up the hill. As Erak had suggested, it would have been impossible to haul a full-size wolfship up to the next level.

"Obviously," Hal said to Lydia, who had accompanied him, "someone's come up this way sometime in the past. But there's no record of it."

The crew set to work lightening the ship, removing all excess weight. The two yardarms and sails came out, and all the oars. The food and other stores were piled on the bank, and Hal allowed the large freshwater tank under the deck to drain away. This close to the river, there was no shortage of drinking water. By the time they had finished, the ship had lost about two-thirds of its deadweight and they were able to haul it onto the bank with relative ease.

Hauling it up the track would be another matter. But Hal had thought of that. He took a set of blocks—wooden pulleys—from the ship and went inland to the beginning of the track. He peered uphill and picked out two solid-looking trees, one either side of the track, thirty meters up the slope, where the track angled to the right. He attached a block to the base of each and ran ropes through them, leading the rope back down to where the ship would be positioned. Instead of shoving the ship up the hill with brute strength, the Herons would be able to haul it up using the ropes. Using two ropes and pulleys would serve to keep the ship moving straight up the hill, rather than being pulled off to the side as it got closer to the top. And the mechanical advantage of the pulleys would virtually halve the effort they would need to exert.

It wouldn't be easy, of course. But it would be a lot easier for the small party than if they had to rely on sheer muscle power.

When he was ready, the crew heaved and shoved the lightened hull until they had it positioned at the bottom of the track. Hal tied the two ends of the ropes to the bow post. But before he set the crew to work, he gestured to the pile of equipment on the riverbank.

"Get your weapons and keep them handy," he said. "We can leave the food and spars and sails where they are for the time being. We'll come back to fetch them later. Lydia?" The girl looked up expectantly, waiting to hear his orders. "Scout the hill for a couple of hundred meters." He jerked his thumb uphill. "I don't want anyone to surprise us when we're busy hauling the boat up."

She nodded and moved swiftly up the track, passing out of their sight when she rounded the point where it angled right. As she went, she moved off the narrow, cleared path and stepped in among the trees. All her senses were alert—sight, hearing and, in the light of her experience at Serpent Pass, her sense of smell as well. If there were Temujai hidden among the trees, that might well be the first she knew of them.

She made her way to the top of the portage track, a distance of some two hundred meters, stopping at the level ground above it. There was no sign of any enemy. She waited several minutes, concealed in the shadows under the trees, watching and listening. Eventually, she was reassured that there was nobody nearby and made her way back down the slope to where the Herons waited.

"All clear," she told Hal. He stooped and took hold of the left-hand rope, gesturing for the rest of the crew to take their places.

They all seized hold of the tow ropes, except for Edvin. He was by the bow, with a pile of six wooden rollers—meter-long pieces cut from sapling trunks. He picked up the first and slid it under the bow of the ship as the crew began to heave. The curved keel section rode up on the roller and slid uphill. After it had gone two meters, Edvin slid another roller under the bow, then another. With the addition of each roller, the task of pulling the ship overland became progressively easier and the ship moved slowly up the track. Lydia, watching keenly, quickly caught on to the idea. She ran to the stern as the first roller came clear. She picked it up and ran back uphill to the bow, placing it under the keel. Edvin nodded his thanks and trotted downhill to retrieve and replace the second roller. As he did, Lydia went downhill again to retrieve the third, carry it uphill and place it under the up-curved keel at the bow once more.

Working in tandem, they kept the ship moving on the constantly renewed bed of rollers, while the rest of the crew heaved and tugged on the ropes.

"Keep it moving!" Hal gasped to his crew. "If we let her stop, it'll be twice as hard to get her going again."

Nobody replied. They had no breath to spare for unnecessary chatter. They strained and heaved, feet slipping in the loose earth and leaf mold as they searched for solid purchase. And all the while, Lydia and Edvin kept up their back-and-forth ritual, constantly renewing the rollers under the ship's keel so that there were always five of them in place.

And slowly, ponderously, *Heron* inched her way up the slope.

After an hour's backbreaking, muscle-straining labor, they reached the top of the first section.

"Rest!" Hal shouted. At least, he attempted to shout. The command came out more like a breathless grunt. But the crew heard and understood it, releasing the drag ropes with a chorus of groans and flinging themselves onto the ground. Hal stood leaning against a tree trunk, his chest heaving with exertion as he studied the slope they had just conquered. He shook his head with relief. He hadn't been sure if his ropes and pulleys and rollers would work as well as they had. He felt a sense of exultation. They had beaten this hill.

"Anyone think to bring a canteen?" he asked, his throat dry. He was met by blank looks. But Lydia stepped forward. There were half a dozen canteens back down the hill, where the food and stores were piled.

"I'll get some," she volunteered, and Hal nodded gratefully as she set off down the hill, running lightly over the ground where they had just struggled with so much effort.

Not that Lydia had enjoyed an easy time, he thought. Constantly running back and forth up and down the hill, retrieving and then replacing the rollers, was an exhausting task and she had probably covered four times the distance the rest of the crew had. But it was nowhere near as exhausting as dragging the ship overland and uphill. Hal slid down the trunk of the tree, resting his back against it as he sat at its base, legs sprawled out in front of him. He gave Thorn a tired grin. The old sea wolf was white-haired and many years senior to the rest of the crew. But his strength seemed endless. He was barely breathing heavily. Nor was Ingvar, Hal noted.

"This is why we go to sea," he told the one-armed warrior.

Thorn nodded. "No hills at sea."

Lydia returned a few minutes later with the half dozen canteens. She passed them around, and the crew drank greedily. Mindful that they still had several sections of track to negotiate, she collected them and headed off through the trees to the river to refill them.

"We'll rest a few minutes," Hal told the crew.

Thorn looked up warily. "Not too long," he cautioned.

Hal nodded agreement. If they waited too long, their muscles would stiffen and it would be difficult to get moving again. There was a delicate balance to giving the crew just enough rest, but not too much.

When Lydia returned with the full canteens, he rose to his feet, groaning slightly.

"Let's get moving," he said, and was greeted by a chorus of complaints. But he noted that they all rose to their feet.

It took them thirty minutes to manhandle the ship around the bend in the track. For this, they relied solely on muscle power, as there was no way they could use the pulleys and rollers to slide the hull up and around. Once they were positioned, with the bow pointing up the next section of straight track, Hal went ahead and found anchor points for the pulleys. He slipped and slid back down the hill. The crew were standing by the drag ropes, and Lydia and Edvin had their pile of rollers ready at the bow. He reached down and took hold of the rope, then took the strain.

"Right," he said. "Pull!"

After a moment's hesitation, when it seemed the ship wouldn't budge, they overcame the inertia and the *Heron* began to slide up the hill once more.

Their progress was measured in inches. Heads down, eyes fixed on the ground in front of them, they heaved on the ropes, feeling the ship moving slowly, ever so slowly, up the steep track. The rollers rumbled under the keel, the noise accentuated by the empty hull acting as a sound box. Their world narrowed down to the sound of the rollers against the planks, the creaking of ropes and pulleys as they heaved, and the groaning of their companions as they fought against the deadweight of the ship, forcing her to keep moving up the hill, cursing her for a stubborn, willful beast.

Hal, leaning almost parallel to the slope of the ground as he heaved on the rope, exerting all his strength for a minuscule amount of progress, thought wryly that if there had been any Temujai in the vicinity, they could have simply strolled in and slaughtered the *Heron*'s crew as they labored.

"We probably would have just kept pulling while they did," he muttered, without realizing he had spoken aloud.

On the other side of the hull, Stig heard him but didn't understand the words. "What was that?" he gasped through gritted teeth.

But Hal shook his head. "Forget it," he croaked. He sensed Lydia hurrying past him to place a roller under the bow. Presumably she'd be keeping a watch so that they weren't surprised, he thought. Then he shook his head. He didn't really care and he didn't have breath to waste asking her.

This section was longer than the first, and they had to stop two-thirds of the way up so that he could reset the pulleys.

As before, the crew sprawled on the ground where they fell. Hal allowed himself a five-minute rest before he started up the hill with the pulleys and drag ropes.

Then they began again, with Edvin and Lydia lending a hand to start the ship moving uphill.

Once more they fell into the mindless exercise of heaving on the rope, measuring the ground they won in centimeters, as they struggled against the stubborn weight of the ship.

How did I ever think she was a lightweight? Hal found himself wondering. Of course, once she was afloat, *Heron* was as light as a gull riding on the water. On land she was a ponderous, stubborn deadweight, trying to slide off in the wrong direction as the slope and camber of the track varied.

But they were fit and strong, with their muscles conditioned to row against the sea and wind for hours at a time, and eventually, they reached the end of the second section. This time, Hal had them manhandle the ship into position at the beginning of the third and final part of the track before he allowed them a fifteen-minute rest. Then they resumed. They groaned. They complained. They protested. But they took their places and hauled, heartened by the knowledge that this was the shortest section of the track and they could see the end above them.

They had started out before midmorning, but it was early afternoon before the *Heron* slid over the lip of the hill and onto the level ground at the top. They fetched the spars, sails and other equipment from the lower level and, after they reloaded the ship, launched her, shoving off from the bank and settling to the oars. After two kilometers, they reached the site of the next portage, and the whole business of unloading, hauling and dragging had to be done once more.

Fortunately, the second portage was shorter than the first, and there was no dogleg, so the work was completed in a much shorter time. They rowed on to the next portage site, which was even shorter and not as steep as the others. But the repetitive nature of the task was aggravating, particularly now they were tired. Once they had launched the ship for the third time and moored her to the bank, Stig leaned back, his knuckles kneading his lower back.

"I'm glad that's over," he said.

Hal glanced at the sky. He estimated there was less than an

hour's light left. "We'll load the ship again in the morning," he said. "I think we've earned a rest."

"I know I have," Stig agreed heartily. "What about you, Jesper?"

Jesper was already stretched out on the grass. His only reply was a soft snore.

Stig grinned at Hal. "He seems to agree," he said.

## chapter fourteen

The following morning, Hal let the crew sleep late, then Edvin woke them with a hearty breakfast of bacon, toasted flatbread and eggs. They had reprovisioned before leaving Hallasholm and the eggs were fresh—a rare luxury for them when they were at sea.

As ever, they washed the meal down with hot, sweetened coffee. Thorn, sitting cross-legged on the ground, regarded his second cup appreciatively.

"It's a good idea putting honey in the coffee," he said to Hal. "Where did it come from?"

"I learned it from that Ranger, Gilan, when he came with us to Socorro," Hal said. "And I agree. It's a good idea."

He held out his cup as Edvin passed by, the large coffeepot in his hand, and allowed him to refill it. He didn't bother with more honey, as he had put plenty in the first cup and the remnants were still sweet. He sipped the fragrant brew, stretching his stiff shoulder and arm muscles. He knew that when he stood up, his thigh and calf muscles would protest violently after the exertions of the previous day. But they'd soon loosen up. Regretfully, he looked around their little campsite.

"All right, lads, let's get the ship reloaded."

There was a chorus of cheerful complaints, inevitably led by Jesper, but the brotherband climbed stiffly to their feet and set to work. They loaded the reduced food stores into the hull—Edvin and Hal had decided to leave most of the food at the first portage—and their weapons and equipment. The oars went back in their racks, running the length of the hull. Stefan, Jesper, Ulf and Wulf heaved the two yardarms and sails into the ship and busied themselves rerigging them.

Lydia had learned long ago that the work of restocking the ship was best left to the crew. "Each of us has a specific responsibility," Stig had told her. "That way, we know that everything has been put back aboard."

She accepted the situation gratefully. She had no wish to heave and lift heavy items into position, and stack and stow them so that they would remain stable even in a pitching, rolling sea. Instead, she scouted ahead upriver, traveling half a kilometer to spy out the land. She returned as the crew were shoving the now-laden ship back into the water.

Hal stood by critically, studying the *Heron* with an expert eye to make sure the trim was correct. He pointed to two large barrels of salt pork stowed amidships.

"Move one of them a few meters astern," he ordered Thorn and Stig.

They tilted the barrel on its side, rolling it along the deck to the position he had indicated. He waved a hand for them to move it farther.

"A little more," he said, then held up the hand for them to stop. "That's fine there."

The ship had been sitting slightly nose down, and the transfer of weight corrected the problem. Hal turned to Edvin. "Use the for'ard cask first," he said. That cask was set virtually on the midpoint of the hull and lightening it gradually would have little effect on the trim. He paced along the bank, occasionally dropping to his haunches to study the ship. She was sitting a little high in the water, but once the crew was aboard and the freshwater tank refilled, that would be taken care of. He nodded, satisfied, and gestured for the crew to board and take up their rowing positions. He noticed Lydia standing by to report and walked over to her.

"See anything?" he asked.

She shook her head. "No sign of the Temujai. But a lot of grass. The trees thin out up here and the terrain becomes rolling grasslands, with occasional clumps of smaller trees. The river begins to widen out as well. I think you'll be able to sail before too long."

She had been a member of the crew long enough to know how much room the ship required to tack successfully against a current.

Hal grunted appreciatively. "The boys will be pleased to hear that. And the wind has backed. So not so much tacking."

The offshore wind of the day before had shifted during the

night. It was now blowing firmly onshore, which meant it would be behind *Heron* as she made her way upriver. She'd still be switching from one diagonal run to another once the river got wider, but not as much as if they were heading into the wind and the current. Another advantage was that the wind had cleared the snow clouds away and the day was clear and bright.

The crew made their way to the plank that ran from the grassy riverbank to the entry port in the ship's bulwarks. They stepped up and ran lightly one after the other across the plank, dropping onto the deck. Jesper and Edvin hauled the gangplank inboard and stowed it as Hal made his way to the tiller.

"Right, lads, oars!" Stig called, and the rowers detailed to the task took their places on the rowing benches and ran out their long oars with a clatter of wood on wood.

Stig stepped up onto the railing for one last look at the campsite, making sure the fire was extinguished and nothing had been left behind. He turned and nodded to Hal, then dropped down and took his own position on the benches.

"Cast off!" Hal ordered. Jesper in the bow and Edvin in the stern released the mooring lines that had been looped around trees on the bank, hauling the ropes in. Released from the bank, *Heron* began to crab sideways under the wind coming over her port quarter.

"Fend off port!" Hal ordered, and the three port-side rowers used their oars to push the little ship out from the bank and into the stream. Now the current, working in the opposite direction to the wind, began to swing the bow out to starboard.

"Give way, starboard oars!"

The three oars on the starboard side dipped into the water

and heaved against the current. The ship's bow swung back to port under the uneven thrust.

"Give way, port!" Hal ordered, and the other three oars now dipped into the river and pulled as well. The ship straightened and began to head upriver, moving out from the bank at a shallow angle. Hal eased the tiller to keep the ship close to the bank. In the center of the stream, the current would be much stronger, he knew. *Heron* steadied on her upriver course, the oars finding their natural rhythm and heaving her smoothly through the water. The wavelets began to chuckle against her hull and a small ripple of a bow wave formed at her prow, where the bow post cut through the water.

Hal grinned at Wulf, who was manning the middle oar on the port side. "This is better than hauling her uphill," he said.

Wulf cocked his head thoughtfully, without losing the rhythm of his stroke. "It is for you," he said. "All you have to do is lean on the tiller all day."

But he was grinning as he said it, and the grin robbed the words of any animosity. Hal smiled back at him, then turned his gaze for'ard. As Lydia had told him, the river was beginning to widen. Already it was fifty meters from bank to bank and the distance continued to grow. As well as making it possible to use the sails, the extra width would reduce the force of the current. It ran faster when it was restricted between narrow banks.

After a few more minutes, he caught Ulf's eye and nodded toward the mast. "Let's hoist the port sail," he said.

The well-drilled crew took only a few minutes to ready the sail and send it soaring up the top of the mast.

Ulf and Wulf hauled on the sheets and brought the sail under control, forming it into a smooth, bellying curve as they trapped the wind. Hal felt the familiar extra pressure on the rudder as the *Heron* accelerated and the tattoo of wavelets against the hull became more and more rapid.

"We'll need to go about in ten minutes," Hal told Stig, then revised the estimate as he realized that the banks were rapidly moving apart and the river widening, as Lydia had foretold. "Make that twenty minutes."

He studied the smooth surface of the river, gauging the speed of the current as small branches sped past them downriver. The water was deep until close in to the banks, so he could maintain this course until they had nearly reached the western shore.

"Coming about," he called some time later, as he judged they had reached the optimum position. He shoved the tiller over and the bow swung to port. As it did, Ulf and Wulf let out the sheets so that the sail was blown out at almost ninety degrees to the hull by the following wind. Then they tightened the sheets to gain more speed. Hal felt the boat surge forward.

They sailed on, staying on the same tack but progressing upriver in a series of diagonal runs. As the river continued to widen, they could hold each diagonal course longer and they were making good progress.

Jesper, as usual, was perched on the lookout position on the bow post. It was midafternoon when he called back to Hal.

"Something ahead!"

Hal frowned. It wasn't like Jesper to give such a vague report. "Something ahead" could be anything from the Great Blue Tortoise of Tarantas to a live volcano spewing lava.

"What is it?" Hal yelled back.

Jesper hesitated a few seconds. "The river seems to be getting much, much wider," he replied eventually. "And I think I can see breakers."

Breakers, thought Hal, this far inland? He had to be mistaken. But then Jesper called again.

"It's breakers, all right. A line of them on the port side. And there's open water beyond them."

Hal glanced at Stig, signaling for him to take the tiller. Then he ran for'ard to the bow. He gestured for the lookout to come down onto the deck and hurriedly took Jesper's place, shielding his eyes with his hand to block the glare of the lowering sun.

Sure enough, he could see a line of white water reaching some twenty meters out into the river. And beyond them, he could see a wide expanse of gray water. He turned and called back to Stig.

"Bring her round to starboard a little." He waited until their course was well clear of the line of broken water, then held up a hand. The ship steadied on course. The breakers were obviously caused by a sandbar, formed by sand and silt carried on the current and piling up in the shallow part of the river. He heard their low rumble as the ship came abreast of them, then, powered by the wind, she shot out onto the broad expanse of a massive lake.

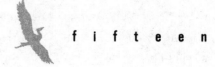

There was a chorus of surprised exclamations from the crew as the size of the lake became apparent. The eastern edge was three kilometers from their current position. It stretched away to the north until it was lost in the misty distance. To the left, the shoreline angled to the west until it too was lost from sight. At the farthest point he could see, he estimated that it was seven or eight kilometers away. Then it receded farther into the distance until there was no sign of a shoreline.

Stig had moved to stand beside him as he studied the lake. "It's more like an inland sea, really," he said.

Hal nodded. "It gives us a bit of room to move," he said. He wasn't in any way awed by the immensity of the lake. On the contrary, he felt a little relieved. Sailing up a river in what might prove to be enemy territory always gave him a sense of confinement, and a feeling that if something went wrong, it would be difficult to escape. This way, he had lots of sea room—or perhaps that should be lake room—in which to disappear.

The crew crowded the bulwarks, staring at the shoreline on either side. Even Kloof was interested—she was always keen to go ashore when they were afloat. She stood on her hind legs, her forepaws propped on the starboard gunwale, with her head thrown back and her nostrils quivering as she sniffed the air, checking out and categorizing all the alien smells she could pick up.

The surface of the lake close to them was dotted here and there with small islets—too small to deserve any real attention. Most weren't much longer than the ship itself and were dotted with solitary trees and small shrubs. But in the distance, Hal could see a larger mass, set perhaps a kilometer off the eastern coastline. He had automatically kept the ship close to the eastern side of the lake, realizing that this was the direction from which they might see any Temujai who were present. The Temujai's lands lay to the east and it was logical to assume that they would approach from that direction.

If they were going to approach at all.

Now that they were in open water, the brisk wind was kicking up the surface into steep, short waves, about a meter high. They drove into *Heron* from her starboard quarter, lifting the stern and rolling the ship to port, then passing under her as she rolled and pitched back. It was a short, sharp motion and not particularly comfortable. It was necessary to keep hold of something—a halyard, a shroud or the gunwale itself—to keep from staggering with the jerky movement. Back in his position on the bow-post lookout, Jesper clung on with two hands, his knees bending and flexing to absorb the abrupt movement. It was a tiring action and Hal made a mental note to relieve him before long.

But not just yet. This was new territory, and any moment, enemies could show themselves. In case that happened, he wanted his best lookout on the job. He called down the length of the deck.

"I'll give you a spell soon, Jes."

Jesper waved one hand in acknowledgment, then hastily grabbed at the bow post as the ship lurched in an unexpected motion. "I'm fine for now, Hal," he said.

Hal nodded in appreciation. Jesper could be a pain at times, and a nuisance. But he understood the need for a good lookout on occasions like this, and he could be trusted to keep his eyes on the job and avoid distractions.

Hal's faith in him was borne out a few minutes later when he suddenly stiffened and pointed to the eastern bank ahead of the ship.

"Riders!" he called. He wrapped his left arm around the bow post to give him a secure hold while he pointed with his right hand to a spot forty-five degrees off the *Heron's* starboard bow. "A dozen of them!"

The ship was currently on a starboard tack, with the sail blowing out to port, so that Hal had a relatively unrestricted view in the direction Jesper was pointing. After a few seconds searching, he sighted movement. A group of riders, traveling in single file, was moving toward the lakeshore, traveling in a southwest direction and about half a kilometer inland. He couldn't make out any details of clothing or equipment at this distance, but they could only be Temujai.

He reacted instinctively, calling out a rapid set of orders.

"Sail down! Everybody out of sight. No noise. No movement!"

There was a good chance that the riders hadn't noticed the little ship yet. But the longer the light gray sail, which would appear white at a distance, was left up, the greater the chance was that they would be spotted. He heard the sail come down with a slithering rush and a clatter as Stefan and Edvin released the halyards. The canvas flapped on the deck for a minute until Ulf and Wulf subdued it by the simple expedient of clambering onto the central deck and lying on the canvas.

Jesper slid quickly down from the lookout post and crouched by the bow bulwark, only his eyes above the timber railing. The rest of the crew dropped into the rowing wells, out of sight. They were too disciplined to make the mistake of raising their heads above the bulwarks to peer at the Temujai. Pale faces were all too visible at a distance, they knew.

As it was, there was a good chance that the *Heron*'s dull green hull would merge with the gray background of the lake's surface and she would remain unseen—particularly since there was no reason why the riders might be studying the lake's surface. They would be more inclined to look for danger on the shore, Hal reasoned.

He himself was hunkered down below the bulwark at the steering position. Like Jesper, he allowed only his eyes to show above the smooth timber railing. He held the tiller in a tight grip to prevent its banging back and forth in the uneven chop—although the noise would hardly be loud enough to alert the riders onshore.

Still, he realized, sound could carry a long way over water and there was no harm in making sure it was kept to a minimum. Not that there was any chance the Temujai could attack them. They were well out of bowshot. But he didn't want them to be aware of the *Heron*'s presence here on the lake.

Conscious that his crew would be wondering what was happening, as they kept their heads bent and their eyes below the bulwarks, he spoke in a low but carrying voice as he detailed the horsemen's movements.

"They're heading toward the bank . . . traveling southwest. If they keep on in that direction, they'll reach the shore about two hundred meters astern of our position."

As he said the last few words, he glanced up at the telltale on the sternpost above him. It was streaming out at an angle off the port bow. That was fortunate. If the wind was in that direction, it would keep the *Heron* drifting away from the eastern shore. It would have been potentially disastrous if the wind had been setting them ashore. If that had been the case, they would have had to row back out, and risk discovery.

"They don't seem to have seen us," he continued as he had that last thought. "Still keeping on in the direction they were heading when Jes spotted them . . ."

He trailed off. It was one thing to keep the crew informed, another entirely to chatter on about unimportant details. It was enough that the crew knew the Temujai were moving closer and that, so far, they hadn't noticed the little ship drifting on the gray water of the lake. The grass was long, he noticed, reaching up to the horses' shoulders as the Temujai warriors rode through it. It gave a strange impression that they were somehow floating on the top of the grass, as the *Heron* was floating on the lake.

"They're abreast of us now. Maybe a hundred meters from the lake . . ."

Instinctively, several crew members' eyes swiveled to the starboard side, as if their owners could see through the solid planking. Hal had a momentary rush of concern as he remembered the crew's shields, arranged along the bulwarks. Unlike the green hull itself, they were painted in various colors that might well stand out if any of the riders glanced in their direction. His own shield was probably most at fault, being painted in a rich blue enamel. He glanced up at the sun. All they needed now was one flash of sunlight reflected from the metal fittings on a shield to catch the attention of one of the riders. But it was afternoon and the sun was sliding down in the west, behind them. There was no way it would reflect a flash of light from the line of shields.

So far, they seemed to have escaped the attention of the patrol. He made a mental note to have the shields stowed inboard as soon as possible.

Across the water, he heard a thin cry of command, and his heart leapt to his mouth as the line of horsemen came to a halt. Had they been spotted?

He held his breath for several seconds—an instinctive action and a relatively useless one, as there was no way the Temujai would hear him breathing. Then he saw the patrol commander rise in his stirrups and peer farther down the shore and the lake itself, shielding his eyes with one hand.

"They've stopped," he told the crew. "But they haven't spotted us. Their leader is looking down the lake behind us. Nobody move." He realized that this was possibly the moment of greatest danger. With the riders stopped and the leader scanning the lakeshore to the south, there was every chance that the rest of the patrol would glance idly about them—and spot the little ship drifting barely two hundred meters away.

The patrol leader settled back into his saddle and raised his hand above his head in a circling motion. Another thin cry of command carried to Hal and the patrol moved off, moving in a long arc until they were headed back in the direction from which they'd come. He heaved a sigh of relief, releasing a pent-up breath that he wasn't aware he was holding.

"They're heading off," Hal told the crew. "Stay down for a few more minutes until they're out of sight."

Gradually, the muted thud of hoofs on soft ground faded away, and the line of riders galloped over a shallow crest and disappeared. Hal counted slowly to ten, making sure the riders didn't suddenly reappear.

"All right, everyone, back to your stations. Let's get that sail up again."

The little ship came to life as the crew rose from their crouched hiding places. Jesper moved to the mast to join Stefan in raising the port sail, while Ulf and Wulf tended the sheets. As the yardarm clunked into place and they hauled in on the sheets, the ship quivered, then began to cut through the water, gathering speed. Hal shoved the tiller over so that they were heading out onto the main surface of the lake, away from the eastern shore. Stig and Thorn moved to stand beside him.

"What the devil are they doing here?" Hal said. "We're miles from the border at Serpent Pass. They've traveled a long way to get here."

"There were only a dozen of them," Stig pointed out.

But Thorn disagreed. "There'll be more. They don't move about in small numbers." He looked at Hal. "To answer your question, maybe they've had the same thought that Erak had. After all, they can read maps as well as we can."

"You mean they're looking to see if they can use Ice River Valley as a way down to the coast?" Stig asked.

"If we can come up it, they can certainly get down it," Thorn said. "What we have to do is find a way to stop them."

Hal thought for a few seconds before speaking. "We may be jumping to a conclusion there," he said. "What we need to do is hole up around here and keep an eye on them for a few days—see what they get up to."

"And where do you suggest we 'hole up' for a few days?" Stig said, looking at the shoreline. "The bank there doesn't have a lot of places we could keep out of sight."

"Maybe not the bank," Hal said. He pointed to the large island he had spotted earlier. "But that island might be just the place we need."

T he island was perhaps six hundred meters long and two hundred across. Unlike the shores of the lake, it was covered in heavy tree growth. They were relatively low trees, but with thick foliage. The island would make a good hiding place, so long as they could find a way to conceal the ship.

As they drew closer, Hal had the crew lower the sails and resume rowing. He steered the ship in closer, studying the island carefully. The banks were steep, dropping off into the water and with trees growing right up to the water's edge. They offered no mooring place or hiding place on the eastern side.

They swung around the northern end of the island and then came back down the western side. Here, the banks were the same, although, at a pinch, Hal thought they could moor and drape the ship with foliage and netting to conceal her. The chances of seeing Temujai on the western shore of the lake were small, and in any event, the shore was almost out of sight, forming a green-gray line along the horizon.

He had just decided that this would be the best choice they had when Lydia called him, pointing to the shoreline astern.

"There, Hal!"

He looked back over his shoulder and saw the mouth of a small inlet in the island's west bank—an opening that was half again as wide as the *Heron* and ran in among the trees for about fifteen meters. It was a perfect hiding place for the ship—as long as the water was deep enough. He had missed it as they sailed past. It was only visible when one looked astern, as Lydia had just done. He nodded his thanks and swung the tiller, taking the *Heron* in a circle to head back toward the little gap.

"Easy all," he warned the rowers. He didn't want to go charging in at full speed. Gradually, the way died off the ship until she was creeping over the water.

"Jes!" he called. "Keep an eye on the depth as we go in."

Jesper, still on the bow post, waved acknowledgment. At the slowest possible speed they could manage and still maintain steerageway, the ship stole forward, edging her way toward the narrow opening. Jesper craned on his toes, peering down at the water for any sign of it shallowing. He made a circular gesture with his hand, telling Hal to keep coming.

Slowly, cautiously, *Heron* nosed into the narrow gap and under the trees. The wind was blanketed here and the choppy waves gave way to smooth water. The external sounds died away as they crept in among the trees. About forty meters beyond their current position, Hal could see that the little inlet petered out in a tangle of reeds and low shrubs. They'd come far enough, he thought. The ship was well and truly inside the concealing arms of the inlet now.

"Stop rowing," he said. There was no need to raise his voice in the shelter of the trees.

The regular, muted splash of oars in the water ceased as the rowers rested on their oars.

"In oars." As ever, the oars rattled against the rowlocks and the stowage racks as the crew hauled them inboard and stowed them. *Heron* came to a halt almost immediately. She had barely been moving anyway.

"Get her moored, Stig," Hal said.

Stig took up the stern line and quickly tied a small grapnel to it. Then he cast it underhand onto the bank, among the thick growth of trees and saplings there. In the bow, Jesper scrambled down from his lookout post and did the same with the bow mooring line. The two of them hauled on the lines and dragged the ship in close to the bank, tying off the ropes when there was barely a meter of open water between the hull and the bank.

Stig ran a gangplank out over the gunwale to the shore, shoving it through the undergrowth and pushing till he found a firm footing for it. He looked around at the curtain of trees that concealed them.

"Do you want the nets rigged?" he asked. The nets were fishing nets festooned with irregular strips and patches of green and gray cloth. Draped over the ship, they broke up her outline and made her more difficult for passersby to spot. Hal considered the idea, then shook his head.

"We're pretty well concealed here," he said. "Get the camp set up ashore. We may as well sleep comfortably."

Stig nodded. They could sleep on board, of course. But it was more comfortable to set up their big tent, where they could roll their blankets out on soft ground rather than the hard planks of the *Heron*'s deck. He called out orders to the rest of the crew and they began unloading the equipment they'd need for the camp.

Hal noticed Edvin standing nearby, waiting to speak. He nodded for the young man to go ahead.

"I should be able to set a cook fire here, Hal," he said. "I'll keep it hot so there's a minimum of smoke. And what there is will be dissipated among the trees anyway."

Hal considered the statement. "What about the smell of smoke?" he asked.

Edvin shrugged. "We're a long way from the shore. And the breeze is blowing to the northwest. That should carry it away."

"Besides," Lydia interjected, smiling, "the Temujai are unlikely to smell anything above their own pleasant perfume of sweat and horse dung. They're not the daintiest people," she added, remembering how she had sensed their presence in the valley north of Fort Ragnak.

Hal knew she was half joking. But he also knew she was an experienced scout and hunter. If she felt there was no risk of their smoke being detected, that was good enough for him. He nodded to Edvin.

"Fine, Edvin. Get a fire going. It'll be good to have a cup of coffee." His mouth suddenly watered at the thought. He turned and saw Thorn waiting expectantly, anticipating Hal's next action.

"Thorn, you come with me. Let's take a look at the eastern shore and see what's stirring."

They left the crew to the business of setting up camp and headed off into the thick undergrowth beneath the trees. There were no paths that they could see. The island was obviously uninhabited by man or beast. From time to time, they had to use their razor-sharp saxes to hack their way through the bushes and vines that clung to them and tried to stop their progress.

For all that, it didn't take them long to reach the opposite bank of the island. They crouched among the trees, making sure they kept in their concealing shadow, and surveyed the eastern shore of the lake.

"Don't see anything," Thorn said.

Hal grimaced at him. "Not yet, anyway. We'll give it a while."

Thorn nodded and slid to the ground, resting his back against the trunk of a small tree. He plucked a long piece of grass and chewed on it thoughtfully.

"Are you expecting anything in particular?" he asked after several minutes had passed. Hal shrugged and lowered himself to the ground, picking a soft, grassy spot and making himself comfortable.

"I'm thinking that if we saw one Temujai patrol earlier, we're likely to see more, scouting out the land. From what you've told me, they're an organized bunch. They wouldn't come this way in large numbers without reconnoitering first. I get the impression they like to know what they're walking into."

"Are they coming this way?" Thorn asked.

Hal considered the question before answering. "Unfortunately, I think they might be. I think they're looking for another way to get down to the coast, and this might well be the way they come. Anyway, we'll have a better idea in a day or two. If we don't see them again, we'll assume I'm wrong and we can head back down ourselves."

"That would be nice," Thorn said. "But I think you might be right. Look."

He pointed with his hook, and Hal, looking in the direction Thorn indicated, saw movement among the long grass on the eastern shore. As he watched, a file of horsemen rode over a low ridge, the long grass reaching to their horses' bellies again and giving that same impression that they were somehow floating over the grasslands.

"Are they the same ones we saw before?" Thorn asked. It was hard to differentiate between one band of Temujai and another. They wore the same clothes, had the same weapons and carried the same banners—horsetails on a crosspiece mounted on a spear handle.

"I think they might be a different lot," Hal said. "The leader of the other patrol rode a black horse. That one is brown and white."

"Or he's the same man and he's changed horses," Thorn suggested.

Hal nodded. "That could be right."

They watched in silence for several minutes before Thorn spoke again. "They're patrolling a different section."

Hal realized he was right. The previous group had ridden on a diagonal course to the shore of the lake, then swung southward. These riders stayed farther inland, sweeping the ground parallel to the lakeshore.

"One thing's the same," Hal observed. "They're coming out of the east and then looking to the south. And if that becomes a trend, it bothers me."

"Maybe they're just looking for a way around the lake," Thorn suggested. "Maybe they plan to continue moving to the west."

"Maybe," Hal replied. But his voice didn't carry any conviction.

They stayed for another half hour and saw no further sign of Temujai riders. The group they had seen moved farther south, then turned to the east and rode out of sight.

"We'll set up a roster to keep watch on them," Hal said. "If we've seen two patrols, I'd expect to see more. But how many of them, and where they're looking, is information I'd like to know."

They headed back the way they had come and found the camp set up and organized. Edvin had prepared a meal and they took a bowl each, eagerly smelling the fragrant fumes that rose from it.

"Salt pork and potato soup," the cook told them. He shrugged diffidently. "Sorry it's a bit ordinary. Looks like there'll be no fresh game while we're here. There's nothing on the island."

Hal shrugged the apology aside as he spooned the soup into his mouth. "This is fine," he said. "And maybe there'll be fish in the lake."

Edvin brightened. "That's true. I'll set some lines before dark."

Hal looked across the small clearing to where Stig and Lydia were finishing their meals and rinsing their bowls and spoons in a basin of boiling water.

"Stig, Lydia," he called, and they turned expectantly. He jerked his head in the direction of the east bank. "Head across and keep an eye on the shore."

Stig nodded and, picking up his battleax, pushed the haft through the iron retaining ring on his belt. The island might be uninhabited, but Stig would never go anywhere without his ax. Lydia had the same automatic reaction, slinging the quiver of darts over her shoulder as she turned toward the path Hal and Thorn had blazed through the trees.

"Are we looking for anything in particular?" she asked.

"You're looking for Temujai," Hal told her. "We saw one patrol while we were watching. That makes two today and that's two too many. I get the feeling that they're scouting out the lakeshore."

"Could be coincidence, of course," Stig said.

"Could be. Or it could be they're planning to make a move this way in force. If they are, I'd like to know."

As Stig and Lydia headed for the trees, Kloof came to her feet and bounded after them. She'd been lying around the campsite for an hour or more and she wanted exercise.

Stig looked at Hal, questioning him. "All right if Kloof comes?"

Hal nodded. "Actually, it's a good idea. She often hears or smells things long before we can see them. I'm not sure which it is, but it's quite uncanny."

Lydia grinned. "Well, the way the Temujai spend their time sitting around those horse-dung fires, I'd say she'll smell them."

For the next two days, they maintained their surveillance over the lake's eastern shore.

They kept watch in pairs, remaining hidden among the trees on the edge of the island, scanning the rolling grasslands that stretched out to the horizon.

It was a boring assignment. Sometimes they could wait for hours before seeing any activity on the part of the Temujai, and it would be easy to nod off, particularly since the last two days had enjoyed typical early spring weather. The skies had been clear and the sun was warm. And in among the trees, sheltered from the prevailing breeze, it was cozy and comfortable. Having two people on watch made sure that they stayed awake.

But in spite of the hours of inactivity, they did see more Temujai patrols. On the second day, they saw three, and on the third day, two more. Generally, the horsemen rode in groups of eight or ten. It was clear that they were studying the land close to the lake, perhaps searching for potential danger, or perhaps, as Hal feared, searching for a path down from the high country to the coastal plain. Each patrol followed the same basic pattern. They would emerge from the east and turn south, sometimes close to the shore, sometimes farther inland. And they would travel farther south each day, judging by the time they were out of sight. Then, after several hours, they would return and swing east again—always east— heading in that direction until they disappeared from view.

"Obviously," Thorn said as they discussed the repeating pattern on the third night, "that's where their main camp is located. They always come out of the east and return there when they're finished."

Hal nodded agreement. "What I'd like to know is, how big is the camp?" he said, poking a green twig into the coals of the small fire. "Is it just an exploration? Or is it the main body of the Temujai on the move?"

"If it's not the main body, it's a big group," Stig put in. "We've seen forty or fifty of them patrolling and they've all been different riders."

Hal had instructed the watchers to note down any distinguishing features of each patrol—the color of the leader's horse, or any unusual colors among the other horses, or distinctive items of clothing or weaponry. While it was often difficult to identify individuals at this distance, the Herons were reasonably sure that they had seen five different patrols, making up the forty or fifty horsemen that Stig referred to now.

"They must be quite a way off still," Lydia said. She made up the fourth member of the party discussing the patrols. "If it's a big camp and they were close, we could expect to see the loom of the light from their campfires at night."

"Maybe they just have good fire discipline," Hal said. "They might be keeping their fires small to avoid giving warning that they're in the area."

"Why would they bother?" Thorn asked. "So far as they know, there's nobody here looking for them."

"We're keeping our fires small," Stig said.

Thorn turned to look at him. "That's because we know they're there," he said. "They don't have any idea that we're here watching."

"We hope," said Hal.

"Yes. We hope."

"The point is," Lydia said, "we can argue back and forth about whether they have small fires or whether they're a long way off. The only way we're going to know is if someone goes and has a look."

"Someone?" Hal said.

"Well, me and someone. I assume you'd want to go and take a look yourself," Lydia said to him. "And you'd be crazy not to take me along. Without me to show you the way," she continued, grinning at him, "you'd be stepping in holes and falling over your own big feet."

"Good to see you have such faith in me," Hal said, returning the grin. "But I agree—"

"That you'd be falling over your own big feet?" Stig asked.

Hal gave him a disparaging look. "No. That Lydia and I should go and see if we can find the Temujai's main camp." He looked back at Lydia. "I suggest we get started tomorrow morning before first light. That should get us clear of the shore before the Temujai start nosing around."

The moon set just after the third hour the following morning. Hal waited another half hour, then signaled for the mooring ropes to be cast off. Ingvar and Stig used their oars as poles, digging them into the muddy bottom of the little inlet and shoving the ship backward into open water.

She slid smoothly out of her hiding place and onto the surface of the lake, the motion slowly falling off as the impetus of the final shove from Stig and Ingvar died away.

"Oars," Hal ordered in a soft voice. "And quietly," he added.

For once, there was no clatter of wood on wood as the rowers raised their oars and slid them out through the rowlocks. The four designated rowers handled the long wooden shafts with exaggerated care, avoiding any unnecessary noise. And the oars themselves were wrapped in rags where they passed through the rowlocks, to muffle any sound. Hal didn't expect any Temujai to be abroad at this early hour. So far as they could see, the riders had confined their patrolling to daylight hours. But you never knew.

"Give way," Stig commanded quietly, and Stefan, Ulf and Wulf all leaned their weight back on the oars, sending the *Heron* gurgling through the water. Tiny lights of phosphorescence gleamed in her wake as she gathered speed and headed for the shore, a little to the north of their current position. During the afternoon, Stig, Hal and Thorn had surveyed the shoreline from their hiding place among the trees and picked out the best place for them to land.

This had been the subject of some debate. Hal was inclined to have the ship drop them off and then return to its hiding place on the island. Thorn had vetoed the idea and Stig had agreed.

"I'm not dropping you off and leaving you," the old sea wolf had protested. "If we go back to the island and you get into trouble, it'll take too long for us to get back to pick you up. We'll find a good spot to moor up and we'll wait for you."

"But if you do that, and a patrol comes by, they'll see you," Hal pointed out.

Thorn, however, was adamant. "So far, they've stayed away from the banks. They've stayed well inland. If we rig our nets to break up the shape of the *Heron*, chances are they won't notice it. After all, they're spending all their time looking south."

"But if they do spot you—" Hal began.

Stig overrode him. "Then we can always shove off and head back out into the lake. But this way, we'll be on hand if you need us."

"They've got a point," Lydia told Hal. "I don't like the idea of being chased by horsemen without any chance of escape."

Reluctantly, Hal allowed himself to be convinced. Thorn was, after all, their battlemaster and the person they looked to for tactical decisions like this. Eventually, they picked out a spot where a small promontory ran out into the lake. It was a narrow spit of land about thirty meters long, where they could moor *Heron* and form a defensive position across the neck of the promontory.

"If we're attacked, we'll form a shield wall with the ship behind us," Thorn said. "And we'll moor with the bow inward, so we can use the Mangler if we need to."

The sky in the east was still dark as they ran the ship alongside the jutting finger of land. Jesper and Edvin hurled grapnels ashore from the bow and the stern, and they hauled the little ship in, parallel to the bank. Once they were in position, Stig heaved the narrow gangplank up onto the bulwark and slid it out until its butt end rested on the soft mud that formed the shoreline.

Hal and Lydia waited impatiently for Stig to set the gangplank firmly. Once it was ready, Thorn slapped Hal on the shoulder.

"Get going," he said. "We'll look for you tonight."

"It might take us more than a day to find the Temujai camp and get back here," Hal reminded him.

"Then we'll look for you tomorrow night too," Thorn replied, and shoved him gently toward the gangplank. "Now get going. It'll be light before you know it."

Hal and Lydia crossed to the shore and headed off into the waist-high grass, Lydia leading the way. Thorn watched them go, nodding approvingly. The long grass, soughing gently in the predawn breeze, would make progress a little difficult as they forced their way through it. But it would provide excellent cover if they had to hide from a Temujai patrol.

He turned to the crew, who were standing by expectantly. "Right, lads," he said, "let's get ashore and set up a defensive position on this spit of land. Edvin, you get the lashings off the Mangler and make it ready for action."

He paused as they began to move about their tasks, then snapped at them. "Get a move on. We could have unfriendly visitors any minute!"

. . . . .

The Herons selected the narrowest part of the promontory as the place to set their defensive position. Here, the eight of them could form an effective shield wall, denying the horsemen access to the narrow spit of land beyond.

As they had seen at Fort Ragnak, they dug a ditch across the spit of land, a meter and a half deep. They threw the spoil behind them, forming it into a low earth rampart behind which they would shelter and set their shield wall. The ditch would discourage the horsemen from riding straight at the shield wall. Their horses would balk at the obstacle and slow any headlong charge. They had cut stakes of wood from the trees on the island and they set these now in the ditch. The upper ends were shaped to a point and they angled them outward, as a further deterrent to the riders. They set more sharpened stakes into the earth wall.

Thorn inspected the finished result with a critical eye and declared himself satisfied.

"That should do it," he said. "Now let's rig the nets over the ship to conceal her."

The fishing nets, covered with irregular shapes of canvas dyed green and brown, were draped over the stumpy mast, and attached to the bow and sternposts.

"Don't haul them tight," Thorn called. "We want the whole thing to look lumpy and irregular."

Once the work was completed, he walked inland for about fifty meters and looked back. The freshly dug earth of the low rampart was still visible, but that would fade in a few hours. More important, the obvious shape of the *Heron* was completely concealed. He half shut his eyes and studied it. Under a cursory glance, he thought, it would pass muster as a low hillock on the promontory.

"Let's just hope they don't give it more than a cursory glance," he said to himself as he walked back to the promontory, the long grass swishing around his legs.

The long grass would provide good cover for Hal and Lydia in case they spotted a party of horsemen. But it had at least one major drawback.

It was wet with early morning dew, and as they walked, they left a trail where they had knocked the moisture off the long strands of grass. Hal turned after the first few hundred meters and looked back. With the sun rising in the east and casting a low-level light over the plain, the two dark trails they had left through the silvery-coated grass were painfully obvious. He pointed the fact out to Lydia, who shrugged fatalistically.

"Nothing we can do about it," she said. "And once the sun's fully up, the dew will evaporate and the trails will be obliterated."

"Let's hope the patrols stay away until the sun is fully up, then," Hal said, a worried tone in his voice.

"We haven't seen an early morning patrol so far," Lydia reminded him.

He pursed his lips. He didn't like taking things for granted. It wasn't in his nature to simply hope for the best. But as Lydia had said, they didn't have any choice in the matter. All he could do was will the sun to rise faster and dry out the grass.

They crested a low ridge about five hundred meters from the shore. As they did, Hal turned to look back at the promontory. He could make out the freshly dug earth of the rampart, and see his crew moving about behind it. The ship itself, draped in the concealing nets, was an amorphous shape alongside the bank. They pushed on and the promontory was lost to sight as they found themselves alone on the massive, grassy plain, swept by the wind and dotted here and there with clumps of low trees and bushes. It stretched from one horizon to the other and again he was aware of the sensation of being adrift in a massive, grassy sea.

The long grass swished about their thighs as they pushed through it. After some time, the effort of doing so became quite intense and strands of the stuff tangled around their legs, trying to trip them. The flattened stalks formed a slippery, uncertain surface underfoot.

"Be nice if we had horses to do all the work," he said.

Lydia merely grunted in reply—a reaction he took as meaning "save your breath."

They trudged on as the sun rose higher in the sky. Glancing behind them again, Hal was encouraged to see the tracks of their passage had virtually disappeared as the dew evaporated. In fact, the rising moisture had formed a low ground mist, which helped conceal them further.

"Stop!" Lydia said. Her voice was quiet, but the urgent tone in the command was obvious. He froze in place, resisting the urge to turn and look at her. On previous occasions like this, she had dinned into him the fact that movement of any kind invited detection. He had been shoving his way through the thick grass with his head down. Now he kept it there, but raised his eyes to scan the land ahead of them.

"What is it?" he said softly.

"Temujai. Maybe a dozen of them, half left, about three hundred meters away."

To be so close without having been spotted sooner, the riders must have been traveling through a patch of dead ground—where the terrain dipped slightly and created a large area hidden from sight. He swiveled his eyes to the left now, while being careful not to move his head at all.

He could see them, just. They were at the limit of his peripheral vision: a line of riders on the shaggy brown and piebald mounts he had become accustomed to seeing.

His eyes were aching with the strain of keeping them swiveled left and up. He relaxed them now. Lydia was in a better position to observe them.

"Have they seen us?" he asked.

She hesitated before replying. "I don't . . . think so," she said. "They haven't changed direction and no one looks as if they're calling attention to us."

"Which way are they heading?" His nerves were shrieking with tension at simply standing here, unmoving, while an enemy passed by in plain sight. But he knew it was their best chance.

"Toward that ridge we just crossed," Lydia said. "If they keep on in that direction, they'll come out pretty well opposite where we left the ship."

"The ship!" Hal said, with a sudden jolt of panic raising the pitch of his voice. "They'll see it! They're bound to."

"Not necessarily," Lydia told him, her voice calm and reassuring. "It was pretty well concealed when we looked back at it. As long as the boys see them and don't move about, they should be fine."

"But if they do?" he insisted. Once again, he refused to simply wait and hope for the best.

"If they do, the crew can shove off and sail out into the lake. Or they can stay and fight. They've got a strong defensive position there and they'll give a good account of themselves. Besides, from what Thorn told me, the Temujai usually underestimate their opposition and that can be fatal. You can relax now," she added. "They've passed behind us."

Without realizing it, Hal had been holding himself tensed in every muscle. He let them relax now and felt a flood of relief through his limbs. He turned slowly and stared after the Temujai as they rode toward the crest in the land. The rolling grasslands might look to be flat and even, but they were covered in low ridges and dips that created dead ground—as witness the sudden appearance of the patrol he was now watching.

"They've stopped," he said as the leader signaled for his men to rein in at the crest.

"Normal procedure when you pass over a ridge. Naturally, the commander would want to check out the ground beyond. But significantly, they didn't seem to worry that they'd be skylining themselves as they passed over the crest. So it would seem they don't expect any danger in the vicinity."

"You say," Hal said.

She smiled at him tolerantly. She was used to moving around on land and staying concealed. Hal was infinitely more at home on the open sea, where he knew the risks and dangers and could allow for them.

"I do indeed," she told him. "Look, they're on the move again."

The patrol leader raised his right hand and made a forward motion with it. The riders urged their ponies forward, trotting in single file over the ridge and down the other side. Hal was relieved to see that they were moving at an oblique angle to the spot where the *Heron* was concealed. It appeared that Lydia was right. Within several minutes, they had disappeared from sight.

"Let's go," Lydia said, turning to the east once more and pushing on through the long, tangled grass. The wind had risen now and it soughed gently across the plain, setting the long strands of grass moving, rolling like waves on the ocean.

Hal shook his head at the soft, pervasive hissing sound. "This place gives me the heebie-jeebies," he said.

Ka'zhak, deputy commander of the Temujai patrol, urged his pony forward until he was level with his commander and best friend, En'tak.

En'tak heard him coming and looked around, surprised to see him. As the deputy leader of the patrol, Ka'zhak's position was in the rear.

"What is it?" he asked. He knew that his friend wouldn't have left his position for the sake of a friendly chat. There must have been something that caught his eye. He held up a hand to command the patrol to halt.

"Don't look right away," Ka'zhak cautioned him. "But there's something down by the water's edge."

"What kind of something?" En'tak asked.

Ka'zhak hesitated. "I'm not sure. But it doesn't look right." He waited, then said, "You can look now. But try not to be too obvious about it. It's off to our right and a little behind us."

Pretending to stretch his back and ease himself in the saddle, En'tak casually stood in the stirrups and twisted his upper body to the left, then to the right, to look in the direction Ka'zhak had mentioned.

"What am I looking for?" he asked.

"There's a shape—a strange shape—on the bank," his friend told him. "A mound of some kind."

En'tak frowned. He could see the odd, irregular shape there. It could be a low clump of bushes. Or a mound in the earth.

Or it could be something else entirely. As he watched, there was a flash of light and movement from the right-hand end of the mound. Something alien. Something not natural.


"They've seen something," Stig muttered. He and Thorn were crouched in the cover of the low rampart. He glanced around hurriedly. None of the crew's shields were visible. They were piled on the port side of the ship, under the concealing netting. The crew were on board as well, under the netting and crouched in the cover of the port rowing wells.

"Maybe," Thorn said. "Or maybe they're just resting. Oh, Loki's ingrown toenail!" He added the curse as he noticed something on the ship. The camouflage netting, draped over the bow post, had been loosely secured. With the recently arisen breeze, one corner had worked its way free, revealing the heron-head mascot at the top of the bow post. Brightly painted and well maintained, it bobbed slightly up and down in time to the ship's movement on the ripples. He glanced over his shoulder at the position of the mid-morning sun. The brightly painted figurehead could have caught its rays and reflected a flash of light.

"They're moving again," Stig said. "Looks like they're satisfied there's nothing here."

"What makes you say that?" Thorn asked.

The big warrior shrugged. "Well, if they saw something, or thought they saw something, they would have come to investigate, wouldn't they?"

Thorn stroked his shaggy beard. He had grown up distrusting the Temujai. Everything he knew about them told him they were a cunning and devious enemy. "Maybe," he said now. "Or maybe they plan to come back later."

"We'll come back after dark," En'tak told his deputy. "That way we can take a closer look."

"What are you expecting to see?" Ka'zhak asked.

The patrol commander shrugged uncertainly. "That strange shape *could* have been a ship. And something caught the light at the front of it. I believe the Skandians often have bird or animal carvings on the front of their ships. It could have been one of those."

"So, you think Skandians were there?" Ka'zhak asked.

"I don't see who else they could be. And if there are, I don't plan to make another mistake."

En'tak had been an *Ulan* commander at the recent battle at the pass into Skandia. It was his *Ulan* of sixty riders that had been so badly mauled by the Skandian defenders. As a result, the Sha'shan had stripped him of his rank. Now he commanded a lowly patrol of ten men. Ka'zhak had been his deputy commander then and had been reduced in rank accordingly. Both men were still smarting from the shame of their demotion and were looking for a way to win their way back into the Sha'shan's good graces.

"But how would they get a ship up here to the lake?" Ka'zhak wondered.

His commander regarded him for a few moments before speaking. In truth, he didn't know. But he knew Skandians were a clever and resourceful people who often managed feats that had been deemed impossible.

"That's what I plan to find out."

The sun was low in the western sky. And still the monotonous grass plains rolled on and on—featureless and unchanging—as Hal and Lydia trudged on toward the east.

They had stopped twice more to hide from Temujai patrols, their hearts in their mouths each time as silent files of riders appeared over the horizon. But neither of the patrols had come close to where they crouched, concealed in the long grass. Now they crested yet another low ridge and surveyed the terrain beyond.

There was no change. The waving grasslands stretched ahead of them to yet another low crest in the distance. They could see several large rock outcrops and a scattering of low trees and shrubs dotted about the plain. But for the most part, the ground was unremarkable and unvarying.

"Better keep an eye out for those patrols heading home,"

Lydia said, conscious that there was barely an hour's daylight left. Hal glanced nervously over his shoulder. This rolling and dipping ground, which allowed the riders to appear suddenly, seemingly out of nowhere, was grating on his nerves. He never knew when the monotony of trudging through the long, clinging stalks of grass would be shattered by the unheralded appearance of a file of silent riders—usually a lot closer than either Lydia or he expected them to be.

"Looks as if we'll be spending the night out here," Lydia said. She looked around, assessing the surrounding long grass. "Could be worse. If we trample down the grass we can form a kind of nest for ourselves. And at least it'll be soft to sleep on."

Hal indicated a small outcrop of rocks about fifty meters away. "Why don't we head for those rocks. We could get a fire going there before the light goes, and have a hot drink. Once the sun's down, we'll douse the fire."

Lydia nodded agreement. In the dark, any small light on the plain would stand out like a beacon. But in daylight, if they used dry, hot-burning wood, there was only a small chance that they'd be spotted. She doubled her pace and set out for the rocks. They were carrying a small supply of firewood with them and Hal quickly set a fire among the rocks, where there was no chance of its spreading to the long grass surrounding them.

They boiled water for coffee and then stamped the fire out, making sure no trace of a spark remained. Hal sat in the long grass, which Lydia had stamped down in a semicircle around the rocks. He cradled a mug of hot, sweet coffee and sighed contentedly as he sipped at it.

"That's better," he said as he felt the invigorating effect of the hot drink flowing through his legs and body. "I don't mind a cold meal, but a cup of coffee does wonders for my spirits."

Lydia grinned. "It's a bad habit I've picked up from you and your crew," she admitted. "But I must say I enjoy it too. And it's just as well you don't mind a cold meal, because that's what you'll be getting."

Hal rose to his feet and peered around at the surrounding horizon. "No sign of those patrols," he said. "I would have thought they'd be heading home by now."

"Maybe they took a different route back," Lydia said. "Or maybe they're like us and they're camping out for the night."

Most of the patrols they had seen that day had returned by a more circuitous route. But the first patrol was still out on the plain and doubling back to the spot where they had observed the strange shape on the shore of the lake.

En'tak led his men back northwest. They had explored to the south, reaching as far as the mouth of the river that ran out of the lake and down through the mountains. Now he called a halt as they reached a low ridge half a kilometer from the spot where they had seen the concealed and camouflaged shape of the *Heron*.

He ordered his men to set up a camp, cautioning them not to light a fire. Then he and Ka'zhak continued on foot, crouching as they crossed the ridge, then staying low as they made their way through the long grass toward the promontory and the strange, irregular shape beside it.

They found a small rise less than a hundred meters from the

site, where they could lie on their bellies and keep watch on it. They lay silently for almost an hour before their patience was rewarded and they saw signs of movement on the bank.

Thorn had ordered the crew to remain concealed throughout the hours of daylight. Most of them remained on board the *Heron*, under the cover of the nets draped over the ship. A few had stayed onshore, concealed behind the low rampart they had built, keeping watch for any sign of the enemy.

Once night fell, however, he decided he could let them relax a little. They had seen no sign of the Temujai operating by night, and he was reasonably confident that they could move about within their small camp without being observed.

Within reason, of course. He still insisted that all movement should be kept to a minimum. Edvin could prepare the evening meal—without a fire, naturally—and the sentries at the rampart could be relieved. But that was the limit of the movement he allowed.

It was enough, however, to attract the attention of the two silent Temujai lying in the long grass.

"There are definitely people there," En'tak breathed, his face close to his companion's ear.

Ka'zhak nodded. "I heard them speaking a few minutes ago. They sound like Skandians."

The patrol commander looked at his friend in some surprise. "I didn't know you spoke Skandian."

But Ka'zhak shook his head. "Only a few words," he admitted.

"It's more the way they speak—sort of abrupt and sharp-sounding."

In contrast to the more staccato tones of the Skandians, the Temujai language was a smooth-flowing tongue.

"How many do you think there are?" Ka'zhak asked now.

His commander shrugged. "Not many. Half a dozen, maybe? Any more than that and they'd make noise. Skandians find it hard to stay silent."

As Thorn had commented, the Temujai tended to underestimate their enemies, treating them with disdain and expecting them to be undisciplined and unruly.

The fact was, they had little experience of a well-trained and disciplined force like the Herons or any of the other Skandian brotherbands.

That was En'tak's first mistake.

"So, what do we do now?" Ka'zhak whispered.

En'tak began to wriggle backward through the grass, looking for the cover of the low rise they had crested some time ago.

"Back to camp," he said. "We'll hit them first thing in the morning."

Ka'zhak mimicked his movement, moving back through the long grass to a point where he could rise to his feet without being seen.

"Maybe we should report back to the main camp and let the Sha'shan know they're here," he said.

But En'tak shook his head forcefully. "This is our chance to win back the Sha'shan's respect—and our former positions," he said. "If we go whining back now to tell him there are half a dozen Skandians on the lake, he'll think we're spineless cowards. On the other hand, if we go back and report that we've wiped out a Skandian war party—and maybe take a prisoner or two along with us—we'll win his respect again. And maybe we'll be reinstated to our former positions."

"I suppose you're right," Ka'zhak said uncertainly. "So, will we attack on horseback?"

En'tak shook his head. "We'll creep in on foot. They'd see us coming too soon if we rode in. If we can get close without being seen, we'll catch them sleeping and unawares before dawn."

And that was his second mistake.

As the sun eventually set, stars began to twinkle in the sky above the massive grass plain. Lydia chewed on a piece of smoked beef wrapped in flatbread. Hal was eating a handful of dried fruit. He took a sip of cold water from his canteen, wishing he had some way of keeping coffee hot after he had made it.

His thighs and calves ached from the hours of pushing through the long, clinging grass. Now that the sun was gone, the night was chilly and he pulled his sheepskin vest tighter around his body and settled back. There was nothing to do but rest, he thought—and after the long day of trudging across the plain, he'd have no trouble sleeping. As he had that thought, he began to nod off.

"Look," said Lydia quietly.

She had risen to her knees and was pointing to the sky in the east. Hal struggled up to a sitting position resentfully. He had been on the point of falling asleep and had found himself a comfortable position in the bed of long grass underneath him.

"What is it?" he asked.

She made no answer but continued to point to the eastern sky. And now he saw it too. With the passing of daylight, and with the moon hours away from rising, he could see a glow of light reflecting from the clouds. It stretched for almost a quarter of the horizon to the east—the reflected light of campfires, hundreds of them.

"It's the Temujai camp," Lydia said. "And it's a big one."

They gathered their equipment and possessions together and rose to their feet. Neither of them spoke but both were driven by a sense of urgency. The Temujai camp must be close by, and they set off through the night toward that glow of light.

If the long grass made walking difficult by daylight, it was twice as hard in the dark. Hal slipped and stumbled repeatedly as he walked into dips and irregularities under the grass. Lydia seemed to have no trouble, he noticed. She seemed to glide across the terrain without any sign of awkwardness. He stumbled and fell to his knees for the fifth time and let out a soft curse.

"Sontod's bad breath!"

Lydia reached back to give him a hand up. "And who might Sontod be?" she asked, with a half smile. The pantheon of gods and demigods that Skandians observed was a constant source of amusement to her. Not, she noticed, that they actually seemed to worship them. They seemed to keep them handy just so they could use them in curses. "And does he have bad breath?"

Hal eyed her balefully. "He's a she. She's the demigod of dance and movement," he told her.

She raised an eyebrow. "You could definitely use a little help from her, then," she said. "Judging by the way you keep blundering around."

Hal drew breath to make a cutting reply. Her earlier remark about his "tripping over his own big feet" sprang to mind. Then a tangle of grass wound around his ankle and he went over again. Lydia waited, all too patiently, he thought, while he regained his feet and moved off again. He decided not to counter her comment about his tripping.

"To answer your question, yes. She does have bad breath. Most demigods and demons do. It goes with their big yellow fangs."

"What attractive gods you have in Skandia," Lydia said. She was yet to hear of one who wasn't ferocious, festooned with long hair and toenails, deceptive or just plain bad-tempered. "Don't you have any who are attractive, pleasant-natured or light on their feet?"

"Sontod is light on her feet. I told you, she'd the goddess of dance."

"But by the sound of her, she's not the sort of dance partner anyone would choose. Not with those big yellow fangs and bad breath."

"Partners don't choose her. She chooses them," Hal pointed out. "And with those big yellow fangs, you don't refuse her when you're chosen."

"I suppose not. Still . . ." Whatever Lydia was going to say next was left unsaid as they finally made their way to the crest of the next rise. Both of them fell silent for a few seconds at the sight of hundreds of campfires on the plain below them, stretching as far as the eye could see.

And now the acrid, harsh smell that Lydia had noted at the

pass was obvious once more. But this time, the camp she was looking at was bigger—much, much bigger—than the one she had seen in the mountains. This wasn't a raiding party or even a war party.

This was the Temujai nation on the move.

An hour before first light, as was his custom when they were in enemy territory, Thorn quietly woke the crew of the *Heron,* moving along the sleeping line of warriors and shaking each one by the shoulder.

Their long training ensured that they woke without any noise, and without speaking. Thorn leaned close to each man's ear and said softly.

"Stand to. Dawn in an hour."

Edvin was the first he woke and he followed Thorn down the line, handing out cups of cold coffee to the defenders. He had brewed a pot the day before, before he had doused the fire at sunset. It would have been better if he had been able to keep it hot. But even cold, the caffeine served to help them wake up. They sipped it gratefully, nodding their thanks.

Dawn was traditionally the time for surprise attacks, which was why Thorn acted as he did. Jesper had been on lookout during the final hours of darkness. Thorn paused beside him, his eyes just above the earth rampart behind which they were sheltering. When the crew had bedded down for the night, he had ordered those who had been on board the ship to take their places at the earthworks. That way, they were all in position, ready to repel any attack that might eventuate. Their shields were beside them, leaning against the inner wall of the rampart. Each warrior also had a spear standing ready and his own personal choice of close-quarters weapon—either a sword or a long-handled ax. Thorn, of course, had his massive club-hand.

"Anything happening?" Thorn breathed, his voice only just audible.

Jesper glanced at him, then looked back at the long grass that lay before them, beginning to wave gently now in the predawn breeze coming off the lake.

"Not sure," he said. "I thought I saw movement out there"—he nodded to his right front—"a few minutes ago."

"The grass moving in the wind, maybe?"

Jesper shook his head. "It was before the wind came up," he told the battlemaster, who considered the report for a moment or two. Jesper was prone to playing silly practical jokes when he was bored. But he was a superlative lookout. In a situation like this, Thorn knew his judgment could be relied on.

"How far out?" he asked now.

"Maybe fifty, sixty meters," Jesper replied. "I've seen nothing since, although I have been watching."

"So, if there is someone there, they haven't moved forward?" Thorn asked.

Jesper shook his head definitely. "No. I've been scanning along that line ever since I thought I saw movement. There's been nothing else."

"All right. I'll warn the others," Thorn said. Better to assume there was an attack in the offing and be ready for it than to dismiss Jesper's uneasy feeling as a false alarm. "Keep scanning that line. Don't fixate on any one spot," he said. He saw Jesper's quick, irritated glance. He hadn't needed to add that last warning. Jesper knew what he was doing. Thorn patted his shoulder apologetically.

"Sorry," he said. Staying in a crouch, he moved back down the line of waiting defenders, warning them that there was a possible enemy in the long grass ahead of them.

"Shields ready," he said, and the Herons slipped their left arms into the straps of their big round shields, ready to raise them and lock them into a defensive wall if required. Thorn took up his own shield and joined the line crouching behind the earth barricade. He considered sending someone—Edvin possibly—back to the ship to man the Mangler, but discarded the idea. Edvin would need help loading the machine after the first shot and that would mean two men out of the shield wall. Thorn couldn't afford to weaken the defenses so severely.

"Stay alert," he said in a gruff whisper. Those near him passed the message down the line. Above the eastern horizon, the sky was slowly turning pink as the sun came close to rising.

If they do hit us, he thought, it'll be just as the sun comes up and the glare is in our eyes.

On the other hand, he knew, the rising sun would backlight the attackers. They'd be silhouetted, but they'd be clearly visible. He moved his club-hand in an unconscious gesture, testing that it was firmly set on the stump of his arm. Waiting was the worst part, he thought. It always had been and it always would be.

"Come on," he muttered. "Let's have you."

He didn't realize that he'd spoken aloud until Stefan, crouched beside him, turned his head.

"What was that, Thorn?" he asked softly. He was concerned that he might have missed some instruction or information. But the shaggy-haired sea wolf shook his head and made a negating gesture with the massive club.

"Nothing," he said. "Stay focused."

As the sun rose, Hal and Lydia could see the Temujai encampment more clearly. Hundreds, perhaps thousands of the hump-shaped felt tents covered the grass plain, looking for all the world like giant mushrooms growing wild. The long grass had been stamped down or cut to make a clear space for the encampment—and, presumably, to provide fodder for the Temujai's horses.

The tents—or *yurts*, as they were called—were roughly organized in groups, with nine or ten tents gathered around a cooking fire. Thin lines of smoke rose from these fires, where the coals of the previous night still smoldered. As they watched, women emerged from the tents and began to stoke the fires into new life. The acrid smell intensified.

Hal wrinkled his nose in distaste. "What are they burning?"

When Lydia told him, he shrugged. "Well, they certainly have an almost endless supply of that," he said, indicating one of several temporary horse-holding paddocks that were set on the perimeter of the camp. Rope fences surrounded the horse lines, enclosing large rectangular spaces, each one with hundreds of horses moving restlessly inside the confining ropes.

"I guess they have so many horses, they had to build three or four containment areas," Hal said softly.

Lydia nodded. She pointed down the slight slope toward the massive camp. "Sentries," she said.

Hal could see them, now that the light was stronger. There was a ring of armed men around the camp, separated by forty meters between each man. They were on foot and armed with bows and swords. Each carried a light shield on his left arm. They all faced outward, but there was a lackluster air about them. They were bored. They didn't expect trouble, Hal thought.

Staying just below the crest and crouching so that only their heads showed briefly above the long grass, Hal and Lydia began to move to their left, skirting the camp. None of the sentries showed any sign that they had seen them. They had gone about fifty meters when Lydia touched Hal's arm and gestured for him to sink to his knees. Hal obeyed, then she led him forward, crawling on their bellies so they could remain unobserved while they studied the camp.

They lay close beside each other, their heads together so they could converse in whispers. Below them, the sounds of the camp awakening were becoming evident. Horses stamped and whinnied. Men and women called out to one another as they greeted their neighbors and the dawn. There was an occasional rattle of cooking implements.

In the center of the camp, they could hear orders being shouted as several parties of men saddled horses and mounted up, riding toward the periphery of the camp. All of them, Hal noticed, were heading south and west.

Closer to the edge of the camp, however, and surrounded by half a dozen guards, was the object that had drawn Lydia's attention.

It was a large wagon, a timber platform mounted on four solid-wood wheels. The body of the wagon was another yurt—but a massive one, perhaps five times the size of those that made up the encampment.

The felt walls rose nearly two meters above the wagon bed before they curved over into the rounded roof. That added another two meters to the height of the structure. As Lydia had noted on her reconnaissance at Serpent Pass, the roof and walls were held in place by rope bindings—seemingly haphazard and untidy but, on further study, forming a tight, secure structure that would survive the severe winter winds of the upper grasslands.

At the rear of the huge wagon, a section had been left open, forming a terrace or porch outside the entrance to the yurt. There was no other structure that they could see that rivaled this in size or grandeur.

Hal looked sidelong at Lydia, a question obvious in his gaze. She breathed a reply.

"The Sha'shan."

He nodded in understanding. "Why not place it in the middle of the camp?"

She shrugged. "This way, it's clear of the cook fires' smoke and the dust from the horse lines."

As she spoke, the tent flap in the rear of the huge yurt was thrown aside and a figure emerged onto the wooden platform. He was short and heavily built, Hal thought. Then he corrected that impression. The man was seriously overweight for his lack of height. He was dressed in a brocaded robe and a pointed felt hat dyed green. His beard and long hair were both plaited and apparently smeared with grease or fat, as the hair stood out from his head in two large pigtails and his beard was also divided in two, with each half curving upward. His mustache was thick and luxuriant.

He walked to the edge of the platform, hawked and spat over the railing onto the trampled grass below. The half dozen guards on duty around the wagon came quickly to attention as they sighted him.

"These guards are a bit more alert than the camp sentries," he observed in a whisper.

Lydia nodded agreement. "I guess if the Sha'shan can pop out any minute of the day and check up on you, it pays to be alert."

"Alert at the yurt," he observed.

Lydia didn't reply, she simply looked at him—and the look spoke volumes. He decided not to share any more lighthearted comments with her. She was too tough an audience, he thought.

"It was a joke," he said finally.

But she shook her head. "A joke is funny," she told him. "Looks like he's going back to bed," she added.

The tubby figure on the rear deck of the wagon-yurt stretched his arms above his head and yawned hugely. Then, with one last glance around, he turned and disappeared back inside.

"Wonder who's in there with him?" Hal said.

Apparently, Lydia had been thinking the same thing. "Maybe we should stay around for a while and see who else comes out."

It seemed like a reasonable idea. After all, Hal thought, they might have to wait here for several hours anyway, as the patrols made their way out of the camp. They might as well keep tabs on the Sha'shan while they were at it. You never knew when that sort of information might come in handy.

Already, a vague idea was forming in his mind. He wasn't ready to give voice to it yet. He thought he'd let it simmer while he considered it—and all the elements that might affect it. He unhitched his canteen from his belt and took a long swig. Then he settled down into the long grass, his chin resting on his hand. His eyes roamed the vast Temujai camp, taking in the clusters of yurts, the riders moving out from the horse corrals and the groups of warriors and women sitting round the campfires, eating the food provided by the women. His stomach rumbled as the breeze wafted the smell of cooking meat toward their hiding place. Then another gust assailed his nostrils with the smell of the dried-dung fires.

His stomach stopped rumbling.

ere they come!"

It was Edvin who saw the first movement and called a warning, as the line of Temujai warriors rose out of the tall grass some thirty meters in front of the Skandian defenses.

Thorn watched them as they rushed forward five meters, then paused as they took arrows from their quivers, nocked them to their bows and drew back. He waited a second, then roared a command.

"Shields!"

As one, the massive Skandian shields came up, linking together and forming a solid wall. A second later, there was a savage rattle as the volley of arrows slammed into the hide-and-wooden shields. Thorn was watching the enemy through a tiny gap between his shield and Stefan's. He saw them preparing to shoot again.

"Keep them up!" he roared, and the second volley rattled harmlessly against the shield wall.

Thorn glanced sidelong at Stefan. "They can keep this up all day but they won't hurt us. They're going to have to come to close quarters."

En'tak loosed another arrow and saw it slam impotently into one of the big round shields. He grimaced in frustration. If they were forced to attack on foot, the Temujai would be giving up their main advantages in a fight—the speed and mobility of their slashing horseback attacks, and their ability to maintain a constant, accurate arrow storm on their opponents' defenses, whittling down their numbers before finally closing with them. They couldn't maintain that speed and accuracy if they were on foot, running over broken, uneven ground, with the long grass threatening to trip them at every stride. In addition, they would be too close to launch any plunging volleys of arrows into the enemy lines, overcoming the solid shield wall that faced them.

But that had been a deliberate decision. He'd wanted to get close to the enemy before launching his attack. Now, as he counted the shields facing his men, he realized he'd underestimated the enemy. He'd expected half a dozen Skandians, no more. But he saw there were eight shields in the wall. So, eight men facing his twelve. They were slightly more even odds than he had counted on.

There was another consideration—one he wasn't aware of. The Temujai were excellent warriors—courageous and determined. But their forte was long-distance warfare, using their bows and shooting from horseback before finally closing to end the battle. They were capable warriors when it came to close quarters, but they were facing Skandians, who were probably the best hand-to-hand fighters in the world.

En'tak didn't know that. But he was about to find out. He tossed his bow aside and drew his curved saber.

"Charge!" he yelled. "Close with them and finish them!"

Shorthanded as he was, he couldn't afford to leave several men back to maintain a steady barrage of arrows as he and the others moved in. That was another standard Temujai tactic—but one he'd have to forgo.

Peering from behind his shield, Thorn felt the deadly rain of arrows cease and saw a warrior in the center of the Temujai line cast his bow aside and draw a long, curved sword. Realizing the shield wall had served its purpose, Thorn rose to his feet and yelled a command.

"Spears!"

Eight spears sailed out from the line of Skandians, arcing up and then down and slamming into the charging Temujai. Two of them went down, hurled backward by the force of the heavy projectiles. The others faltered, seeing the line of shields, axes and swords ready to receive them. But while En'tak was a poor leader and tactician, he was a brave man. He screamed at his troops now to close with the enemy.

He picked out a huge Skandian on the left of the line. The warrior had strange dark circles over his eyes and was armed with a long weapon that looked like a cross between a pike, a spear and an ax. He stepped up onto the rampart to receive the charging Temujai, dropping his huge circular shield to the ground as he did so, in order to hold his weapon in both hands.

En'tak stumbled slightly as he crossed the ditch, which was filled with loose material—brushwood, branches, loose rocks and bundles of grass. He recovered and bounded nimbly up onto the earth rampart beside the giant Skandian, swinging his saber in a deadly overhead arc as he did so.

The Skandian calmly blocked the blow, trapping the blade in the gap between the ax head and the spear point on his weapon. Then, quickly, he twisted the trapped sword out of En'tak's hand, withdrew and then lunged forward—all in the space of a heartbeat.

En'tak reared back, lost his footing and tumbled off the rampart into the ditch. As he struggled to regain his footing in the loose, shifting material that filled the ditch, he heard his friend's voice close by him.

"We're losing!" Ka'zhak shouted. "You need to get back to the camp and tell the Sha'shan that the Skandians are on the lake. Go now! We'll keep them busy while you get away!"

The patrol commander looked around desperately. He saw two of his men facedown on the earth wall. As he watched, another was hurled backward. A shaggy-haired, bearded Skandian, with a huge club in place of his right hand, had slammed his weapon onto the Temujai's midsection in a savage thrust, smashing ribs and sending the slightly built horseman sailing backward. En'tak shook his head in confusion. How had it all gone so wrong?

Ka'zhak was tugging at his arm, spinning him round so that he faced away from the battle and shoving him back toward their camp.

"Go! Go now!"

Numbly, En'tak realized his deputy was right. The Sha'shan had to be warned about this Skandian incursion onto the great lake. If there was one ship, there might well be others, and Pa'tong, the leader of the Temujai nation, must be made aware of the fact.

He began to run. Then he heard a cry of pain behind him and turned to see his friend falling under an ax blow from the massive, black-eyed Skandian. Ka'zhak rolled down the earth wall into the ditch and lay still. Sobbing with frustration and sorrow, En'tak began to run again, trying to shut out the sound of the fighting behind him.

He made it to their camp, where the horses were tethered in a temporary rope corral. He untied his own horse, looking at the saddle on the ground nearby. The horse's rope bridle was already in place. He decided there was no time to saddle the horse and leapt astride, riding bareback. He was barely astride, hauling at the bridle, when the horse pirouetted on its back feet, turning toward the east. By the time he crested the nearest low ridge, the horse was already at a full gallop. Behind him, there was an ominous silence. The clash of weapons and shouts of the wounded had ceased.

Lydia and Hal lay concealed in the long grass above the Sha'shan's massive wagon-yurt. In the time they had been keeping watch, they had seen the Temujai leader emerge once more to confer with the commander of his guards. Then, half an hour later, a woman came out onto the rear platform of the wagon, a bowl of water in her hands. She tossed the water over the railing, looked idly around and returned to the interior.

"Two of them," Hal said. "Do you think there are more?"

Lydia shrugged. "Could be. It's hard to tell."

Shortly after, the question was answered as three of the women who had been preparing food at one of the cook fires approached the wagon, carrying bowls of food.

They paused at the bottom of the steps that led up to the rear platform and called a greeting. A male voice answered them, and they climbed the stairs and stood waiting. The tent flap opened, and the Sha'shan and the woman they had seen emerged. The woman carried two low stools. She set them down on the platform and motioned for the Sha'shan to sit on one. The rotund leader did as she suggested and the other women proceeded to serve him, placing several bowls of food in front of him on the timber decking.

"Breakfast in the fresh air," Hal observed. Lydia said nothing. When the Sha'shan was served, his companion received a bowl of food as well. She sat on the second low stool and began to eat.

Hal smiled. "One bowl for her. Three for him."

"That's obviously how he keeps his trim figure," Lydia said dryly.

Time passed and they continued to observe. While they had been watching, several patrols had left the camp and headed south and west. There seemed to be no further activity of this kind as the camp went about its workaday tasks—airing bedding, beating the dust out of rugs and blankets, and tending to washtubs set over some of the larger fires. Lydia noted that the majority of these tasks seemed to be carried out by the women of the camp. The men sat idly in the sunshine outside their tents, fletching arrows or sharpening their curved sabers. Several of them were busy making new bows—the short, laminated recurve bows that they shot from horseback. Hal strained his eyes but could see little in the way of detail.

"I'd like to see how they do that," he said quietly. He was always fascinated by weapon-making techniques.

Lydia grinned at him. "Maybe you could stroll down and ask them to show you."

Hal regarded her bleakly. "I don't think so," he said. He glanced around, noting the position of the sun. It was well up now and the dew on the grass would have evaporated. That meant they would leave no telltale path when they left.

"Might be time for us to go," he said. "I'm not sure what else we'll find out here."

Lydia nodded agreement. "Thorn will be getting worried about us," she said. "He's such a mother hen."

They began to inch their way backward, away from the crest they had been on to observe the camp. Once they were out of sight of the sentries, Hal started to rise to his knees. But Lydia shot out a hand to stop him.

"Listen!" she said urgently. He froze in a half crouch. Faintly, he heard the sound of galloping hoofs behind them, coming from the west. He sank back down into the grass and turned toward the direction of the hoofbeats.

"A patrol coming back?" he suggested.

But Lydia shook her head. "It's just one horse," she said. Then she pointed to a ridgeline south of them as a single horse and rider came into view. The rider was urging the horse on, in spite of the fact that it was running as fast as it could. Its sides were white and lathered. They passed out of sight, heading for the camp.

Hal and Lydia exchanged a look. Quickly, they scurried back to their former vantage point.

"Something's happened," Lydia said.

"He came from the west," Hal said, a worried tone in his voice. Lydia looked at him, a question on her face, and he explained further. "He didn't come from the south. He came from due west. That's where the *Heron* lies."

She thought about what he'd said, then replied, "That's not to say that he had anything to do with the ship."

"Maybe not. But what else could it be?"

They fell silent as they watched the new arrival stop outside a large yurt set in an open space past the first few rows of accommodation tents. They'd seen riders coming and going from this tent during the morning. It was clearly a command tent.

Several minutes later, the man reemerged, being dragged by the arms by two Temujai, while a third—an older man and presumably a senior officer—strode purposefully ahead of them, leading the way to the Sha'shan's wagon. The prisoner, for that was obviously what he now was, struggled in vain against the two men frog-marching him. The older man turned and spat a few curt words at him. His struggles ceased, and he stood erect and walked more willingly.

"I'd say he doesn't have good news to report," Lydia observed. "That augurs well for the crew."

"Let's hope so," Hal replied.

The small party had reached the wagon-yurt now. The two guards and the prisoner halted at ground level, while the leader mounted the steps and stood outside the yurt, calling out. After a minute or so, the Sha'shan emerged. The senior officer bowed—a short, cursory head movement—and spoke rapidly. Even from a distance, the Sha'shan's growing rage was all too evident. He made a few interjections, asking for more details. Then he pointed at the prisoner and made a peremptory motion for him to be brought up to the wagon deck.

An angry discussion followed, with the Sha'shan firing questions at the forlorn man, often cutting off his answers with yet another query. The prisoner stood, head down, answering in a low voice. Lydia and Hal could hear the Sha'shan all too clearly. The mumbled replies were inaudible to them.

Finally, the Temujai leader made a dismissive gesture and the prisoner's escort shoved him back down the stairs, where his arms were pinned by the other two troops. The Sha'shan shouted a furious order at them, at which the prisoner cried out in fear, seeming to beg for mercy. The Sha'shan waved him away and the two guards dragged him back through the camp to the command tent.

"I don't think I want to know what's about to happen to him," Hal said. Lydia remained silent, although she echoed the thought.

The Sha'shan and his officer continued to talk for several more minutes. Their words were accompanied by much arm waving and pointing—sometimes to due west, and sometimes to the south.

Then the officer bowed once more and turned to the stairs, while the Sha'shan reentered his yurt.

As the officer strode quickly back through the camp, Hal turned to Lydia.

"I think it's time we weren't here," he said.

They had gone barely fifty meters when they heard voices shouting and bugles sounding within the camp. Lydia put a hand on Hal's arm, signaling for him to stop, and they looked back up the slight rise.

A few minutes later, a party of sixty riders, riding in two files, appeared over the rise on their right, heading southwest. The two Herons dropped into the cover of the long grass and watched as the riders went over another crest and passed out of sight.

"That's not a patrol," Hal said. "That was a full *Ulan*."

Lydia had no time to reply before they heard more pounding hooves and another two *Ulans* appeared in the distance, riding hard from the camp. Like the first sixty, they headed southwest as well.

"They're on the move," Lydia said.

Hal shook his head. "Not the whole camp. It'll take at least a day, maybe two, for them to get underway. But that's a sizable war party: one hundred and eighty riders."

"I would have thought they'd head due west, toward where the ship was moored," said Lydia.

But Hal shook his head. "They're playing it smart," he said. "They know a ship wouldn't wait around there once she'd been discovered. She'd head off across the lake, where the Temujai can't follow. And it's a huge lake—so there's plenty of room to get lost. That's certainly what I'd have done if I were on board. What they need is a chokepoint—somewhere they can stop the ship if she tries to get back to the low country."

Lydia's eyes narrowed as she followed his reasoning. "Like the point where the river flows out of the lake?"

"That's what I'd do in their place. If they can block that off, they'll have us trapped up here."

"Which means we'd better get a move on."

"Exactly."

They resumed their trek with a new sense of urgency, moving the pace up to a slow jog, which was the best speed they could maintain through the clinging long grass that dogged their every step. They sighted no more *Ulans* heading southwest. The grasslands seemed deserted as they forced their way through the long growth. The only sound was the whisper of the wind through the tops of the grass.

It was well after midday when they finally crested the small rise above the spot where the *Heron* had been moored. As he stopped to study the small promontory, Hal's heart sank.

The ship was gone.

They exchanged a despairing look. Hal scanned the shore of the lake to the north and south, searching for some sign of the ship. He stared closely at the island, trying to see if the *Heron* was there.

Nothing.

Then Lydia grasped his forearm, pointing with her free hand to the bank by the little promontory.

"Down there," she said. When Hal followed the direction she was indicating, he saw a familiar figure rise from the long grass and wave to them.

"It's Thorn!" he said, the relief evident in his voice. He began to run down the slight incline to the waiting figure. Lydia followed, a few paces behind him. They blundered through the grass, and as they went, Hal saw two brilliant flashes of light, as Thorn struck a flint with the blunt edge of his saxe. It was their standard method of signaling on board the ship.

They were halfway down the slope and only thirty meters away from Thorn when Lydia cried out again. Hal, who was intent on keeping his footing and had his eyes on the uneven ground ahead of him, looked up to see a lean, low shape emerging from behind the island. The *Heron*, under oars, swung its bow toward the shore and sped toward them, a ripple of white water under her forefoot as she came. A bone in her teeth, Hal thought, as sailors liked to describe a ship moving at speed.

He reached Thorn and threw his arms around the grinning sea wolf, causing him to stagger a pace or two under the impact of Hal's arrival.

"So, you're back!" Thorn said, returning Hal's hug. He received Lydia, who was a little less demonstrative. "Good to see you, girl!"

Lydia disengaged herself from him, her nose wrinkling. "Don't you ever bathe?" she asked. She knew that when they were at sea, freshwater was strictly rationed. But here, Thorn had a whole lake full of freshwater at his disposal. He grinned at her, by no means insulted.

"Bathing is for them who's dirty or smelly," he said cheerfully.

"And you qualify on both counts," she told him. But before the discussion could continue, Hal intervened.

"What happened here?" he asked. He could see evidence of burial mounds on the shore of the promontory. "Is everyone all right?" he asked, suddenly fearful.

Thorn patted his arm reassuringly. "We're all fine. Ingvar took a small cut on the arm—an arrow that nearly missed him. Otherwise, no injuries. Those"—he nodded toward the fresh graves—"are Temujai. We ran afoul of one of their patrols."

Hal nodded. "We thought something like that might have happened."

"Thankfully, it was a small one and their commander wasn't too good at his job. He chose to attack us on foot, which wasn't a great idea. Temujai may be many things, but they're not infantry."

"Is he one of those?" Hal asked, indicating the graves.

Thorn shook his head. "He got away. He was the only one who did. Last we saw, he was heading back to the Temujai camp as if all the fiends of hell were after him."

Hal and Lydia exchanged a quick look. "That'll be the one we saw," Hal said. He turned back to Thorn to explain. "We saw a rider come in this morning. He was obviously reporting bad news to the Sha'shan—"

"You saw the Sha'shan?" Thorn interrupted, but Hal held up a hand to silence him.

"I'll get to that. But a few minutes after he reported, the whole camp went wild. There were warriors riding out and heading south—lots of them."

"South," Thorn mused. "Not west, where we were."

"Hal thinks they're hoping to seal off the exit from the lake," Lydia said. "And keep us bottled up here."

Thorn nodded thoughtfully. "That could be right," he said. "They'd probably assume that we'd have moved on from here. How big is their camp? If the Sha'shan is with them, it must be pretty massive."

"It's huge," Hal told him. "There are thousands of them. It's more than a camp. I think it's the entire Temujai nation."

An eager voice hailed them as the *Heron* ran her prow up onto the bank. Stig vaulted over the rail at the bow, splashing down in the shallow water, and ran toward them.

"Are you all right?" he said as he came closer.

Hal reassured him. "We're fine. But we don't have time to stand here nattering. Let's get aboard and I'll fill you in on what's been happening."

They ran down to the ship, where Jesper and Stefan were leaning over the bow railing to help them aboard. Stig waited until the other three were aboard, then put his shoulder to the bow of the little ship, pushing her back through the soft mud until she floated free. Then he grasped the railing and sprang up, rolling over the railing onto the deck. Jesper grabbed the back of his belt and helped him aboard.

"Thanks," Stig told him, running aft and calling out orders to the rowers. Ulf, Wulf, Stefan and Ingvar backed water for three strokes, then the starboard two went ahead while the port side continued to back water. The ship spun in its own length in a turn to port.

Hal had reached the tiller and was glancing at the telltale when Stig began to bark more orders at the rowers.

"Belay that," Hal told him. "Hoist the port sail."

The breeze was fresh and was on their starboard beam—an excellent point of sailing. Oars came in with the usual clatter—there was no need for stealth now—and Stefan and Jesper made their way to the halyards while Ulf and Wulf took up their positions at the sheets.

The yardarm shot up the mast and clunked home into the retaining socket. The sail billowed out momentarily, then hardened into a tight curve as the twins hauled on the sheets and brought it under control. *Heron* accelerated eagerly, the *tonk-tonk, tonk-tonk* of wavelets beating a rapid tattoo on her planks as she surged through the water.

As she flew down the lake, parallel to the eastern shore, Hal filled the crew in on events at the Temujai encampment. At the same time, Thorn described the battle on the lakeshore.

"We were lucky," he said. "The patrol leader wasn't the sharpest tool in the kit. I doubt we'll be that lucky again."

"You could be right. But if we do have any luck, it'll be to get to the river before the Temujai can seal it off and trap us."

Edvin moved aft to the steering platform, a worried expression on his face. Hal noticed him standing awkwardly by and gestured for him to come closer.

"What is it, Edvin?" he asked.

Edvin shrugged apologetically. "We've left all our camping equipment on the island," he said. "The big tent, your smaller tent and my cooking equipment. Plus we left the provisions there as well. I've got nothing on board. Sorry, Hal. I had no idea we'd be taking off directly you came back aboard. None of us did."

Hal waved the apology aside. "Don't worry, Edvin. If we don't beat the Temujai to the foot of the lake, that'll be the least of our problems. If we beat them to it, we can always pick up the food we left at the bottom of the first portage. If they do get to the river before us, we can sail back to the island and pick up the stuff we've left."

Edvin looked relieved for a few moments, then he frowned. "If they get there first, what are we going to do?"

Hal shook his head. "I have a vague idea," he said. "But let's face that when we see if they've beaten us to it."

Mindful that they could sight the Temujai at any moment, he steered the ship out away from the east bank and more in the center of the lake, keeping her two hundred and fifty meters away from the shore—well out of bowshot.

The shore began to curve back to the west, indicating that they were approaching the bottom of the lake, where the river ran out and, eventually, down Ice River Valley. Silence fell over the little ship as the crew moved to the bow, peering ahead, trying to see the first sign of Temujai troops on the shore.

"We might have made it," Hal said, earning himself a grim look from Thorn. The old sea wolf was superstitious enough to believe you should never tempt fate with good news until you were certain. Hal saw the look and shrugged. If the Temujai were there, talking about it wouldn't make matters worse. If they weren't, saying so wouldn't suddenly make them appear.

They could see the river mouth now, and the small line of breakers on the western side. Still there was no sign of anyone waiting on the bank.

Then a silent line of riders appeared out of the grass on the eastern bank, riding toward the point where the river flowed out of the lake. Hal's heart sank. Maybe Thorn was right, he thought. Maybe you shouldn't voice your wishes.

The river mouth was eighty meters wide. On the western side, the shallows over the sand bar and the line of breakers restricted the width they could use to sixty meters. So, they would be well within range of the Temujai bows if they tried to sail downstream. With about two hundred Temujai lining the banks, the *Heron* would be vulnerable to a continual barrage of arrows as she sailed past. And the Temujai could keep pace with them as they sailed downriver, maintaining constant volleys of arrows as they went. Effective as the Skandian shields might be, they couldn't hope to weather such a nonstop onslaught without taking casualties. And the Temujai would be ready and waiting for the moment when they had to land at the first portage point. He reluctantly faced reality.

They were trapped on the lake.

## chapter twenty-three

Gorlog rot you." Hal directed the curse at the horsemen sitting motionless on the bank. Lydia looked at him in surprise. It was rare for Hal to let his emotions get the better of him like this. As they watched, more horsemen rode over the crest and joined their comrades. There were now over one hundred of them, and more to come. Kloof, standing with her forepaws on the railing, barked defiantly at them.

"That's fine for you," Hal told her bitterly. "You have no real grasp of the situation. And barking won't make them go away." Kloof, sensing the anger in his tone, dropped her forepaws to the deck and lay down, curling up and keeping a watchful eye on her master.

"What now?" Stig asked. A grim silence had fallen over the ship.

"We go back to the island," Hal told him.

He put the ship about and they headed north. The southern shore of the lake, with its row of silent, watchful horsemen, gradually sank into the distance. Stig was about to ask Hal what his plans were. But seeing his skirl's angry, fixed expression and receiving a warning shake of the head from Thorn, he remained silent.

They moored at their original landing place on the island, and Stig shoved the gangplank over the side. He moved toward Hal, who had remained silent, apart from passing necessary orders, since they had left the southern shore of the lake.

"Will we rig the nets?" he asked.

Hal shook his head. "No point. They can't see us from the eastern shore."

Stig paused uncertainly. He wasn't sure if he should order the crew to strike their camp on the island, or whether Hal was planning to spend the night here. Hal noticed his hesitation and put a hand on his shoulder.

"Sorry, Stig. Didn't mean to take it out on you. We'll stay here tonight. May as well be comfortable. Tomorrow, we'll see what we're going to do."

In fact, it was later that evening when he came to a decision. Edvin had prepared a meal for them, and the crew were sitting around their campfire drinking an after-dinner cup of coffee. Hal was continually surprised how Edvin could keep conjuring up interesting, appetizing meals with the scant resources he had at his disposal. The young man had a definite gift, he thought—that alone was worth three additional fighting men. His cooking kept the crew's morale high and their enthusiasm undiminished.

Hal looked around the circle of faces now as they conversed quietly, leaning into the warmth of the fire. It was a chilly night and they had built the fire up. As he had observed earlier, there was no point in maintaining secrecy. The Temujai knew they were here on the lake. And it wouldn't take much for them to figure they had a base on this island.

He listened in on the various conversations around the fire. Ulf and Wulf were discussing snowflakes again, while Stefan interjected in their conversation from time to time to ask pointed technical questions—which neither of the twins could answer. Stig and Thorn were reviewing the battle at the lakeshore and analyzing where the Temujai patrol commander had gone wrong. Ingvar and Lydia, sitting close together with a blanket wrapped around their shoulders, listened keenly to that discussion. Lydia was particularly interested in the fact that the Skandians had hurled a volley of spears at the charging Temujai. She had never seen the Skandians employ that tactic before and she said so now.

Thorn grinned at her. "We usually don't have to do that when you're around," he said. He looked at Stig. "Still, I noticed that we only hit two of the horsemen. Our accuracy left something to be desired."

Stig nodded. "I'm assuming this means you're going to put us through more spear-throwing practice?"

Thorn nodded. "I admit I've neglected it lately." As the battle-master for the crew, Thorn was responsible for weapon training and tactical drill. He was a hard taskmaster, but all the Herons knew that his insistence on "getting it right," as he put it, had saved their lives many times over. They were a small unit. Most brotherbands numbered around twenty, and most wolfship crews over thirty. But the Herons' skill and well-drilled efficiency made them one of the more effective fighting units in the Skandian fleet.

There was a momentary lull as both conversations came to an end at the same time. Hal rose from where he had been sitting, a few meters away from the circle around the fire, and walked in to join them. The crew had left him alone to his thoughts, knowing he was working on a plan of action. They were used to their skirl coming up with ideas to get them out of tight spots. They had faith he would find a way out of this one. They fell silent as he stepped into the circle of firelight, waiting expectantly to hear what he had to say.

"All right," he said, "you've been wondering what we do next, I'm sure."

There was a mumble of assent. He paused, looking round their faces, seeing their confidence in him. He had a momentary flash of uncertainty, hoping their confidence might not be misplaced. His idea was risky, there was no doubt about it.

"We've got about two hundred Temujai blocking our exit from the lake," he said, summarizing the situation. "We could sail past them, but we'd be exposed to their arrows and we couldn't hope to get past them unscathed."

Several of the crew nodded. They looked at one another, each one wondering which of his friends might be hit by a Temujai arrow. As was the way with warriors facing a battle, none of them thought that the victims might include themselves.

"On top of that, they can keep pace with us down the riverbank until we make it to the first portage. They'd be shooting at us all the way and we'd be exposed while we're working the ship."

"We'd be sitting ducks," Stig put in.

Hal nodded at him. "Exactly. Then we have to look at what might happen when we reach the portage. They're not going to be sitting on their hands while we haul the ship ashore and drag her down the track to the next level."

"They'll be on the opposite bank, of course," Thorn said.

Hal glanced at his shaggy-haired mentor. He was right. The Temujai were gathered on the eastern bank of the river. The portages were on the western bank.

"It won't take them too long to find a way across the river," he said. "There may not be any fords, but I wouldn't assume they couldn't make it."

"No. They're not people you should underestimate," said Thorn.

"On top of that, consider how exposed we'll be while we're dragging the boat ashore, lightening her and getting her ready for the downhill portage. We'd be well within bowshot, even if they don't get across to the western bank. And the one thing we know about the Temujai is that they're good shots. With about two hundred of them shooting at us, it could be quite uncomfortable."

"So, what's your plan?" Stig asked. After all, he thought, they knew the problems facing them. What they needed to know was how Hal planned to circumvent those problems.

Hal took a deep breath. "We need a hostage," he said. "Someone who they won't be willing to risk killing. Someone who they won't take the chance on a stray arrow hitting."

Lydia looked doubtful. "They're ruthless people," she said. "We know that. Look at the way they threw men away at Fort Ragnak, just to test our defenses there. If we capture one of them and hold him hostage, they won't hesitate for a second. They'll shoot at us, and if the hostage gets hit, that's just bad luck for him."

Hal smiled at her. "Not if it's the Sha'shan."

Instantly, a chorus of questions broke out, as he had known it would. Stig was looking at him as if he was crazy. Thorn, on the other hand, was considering the idea, his head to one side and a grim smile on his lips. Stig rose to his feet and gestured for the rest of the crew to be silent. The babble of questions died away, and Stig faced his skirl.

"You can't be serious?" he said. "Kidnap the Sha'shan? Hold him as a hostage? We'd never manage to pull it off."

"On the contrary," said Hal, with a calming gesture, "I can't think of a better time to do it."

Stig shook his head, puzzled. "I think you'd better explain that."

"Look, the Sha'shan lives and sleeps in a huge tent on a wagon. It's set close to the edge of the camp to keep it clear of the smoke and the noise."

"But he must have guards?" Stig said.

Hal glanced at Lydia for confirmation. "We saw six, right, Lydia?"

The girl nodded slowly. "Yes. Six, placed around the big wagon."

"And they weren't too alert when we saw them, right?" Again, Lydia nodded agreement and Hal continued. "The thing is, they don't *expect* anyone to attack the Sha'shan. They've spent too many years secure in their encampment, with no real threat, no enemy who might be bold enough to raid the Sha'shan's wagon."

"It's a good point," Thorn said thoughtfully. "The Temujai are used to attacking other people, not having other people attack them."

"That's right," Hal said. He could see the doubt and uncertainty disappearing from the faces of the crew as he spoke. "And on top of that, at the moment, they're highly disorganized. They've sent at least three *Ulans* to the lake entrance, and the rest of them are busy getting the encampment ready to move. And believe me, that's going to be a big undertaking. There's going to be a lot of disorganization and disruption in that camp for the next two or three days. I'm suggesting we take advantage of it, sneak in and grab the Sha'shan."

"How many in the raiding party?" Thorn asked. The others leaned forward expectantly. And with that question, and the crew's reaction, Hal knew that they had accepted his idea. Moreover, he realized that it had stood up to Thorn's expert scrutiny, and that removed any lingering doubts he might have had himself.

He glanced quickly at Stig. The tall first mate had been the first to voice an objection to the idea—and a vehement one at that. But now he could see an expression of eager acceptance on his friend's face. Stig was grinning broadly, shaking his head in admiration of Hal's thinking.

"Four of us," Hal said, answering Thorn's question. "Stig . . ." He paused, his gaze meeting Stig's and seeing a nod of agreement before continuing. "Thorn, Lydia and me."

Ingvar stood suddenly, his giant frame towering over Hal. "Me," he said. "You said six guards. I want to go too."

Several other voices echoed his sentiment as Stefan, Ulf and Wulf all stood, clamoring to be part of the attack group. Hal held his hands up to stop their protests.

"Four of us will be enough," he said firmly. "We'll have the advantage of surprise on our side. And if more of you come, there won't be enough to handle the ship. Believe me, we're going to need the ship ready and waiting to help us get away.

"Grabbing the Sha'shan won't be the hard part. Getting away with him is going to be another matter altogether. We'll need the ship manned and ready to pick us up before word can reach the southern shore and alert the Temujai there. We want to take them by surprise. I don't want them to have any time to figure out a counter-tactic."

Ingvar looked as if he were about to argue further. But Lydia rose and put a hand on his arm.

"He's right, Ingvar. Four of us will be enough. The rest of you will be needed on the ship."

Ingvar went to speak, thought better of it and shook his head, swaying slightly from side to side, for all the world like an angry, confused bear.

Hal moved a pace closer to him and said quietly, "I can make it an order, Ingvar. But I'd rather you agreed with my decision." As the skirl spoke, he saw Lydia's hand close on Ingvar's massive forearm, squeezing it gently.

Finally, Ingvar nodded. "All right, Hal. Whatever you say."

## chapter twenty-four

Hal and Thorn stood among the concealing trees of the island, studying the rolling grasslands that stretched out to the low horizon. During the day, they had seen several small patrols riding along the eastern shore of the lake, presumably searching for some sign of the ship.

"Not many of them," Thorn observed.

"Most of them will be at the lake entrance. Or getting ready to move the camp," Hal replied.

Thorn nodded. "As you said, they'll be distracted. This is an ideal time to grab the Sha'shan. When do you want to get going?"

Hal glanced at the sun. He estimated that there were still a few hours of daylight left. "We may as well move out now. No sense in wasting time. We can get most of the way to the Temujai camp before it's full dark."

They hurried back to the campsite. While they had been gone, Stig and the crew had packed away the tents and camping equipment, stowing them back aboard the ship. The site looked strangely bare, with only a burned circle of grass where the fire had been.

"Ready to move?" Hal asked. When Stig nodded in confirmation, Hal raised his voice to address the rest of the crew. "We'll go ashore now and strike out for the Temujai camp. Edvin, you'll be in command while we're gone."

The slightly built Edvin nodded his understanding. He was the logical choice as a commander in Hal's absence. He was an experienced helmsman and a good thinker. Most important, he had a stable temperament. Jesper, Ulf and Wulf tended to be mercurial and make hasty decisions. Stefan and Ingvar had no experience of command, or any wish to gain any. They all accepted Hal's decision readily.

"Drop us off on the shore, then get back here to the island," Hal said. "You can moor up on the eastern bank, where you can keep an eye out for us."

"Won't the Temujai see us there?" Jesper asked. "Wouldn't we be better round this side?"

Hal shook his head. "There's no sign of the Temujai and it'll be dark in a few hours. You'll be relatively well concealed on the east side—certainly not as obvious as if you were out on the lake surface. Just make sure you don't show any lights. I want you there because you need to be ready to take us off without delay when we come back. Chances are, we'll be in a hurry."

Jesper and several others of the crew expressed agreement.

"When we reach that first crest," Hal said, pointing to the farthest point in the rolling grasslands, "we'll signal you with three flashes of a flint. Four flashes if there's danger. Keep a good eye out for us. When you see the signal, shove off and head for the shore to pick us up."

"And don't take your time about it," Thorn put in.

Hal glanced at him and smiled. "No. We don't want to be sitting there twiddling our thumbs waiting for you."

"We'll be there when you want us, Hal," Edvin said quietly.

Hal paused, checking to make sure there was nothing more he needed to add. He decided that he'd covered everything. In a situation like this it didn't pay to be too rigid. It was better to keep things flexible and adapt to situations as they arose. He gestured toward the ship.

"All right. Let's get underway."

The *Heron* nosed into the soft mud of the bank, held there under pressure of two of the oars. Hal, Thorn, Stig and Lydia were waiting in the bow as she touched land. In a few seconds, they slipped over the railing and splashed ashore through a few centimeters of water. They had barely reached dry land when Edvin's soft order had the oars reverse and the ship backed away from the bank.

Hal watched her pulling away, turning in a wide arc to head back to the island. He felt a strange sense of helplessness, away from the comforting and familiar surrounds of his ship.

"Let's get going," Thorn said, sensing Hal's sudden feeling of vulnerability and snapping him out of it. Hal shook himself—mentally and literally—and turned toward the east.

They walked in single file through the long, clinging grass, taking it in turns to lead the way and break a trail for those following behind. As they reached each low crest in the land, they sank to their knees and the leader went ahead, checking to make sure the way was clear over the next section. But they saw no sign of Temujai patrols this time.

It was just as well, Hal thought, glancing behind and looking over the seemingly endless rolling grasslands. With four of them walking one behind the other, they were leaving an all too easily noticed trail where they flattened the long grass as they passed. He considered suggesting that they walk in line abreast, leaving a less obvious track. But he realized that, this way, they were making much better time than he and Lydia had managed on their first trek through the grasslands.

Besides, he thought, it would be dark in an hour or so and the trail would be much less visible—even if there were anyone to see it.

"At least it'll be easier going back," Stig said after they had been traveling for over an hour. "The trail will be already trampled down."

"Save your breath," Thorn told him gruffly. He was currently in the lead, cursing occasionally as the long grass tangled round his legs, threatening to drag him down, or when he stepped into a dip or hole hidden by the grass.

Stig smiled to himself, taking no offense. But he obeyed and they continued on in silence, aside from the occasional soft curse or exclamation over the irregularities in the ground beneath their feet. As the sun dipped lower to the western horizon, their shadows lengthened, rippling and moving ahead of them like grotesque parodies of their true shapes. There was a short period of twilight once the sun was down, then the stars began to twinkle in the clear, cold sky above them. Hal, who was currently leading the line, held up his hand in a signal to halt.

"We'll stop here for a while," he said. "Moonrise is in an hour. We'll get going again then."

"We could keep going now," Stig observed, but Hal shook his head.

"Not over this ground. We need a little light to see where we're going. And there are so many dips and undulations, it's hard to keep your feet in the full dark. It'd be all too easy for someone to twist an ankle or a knee. Then we'd be in real trouble."

They sank gratefully to the ground where they stood, resting tired muscles and limbs. Even with one of their number breaking trail for them, it was exhausting work trudging through the long grass. Edvin had provided them with canteens of coffee before they left and the contents were still lukewarm. They drank it eagerly, feeling the energizing hit of the caffeine.

"What's the plan when we get there?" Stig asked.

"We'll check out the situation once we're on the hill above the wagon-yurt," Hal replied. "There should be six guards, so we'll need to take out two before we move in. Then we'll take one each and silence them. Once they're accounted for, we'll walk in and nab the Sha'shan."

"Easy as that?" Stig grinned.

"Easy as that," Hal replied.

Lydia slapped at an insect that was crawling on her face, removing its crushed body with her finger and thumb. "Have you thought about what we do with Mrs. Sha'shan?"

Stig looked at her. "Mrs. Sha'shan?"

"His wife. She lives in the wagon-yurt with him. Or at least, it looked that way when we were here before." She looked directly at Hal now. "We can't leave her behind to raise the alarm," she said meaningfully. "Or were you planning on bringing her along with us?"

Hal didn't answer for several seconds. He had been thinking over the problem of the Sha'shan's wife for the past few kilometers.

"We can't take her with us," he said finally. "There aren't enough of us to secure her and the Sha'shan—and keep them both quiet while we get away."

"Well, we can't leave her behind to raise the alarm," Lydia said.

There was another awkward silence before Hal replied.

"Are you suggesting we kill her?" he said, with some distaste.

Lydia shook her head vehemently. "No! Of course not. I'm asking, have you considered the problem. Do you have any plan as to what we'll do with her?"

"We'll tie her up and gag her," Hal said. "That'll have to do."

"Mind you, if anyone finds her before we get back to the ship, she'll be able to tell them exactly what's happened," Thorn said.

Hal looked at him in exasperation. "Well, that'll be too bad. It'll just have to do." He turned back to Lydia. "It'll be your job to keep her quiet when we break into the yurt."

Lydia reared back a little. "Me? Why me?" she challenged.

Hal indicated Stig and Thorn with a vague gesture. "Because none of us want to knock a woman unconscious," he said, adding with a malevolent smile, "and because you brought the subject up in the first place."

"So, it's all right for me to knock her out because I'm a woman too? Is that what you're saying?" Lydia asked with some heat.

Hal shifted uncomfortably. "No. You're a woman and you're ingenious. I'm sure you'll find a nonviolent way of silencing her."

Lydia was about to object further, but Hal gestured to the eastern horizon, where the yellow disk of the moon was showing itself.

"Moonrise," he said. "Time we were moving again. Lydia, you take the lead."

"Because I'm ingenious?"

He shook his head. "No. Because it's your turn. Let's go."

They plodded on through the night, heads down, legs trudging as they concentrated on making one step follow another. The land around them was empty and monotonous. Their muscles ached. Their throats were dry and they drank from their water canteens regularly. Each of them carried two canteens—one filled with freshwater and the other with lukewarm coffee. But they knew that the coffee, heavily sweetened with honey, would do little to assuage their thirst—in fact, the sweetness would only accentuate it.

They were disciplined campaigners and they contented themselves with small sips of water at a time, making sure they left plenty in reserve for the return trip. After several more hours, Thorn called their attention to the light in the eastern sky.

"We're getting close," he said. "That'll be the camp."

Stig whistled softly at the extent of the loom of light. Hal and Lydia had told them of the size of the Temujai camp. But this was bigger than he'd expected. It seemed to stretch from one horizon to the other.

"There must be hundreds of fires," he said softly.

Lydia looked at him. "There are."

The light was so bright and so widespread that it seemed the camp must be over the next horizon. But they crested another low ridge and still the featureless grass plain stretched out before them.

"Let's pace it up," Hal said, and they increased their speed, stumbling occasionally as they crossed the plain, leaving a clear trail behind them. As they approached the next rise, Hal, who was in the lead once more, held out a cautioning hand.

"Take it easy," he said, crouching, then dropping to his knees as he reached the crest. The others followed suit, then crept forward, staying low.

And there was the massive Temujai camp once more.

They paused for several minutes, studying the giant encampment, with Hal and Lydia making sure there were no significant changes since they had seen the camp before.

There were several empty areas where there had previously been yurts, and one of the horse corrals was half empty. Otherwise, nothing had changed. Hal indicated the depleted horse paddock and the bare spaces.

"They'll be the *Ulans* that have gone to the south bank," he said in a whisper.

Thorn nodded. "Still leaves a lot of them here. Where's this wagon the Sha'shan lives in?"

Hal pointed to the left and, dropping back below the crest so that he wasn't visible from the camp, led the small group several hundred meters to a spot opposite where the Sha'shan's wagon-yurt was positioned. They moved up to the crest on hands and knees and lay in a line, studying the situation.

"Still six sentries," Lydia said.

Hal nodded and pointed to the outer ring of guards surrounding the camp. "And the perimeter guards," Hal pointed out. "We'll have to get past them before we take on the Sha'shan's guards."

The nearest of the perimeter guards was thirty meters away. He stood facing out from the camp, resting his weight on his grounded spear. His small, hide-covered shield was on the ground beside him, leaning against his left leg. As they watched, they saw him raise his left hand to his mouth and heard him yawn. As ever, Hal fought down a ridiculous urge to emulate the action. Yawns were highly contagious, he thought.

"He doesn't look too lively," Stig said.

Hal nodded. "I'll wager that a Temujai camp hasn't been attacked in living memory," he replied. "As Thorn said, they don't get attacked. They attack other people. I wouldn't be surprised if half the perimeter guards were asleep on their feet."

"Can you do that?" Stig asked. "Sleep on your feet?"

"On your feet and with your eyes open," Thorn said. "It shouldn't be too hard getting by them. Getting out again might be a different matter. We'll need to make sure we keep the noise down. How do you propose we get past the Sha'shan's sentries?" he asked Hal.

Hal studied the situation for several seconds. He'd formed a plan for taking care of the sentries. Now he made sure that they hadn't changed positions since the last time he and Lydia had observed them.

They were situated in a ring around the wagon, each man about four meters from the large structure. There was a man posted at either end, and the other four were placed opposite the corners of the wagon. Each sentry was visible to the two men on either side of him.

"Lydia," he said, "have you got any of those blunt darts with you?"

It was an unnecessary question. He knew she always carried two or three of the blunts in her quiver. They were darts fitted with a blunt lead-filled warhead instead of the razor-sharp points they usually carried. They were designed to knock a man unconscious rather than kill him. Somehow, the idea of killing the sentries in cold blood didn't appeal to him.

"I've got three," she said. "Not enough to take care of all of them." She made a sweeping gesture, encompassing the ring of sentries.

"I only need you to take down one," Hal told her. "The one opposite the steps at the front of the wagon. Can you manage that?"

Lydia measured the distance to the sentry Hal had nominated, her eyes slitted as she imagined the shot she would have to make. After several seconds, she replied.

"No problem."

But Hal wanted to make sure. "You're sure? The light isn't so good."

They were eighty to ninety meters away from the sentry as they lay on top of the low rise in the ground.

Lydia looked sidelong at Hal. "Did you want me to hit him from here? I assumed we'd move a little closer."

"We will. I figure you'll be throwing from about forty meters away," Hal told her, and she nodded emphatically.

"Then, as I said, no problem. When do you want me to do it?"

"We'll work our way inside the outer ring of sentries, then give Stig and Thorn time to get close to your target. When they're in position, you let fly and knock him out."

"All right," Lydia said, but she was frowning. "But if Stig and Thorn are in position near him, why don't they do it?"

"Because they might be seen by the two men at the front of the wagon. This way, if they see anything, they'll see their comrade collapse for no apparent reason. My guess is, they'll move in to investigate. That's when Thorn and Stig take care of them." He looked now at his two friends, who were watching him intently. A small smile played around the corners of Thorn's mouth. He loved this sort of thing, Hal realized.

"If they don't see him go down, lay him out as if he's sleeping," he told the old sea wolf. "They'll notice he's missing after a while and come to investigate. If he looks like he's asleep, they won't be too suspicious."

"What about if they don't come to investigate?" Stig asked. "What if they just raise the alarm?"

"I'm guessing they won't do that. They'll make sure there's a problem first before they risk ruining the Sha'shan's beauty sleep. He wasn't too thrilled the other morning when they woke him up."

"Does the Sha'shan have a beauty sleep?" Stig asked, grinning.

Hal shook his head. "He doesn't look as if he does. But he

should. Anyway, once you've taken care of those two sentries, we'll skirt around the wagon to the other three. We'll take one each. Lydia, you stay back and be ready to take down any of them that get away or try to raise the alarm."

Lydia nodded her understanding. Hal waited several seconds, then said: "All right. Everyone clear on what we have to do?"

There was a muted chorus of grunts. Taking them as affirmative, Hal slid forward on his belly, over the grassy crest where they were lying.

"Then let's get into position."

They snaked their way downhill through the long grass, Hal in the lead and the other three following. Within a few minutes, they had passed through the outer ring of perimeter sentries, leaving them behind them, facing outward. The risk now was that one of the Sha'shan's guards might see them coming. But, judging by their general lack of vigilance, that seemed unlikely.

Strange, thought Hal. They knew there was an enemy present on the high grasslands and the lake. He would have expected them to be more on their toes. Then he amended the thought. They knew there were a dozen Skandians somewhere on the lake. And there were thousands of armed men in the Temujai camp. They obviously felt there was little to fear. The Skandians might be a nuisance, but the Temujai thought they posed no actual threat.

They reached a point forty meters from the sentry Hal had selected. He held out a hand to stop Lydia going any farther, and gestured for Thorn and Stig to continue slipping on their elbows and knees through the long grass.

He and Lydia watched as the two warriors crawled toward their target. They could see the grass waving slightly to mark their passage, but on the whole, the warriors moved quickly and quietly into position without too much visible movement to give them away. Any movement could be put down to the ever-present evening wind stirring the long strands.

Hal waited several minutes to make sure they were in position. Then he gave it another two minutes, counting the seconds slowly. Finally, he touched Lydia's forearm to gain her attention and nodded toward the sentry, who was leaning on his spear, looking bored.

Lydia slid one of the blunted darts out of her quiver and unclipped the bone-handled atlatl from her belt. Slowly, she rose to one knee, fitting the notched end of the dart into the hooked end of the thrower. She waited until a stronger-than-usual gust of breeze swept across the grass, setting it waving and moving. Then she rose smoothly to her feet, sighted, and threw.

Instantly, as soon as the dart was away, she sank back to her haunches in the grass, still moving smoothly and without any sudden, jerky action.

A second later, Hal heard the dull thud of the blunt hitting the skull of the Temujai sentry. The man gave a low, strangled grunt of surprise. Then his knees buckled and he fell to the grass, disappearing from their sight.

Hal and Lydia remained motionless, hardly breathing, as they waited to see if there was any reaction from the other sentries. Concealed in the long grass close to where Lydia's dart had knocked the man unconscious, Stig and Thorn waited as well. Their pulses raced as they waited for some reaction, some indication that the other two sentries had seen their comrade go down. Seconds passed.

Nothing.

"Let's go," Thorn breathed.

He and Stig slid forward on their bellies, emerging from the grass into the cleared space around the wagon. They moved quickly to the side of the unconscious sentry. He lay facedown, crumpled on the grass, one arm thrown out and his right leg buckled underneath him. His spear was a few meters away, where it had fallen from his hand. Lydia's dart lay on the ground beside it.

Quickly, they rolled him over onto his back, Thorn checking to make sure he was still alive and breathing. His fur-trimmed felt hat had flown off with the impact of the dart. Stig retrieved it now and placed it under his head, while Thorn folded his hands across his chest. There was a massive bruise on the side of his head but from a distance it shouldn't be too noticeable. Thorn retrieved the dart while Stig arranged the spear and shield beside the unconscious man.

Stig studied him for a few seconds. "Do we need to tie his hands?" he asked, but Thorn shook his head.

"He won't be coming round for quite a while yet. That girl is downright dangerous with her darts."

Stig shrugged. "Could have been worse. She could have used one of her killing points." He looked at the recumbent sentry, trying to see if there was any more they could do to make him look at rest. Deciding there wasn't, he raised his head carefully and peered at the sentry on their left. So far, the man had shown no sign that he had noticed his comrade was missing.

"What now?" he asked Thorn. The one-handed warrior gestured to the long grass a few meters away.

"Back into cover and wait to see if they notice their pal has gone missing," he said, and the two of them slid quietly back into the long grass, moving a few meters apart so that they'd be close to and behind the two other sentries if they came to investigate.

They waited for a minute or two, then the sentry on Thorn's side called in a low, anxious voice. He spoke in the Temujai tongue, so they couldn't understand the exact words. But the intonation indicated it was a question and the meaning was all too obvious: *Where are you?*

Hal was right, Thorn thought. They weren't going to risk the Sha'shan's anger by raising the alarm until they were sure there was a problem. Perhaps the man thought his comrade had simply gone off into the long grass to relieve himself.

A short time passed and the sentry called again, a little louder this time but still voicing a question, not sounding the alarm. This time, the sentry on Stig's side of the wagon replied, also in a low voice. A short conversation followed. Thorn, with his head just above the grass, saw the two men start to walk toward the position where the missing sentry should be. He slowly lowered himself back into hiding and said in a low voice:

"They're coming."

The two sentries approached the point where their companion was laid out on his back, seemingly asleep. As they came closer, the sentry from Thorn's side saw the unconscious man's feet protruding from the long grass and stopped with an exclamation of annoyance. He called softly to the other sentry, who increased his pace now and joined him, standing over their comrade.

The second sentry gave a snort of disgust. He said something to his companion, then kicked the unconscious man's feet, none too gently.

The man on the ground stirred and groaned, but didn't awaken. The kicker frowned, puzzled, and leaned closer to study the unconscious man. The two sentries were grouped close together.

"Now," said Thorn quietly, and rose from the long grass behind his man. He wasn't wearing his huge club-hand, but he had his hook in place, made of hardened wood. He brought it down on the back of his man's skull. There was a dull thud and the Temujai sentry went down, never knowing what hit him.

The second sentry had been shocked by Thorn's sudden appearance from the long grass. For a moment, he struggled to comprehend what was happening. But a moment was long enough.

As he drew breath to shout an alarm, Stig's muscular arm went around his neck from behind, cutting off air and sound. The sentry struggled briefly but Stig was bigger and stronger. The Skandian warrior lifted the smaller man off his feet, maintaining the choke hold as he did so. The effect was that the Temujai's own weight added to the pressure on his windpipe. He writhed wildly, trying to shout, but no sound came. He kicked futilely against the Skandian's shins but his soft felt boots made no impression. Finally, his eyes glazed over and he went limp in Stig's grip. The tall warrior maintained the pressure for another ten seconds, in case the Temujai was foxing. Then he gently lowered him to the ground.

"You took your time," Thorn said.

Stig shrugged. "I didn't have a big wooden hook to hit him with."

"True. You can't beat a right hook in a situation like this," Thorn replied. He turned as there was a rustle in the grass behind them, and Hal and Lydia emerged, rising to their feet as they moved onto the cleared patch around the wagon. Hal nodded approvingly at the three unconscious sentries.

"Nice work," he said. "Let's take care of the others before they notice these fellows are missing from their posts."

Stig turned to head back into the long grass. But Hal stopped him, indicating the huge wagon.

"We'll go this way," he said. "Under the wagon. That way, we'll come out behind them."

Stig nodded. "Good thinking," he said, and followed as Hal led the way toward the massive wagon-yurt, dropping to his knees to crawl underneath it, then leading the way to the rear, where the remaining three sentries were standing guard.

As Hal had anticipated, when they reached the far end of the wagon, they found themselves behind the three sentries, who were all facing outward. So far, none of them had noticed that any of their counterparts weren't at their posts. But then, Hal thought, they were all keeping watch outward, not checking up on one another. However, that situation wouldn't persist for too long. Sooner or later, one of the outer pair would glance toward their companions and see them missing. He waited until Stig and Thorn had crept forward to join him, the three of them lying on their elbows under the edge of the wagon. Hal indicated the left-hand sentry and tapped his own chest. Then he pointed to the center man and then to Stig. Finally, he indicated that the right-hand sentry would be Thorn's target. Receiving nods of understanding from his two friends, he began to crawl toward the left-hand wheel, as Thorn moved toward the right-hand side. Stig, who was already in position behind his man, remained waiting until the others were in place.

Lydia lay on the ground behind them, a dart drawn from her

quiver and fitted to the throwing handle. This time, she had selected one with a razor-sharp iron warhead. If anything went wrong and one of the sentries made a break for it, she wouldn't have time to be bothered with the niceties of knocking him unconscious.

Hal peered into the shadows under the wagon. He was ready, behind one of the massive wooden wheels. He could see that Thorn had reached a similar position. His face was turned toward Hal, waiting for his command. Stig was watching as well.

Hal drew his saxe and raised it, turning it back and forth in the clear space beyond the wagon so that the blade caught the dim starlight. Then he gestured forward with it and began to crawl out from under the wagon, heading for the Temujai, who was silhouetted against the sky.

He kept his eye on his target, resisting the urge to check and make sure Stig and Thorn were moving to the attack as well. The Herons had been working and fighting together for years. They trusted one another and he knew they would be moving.

Slowly, he rose to his feet behind the sentry. But his clothing must have made some noise as it rustled in the grass and the man started to turn toward him.

Hal brought the brass hilt of his saxe down in an overhand arc, slamming it against the man's skull. The sentry gave a small whimper of sound and collapsed to the ground, his spear falling one way, his shield the other. But they landed on soft grass and the noise was minimal.

Almost at the same time, Hal heard a similar thud and a slight groan as Thorn brought his hook down on his man, and a catch of breath as Stig's arm went round the middle sentry's neck in the same choke hold.

Hal crouched over the fallen sentry before him, saxe ready, looking uphill to the outer ring of guards. The nearest was fifty meters away and had heard nothing suspicious. He remained staring stolidly outward into the night.

Lydia emerged from under the wagon and rolled the unconscious sentry on his stomach, pulling his hands behind his back and fastening them with a pair of leather thumb cuffs. She whipped a short length of cord around his ankles, quickly binding them, then removed his long, flowing wool scarf and wrapped it around his head and face to muffle any attempt to call for help or sound an alarm.

Hal nodded his thanks. He looked at the others and saw they were tying and gagging their men as well. He waited till they finished and looked at him, then gestured under the cart for them to make their way back to the front of the yurt.

They bound and gagged their three earlier victims lying in the grass near the entrance to the yurt. None of them looked as if he was likely to regain consciousness in the near future, Hal thought. But it didn't hurt to make sure.

Then, bent double, he led the way to the wooden steps leading to the rear platform of the yurt.

The stairs creaked slightly under their weight as they mounted them. But the sound was lost in the creaking and groaning movement of the yurt itself as the wind stirred its fabric.

Moving silently, Hal crossed to the entrance, which was secured by a heavy felt flap. The flap was tied in place and he slid his saxe into the gap between it and the main structure and sliced through the fastenings. He pulled an edge of the flap aside several centimeters and put his eye to the gap.

He let out a sigh of relief when he saw that the interior of the yurt was dimly lit. In the far corner, there was what appeared to be an altar or shrine, and several small oil lamps were burning in front of it. They cast a red light through the interior. It was dim, but not the stygian blackness he had feared it might be. He signaled for the others to wait, pulled the flap aside and slipped inside the yurt, letting the flap fall back into place.

He pressed his back against the felt wall inside the doorway, waiting till his eyes became adjusted to the dimness. Gradually, he began to make out detail.

The yurt interior was one large room. In the center was an iron stove, with a chimney pipe that went up and out through the roof. The stove was currently unlit. To one side, a low table was surrounded by thick cushions for seating. Around two of the walls, robes and cloaks were hanging from wooden racks. Set against the third wall was a large bed—basically a thick mattress placed on the wooden floor, covered in rugs and furs. As his eyes became more accustomed to the dim light, he could make out two figures under the bedclothes. One of them was snoring softly. Hal's lips twitched in a grin. He assumed that was the Sha'shan.

He waited a minute longer, making sure that he hadn't disturbed either of the bed's occupants and that both were still sleeping soundly. Finally, he twitched the door covering aside and motioned for Stig and Lydia to join him. As prearranged, Thorn would stay outside, keeping watch.

The other two slipped through the doorway and he let the flap fall into place once more, ushering them to one side, along the wall where he stood. He pointed out the stove and the table and cushions. He didn't want either of them blundering into the furnishings. Then he pointed to the bed.

They both nodded, but Stig cocked his head to one side in a question. Hal guessed he was asking, *Who's who?* as it was impossible to distinguish between the occupants of the bed. He gave an exaggerated shrug. They'd just have to deal with that when they hauled the bedclothes back.

He held up a hand in a *wait* gesture. He wanted to give his friends time to become used to the dim light in the yurt before they acted. They had discussed this when they were planning the raid. After a minute or so, both Stig and Lydia signaled that they were ready. Hal started toward the bed, drawing his saxe. But Lydia held up a hand to stop him. She moved to one of the racks holding clothes and selected a heavy shawl, testing its weight and thickness before nodding to herself. Then she moved back to join her companions, holding the shawl ready in both hands. Guessing what she intended, Hal mimed a movement where he lifted the bedclothes aside, pointing to the two of them, indicating that they were to take care of the bed's occupants. Again, this was something they had discussed earlier in the evening, and they signaled their understanding.

Moving together, they ghosted across the wooden floor of the yurt and stopped beside the bed. Glancing to either side, Hal made sure that his friends were ready. He leaned in, listening to the soft snoring, and determining that it came from the figure nearest them. He pointed to it, and then to Stig. The tall warrior nodded understanding. Lydia, who would have a little farther to go to reach her quarry, moved a pace forward, the shawl held ready in front of her.

Hal held up his right hand, with three fingers extended. One after another, he closed them, signifying a count of *one, two, three.*

Then he took a firm grip on the fur and blanket covering the two bodies and hauled them aside.

The Sha'shan stirred groggily. He was lying on his side, facing away from the three intruders. But before he could wake up fully or call out, Stig's big left hand clamped over his mouth and twisted him onto his back, while the point of his saxe touched the Sha'shan's throat.

The Temujai leader's wife responded even more slowly. She muttered angrily in her sleep and tried to pull the bedclothes back over herself. Hal couldn't help grinning at her automatic reaction. She was probably used to having her husband steal the covers for himself on cold nights, he thought, and she was used to responding without fully awakening.

Then something must have warned her and her eyes flew open, a startled expression on her face. She started to sit up, opening her mouth to cry out. But Lydia was too fast for her. She dropped onto the bed on her knees, scrambling over the Sha'shan's immobile form, and hurled the heavy shawl over the woman's head and face, sealing off her incipient cry of alarm. All that emerged from under the thick shawl was a mutter of sound.

The Sha'shan was awake now and aware of the situation, if not how it had come about. His eyes angled down to the razor-sharp point of the saxe at his throat, bulging slightly in fear as he took in the tall, shadowy figure leaning over him.

Knowing that the man spoke the common tongue, Hal spoke, enunciating carefully.

"Don't either of you make a sound or you're dead."

## chapter twenty-seven

The woman continued to struggle until a sharp word from the Sha'shan silenced her.

Stig moved the blade of his saxe a few centimeters away from the man's throat. The Sha'shan nodded in appreciation, then spoke, also enunciating carefully.

"My wife does not understand the common tongue."

The woman was pinned down by Lydia's weight. Her legs were still tangled in the bedclothes and the heavy shawl wrapped round her head and face kept her upper body confined. Hal saw her try to turn her head toward the sound of her husband's voice.

"Tell her," Hal said, "that she will not be harmed if she remains silent. We'll take the gag off her face. But if she makes a sound or tries to cry out for help, we will kill you both."

He knew that it was a threat he would never carry out. None

of them could bring themselves to kill an unarmed, helpless woman. But the Sha'shan didn't know that, and from what Hal had learned of the Temujai's merciless ways, he would believe the threat. It was the sort of thing that he and his men would do without a second thought. The Sha'shan looked up at Hal now, trying to see his expression. But the dim light in the yurt defeated the attempt.

"Tell her," Hal repeated. His voice was quiet but he contrived to make it as full of menace as he could manage. Apparently, he succeeded. The Sha'shan spoke again, at length, and the woman, who had been tense and rigid on the bed, slowly subsided. Her voice, heavily muffled and barely audible, came from under the shawl.

"She understands," her husband said. Hal nodded to Lydia, and the girl carefully unwrapped the shawl from the woman's head. The Sha'shan's wife emerged, her hair wildly tousled and her face red. She gasped as she filled her lungs with air. Apparently, her breathing had been constricted under the shawl. She raised her head and glared at Lydia, then turned her wild gaze to her husband, who spoke again, a calming tone in his voice. She relaxed, letting her head fall back on the pillows. Lydia, who had been poised with one hand ready to clap over the woman's mouth, lowered it.

"Let's get some light in here," Hal said. He had noticed an oil lamp on the low table, with a taper beside it. He took the taper and crossed to the shrine, lighting it from one of the red lights burning there and returning to the table, where he placed the tiny tongue of flame against the lamp's wick. The yellow light flared up inside the tent, letting them see more detail.

"Let's get you up," Hal said to the Sha'shan.

Stig nodded and hauled the Temujai leader to his feet with his left hand wrapped in the man's collar. His right hand, still holding the saxe, stayed ready. The Sha'shan's wife made a move to join him, but Hal held out a hand to stop her. "You can stay there," he said. She was relatively immobilized lying in the bed with the bedclothes tangled around her lower body and he thought it would be best to keep her that way. She didn't understand his words, but the meaning of the gesture was obvious. She lay back again. Lydia sat on the bed beside her, ready with the shawl in case the woman tried to cry out.

The Sha'shan looked to be around forty years old. He was short and stocky, like most of the Temujai. But it had been many years since he had ridden hard and led warriors in battle. Life as the Sha'shan was an easy one and he was seriously overweight. His face was fleshy and he had a double chin. He was dressed in a linen nightshirt that came down to his knees. The rounded paunch of his belly was all too obvious.

"Been living the good life, have you?" said Stig.

The Sha'shan looked at him curiously. But Stig had spoken in Skandian and the man didn't understand him. He looked back at Hal now.

"You're the ones from the lake," he said. "The ship-men."

"That's right," Hal told him. "We're Skandians."

The Sha'shan nodded, then frowned. "How did you get to the lake?"

"We flew," Stig said, also using the common tongue.

The Temujai looked at him, puzzled. Humor didn't seem to be one of his fortes. Stig smiled and mimed a bird flying with his hands. The Sha'shan realized he was being mocked and dismissed Stig with an angry hand movement.

"What do you plan to do with us?" he asked, turning back to Hal.

"You're coming with us," Hal told him. "We need you to get us past your men at the south end of the lake."

"They'll never let you pass," the man told him.

Hal smiled easily. "Oh, I think they will," he said. "We'll just have to see, won't we?"

"And what of my wife?" the Sha'shan said, nodding to the woman. "What are you planning to do with her?"

"She stays here. We have to get past the sentries around the camp and dragging two of you along with us would be too much to manage."

The woman's eyes flicked from her husband's face to Hal's. It was obvious they were discussing her and her eyes betrayed her fear. She began to struggle once more and Lydia moved to still her. But her husband spoke a sharp command and she subsided again.

"So, you plan to kill her?" the Temujai leader asked Hal. His voice was matter-of-fact. It was, after all, what he would do if their positions were reversed. He went on. "If you leave her, she'll raise the alarm the moment we're gone."

Hal shook his head. "We'll tie her up and gag her," he said. "That should give us four or five hours' lead before she's discovered. Plenty of time to get back to our ship."

The Temujai leader's lip curled at the statement. "You'd be better to kill her," he said.

"I'll tell her you said so," Hal told him. "Nice to see you're so fond of her."

The Sha'shan shrugged. It was a matter of practicality. The woman would be a risk to the Skandians. They would be wiser to make sure she couldn't get free and raise the alarm.

"If she gets loose, she'll send my men after us," he said.

"She won't get loose," Stig told him. "We're sailors. We're very good at knots." The Sha'shan looked at him for a few seconds.

Hal frowned. "You sound as if you'd prefer it if we killed her," he said, finding it hard to understand the Sha'shan's attitude.

The leader shook his head. "I don't prefer it. She's a good wife and I love her. But this sort of softness is why you will lose to us in the end. The Temujai do what is necessary, no matter how distasteful it might be."

"Well, to us, it's distasteful to drag you along. But we need you. So, let's get going."

He stepped away from the Sha'shan and leaned down over the woman. He spoke softly to her, trying to keep any sense of threat out of his voice. He knew she wouldn't understand the words, but perhaps his reassuring tone would allay her fears.

"We're going to tie you and gag you—" he began.

The Sha'shan started to interpret and Hal rounded on him instantly.

"You shut up!" he ordered. He had no idea what the Sha'shan planned to say to her and he didn't understand his language. For all Hal knew, the man might be telling his wife to yell for help, regardless of the fact that they might kill her. He had already shown a distinct indifference to her safety.

The Sha'shan gave him a superior smile. But he stopped talking. Hal turned back to the woman.

"We're not going to harm you. You'll be left here while we take your husband with us." He used hand gestures to illustrate *left here* and that the Sha'shan would be going with them. She frowned and he knew she hadn't understood. He shrugged and gave up the attempt.

"Get her up," he said to Lydia. "Do it gently. Tie her hands and feet and gag her. But make sure she can breathe."

Lydia rolled off the bed and pulled the bedclothes back. The Sha'shan's wife looked to be in her thirties. She was short and stocky, but not unattractive. Her hair was pulled back into a tight pigtail behind her head. Like her husband, she wore a knee-length linen bedshirt. It had ridden up past her knees and she hastily rearranged it to cover them.

Lydia put a hand under her arm and helped her rise from the bed. She smiled at her and the smile probably did more to reassure the woman than any of Hal's attempts at communication.

"Hands in front, or behind?" Lydia asked.

Hal hesitated for a second or two. In front would be less intimidating, he thought, and more comfortable. But it would also make it a lot easier for the woman to work her way loose. Reluctantly, he decided.

"Behind," he said.

Lydia shrugged apologetically at the woman, turned her around and drew her hands behind her back. The girl was making all her expressions and movements as encouraging as possible, understanding Hal's intention to keep the woman reassured that she was going to come to no serious harm. As long as she believed that, she would be less likely to struggle or resist, or make excessive noise.

Lydia took a length of cord from inside her sheepskin vest. The four Skandians had equipped themselves with thumb cuffs and lengths of cord before they left the ship, knowing there would be occasions where they would have to tie up captives or unconscious sentries.

"Sorry, Mrs. Sha'shan," she said gruffly as she circled her wrists quickly with the cord. The Sha'shan's wife gasped quietly as Lydia pulled the bonds tight. The rope had to be uncomfortable because it had to be tight. Otherwise she might wriggle free before they established a good lead over any pursuit.

"Sorry again," she said, and the woman seemed to understand. She shrugged slightly, although she still pulled a face as she moved her wrists and felt the cord cutting into her flesh.

"Now the gag," Hal said. Lydia found a large silk kerchief and a long neck scarf of the same material. They would serve as a suitable gag and be a little less irritating or uncomfortable than the coarse woolen garments that were the alternatives. She wadded the kerchief up and placed it against the woman's lips.

"Open," she said, then demonstrated what she wanted, opening her own mouth. When the woman complied, she pushed the wadded kerchief into her mouth, then bound it firmly in place with the neck scarf, wrapping it several times around the woman's mouth and neck, making sure she could breathe through her nose. She quickly bound her ankles with another length of cord, and stood back. The woman's eyes followed her above the gag, angry and accusing.

"Well, at least you're alive," she told her.

Hal snapped his fingers impatiently. "Forget it," he said. "Let's get her husband ready to travel."

He selected a pair of woolen trousers and a thigh-length red jacket in heavy, brocaded material from the available clothes and thrust them at the Sha'shan. "Put them on," he ordered.

The Temujai leader complied, stuffing his nightshirt into the trousers. There was a pair of felt boots by the bed and he pulled them on as well. Then, at a word from Hal, Stig stepped forward and tied the Sha'shan's hands firmly in front of him, looping the end of the rope down between his legs and up his back again, then round his throat. If he moved his arms too violently, he would choke himself. Stig found a linen shirt and tore off the sleeves, wadding one up to form a gag, and holding it in place with the other sleeve wound round the man's neck.

Hal studied the dimly lit interior of the yurt, making sure there was nothing else they needed to do. The woman wriggled angrily on the bed. She mumbled something through her gag, but the volume level was very low. He doubted that it would be heard through the thick felt walls of the yurt. Nonetheless, he raised a warning finger to her.

"That's enough," he said, and she settled back, although her eyes flashed with anger. "Stig, take a firm grip on our friend here," he ordered, and Stig took the end of another rope looped around the Sha'shan's neck, twitching it experimentally.

"Remember," he told the Sha'shan, "make a sound and you're dead." He raised the gleaming blade of the saxe that he held in his other hand.

The Sha'shan nodded, understanding.

"Right," said Hal. He blew out the lamp and pulled back the door flap. "Let's get out of here."

He slipped through the gap in the doorway and pressed back against the outer wall of the yurt. Thorn, standing watch outside, nodded a greeting to him. Then Hal held the door flap open so that Stig could emerge, his hand wrapped in the back of the Sha'shan's collar in a grip of iron. He urged the portly Temujai leader out onto the rear deck of the wagon, then stopped him before he could move too far into the open. Lydia followed, moving as silently as a ghost.

Quickly, Hal moved to the top of the steps and checked the three sentries they had knocked out and left bound and gagged. The three forms still lay motionless in the long grass. He looked up at the outer ring of sentries. They were some distance away and seemed to be taking no notice of the camp itself. All of them were facing outward. He estimated that they would have to pass close by the nearest one.

That way, they would be a reasonable distance from his two immediate neighbors. He gestured the others forward and went swiftly down the stairs. Stig followed, with the Sha'shan. Thorn came next and Lydia brought up the rear. They moved to the long grass and knelt, semi-concealed. So far, the Sha'shan had behaved himself. But that wasn't to say he would continue to do so if they passed within a few meters of one of the sentries. Without him, and with the cover of the long grass, the four Skandians could easily break through the ring. With him, it might be a different matter. Hal beckoned Lydia to his side and indicated the nearest sentry.

"We're going out that way," he breathed. "Can you take him down?"

She studied the man's position for a few seconds, eyes slitted as she calculated angles and distance.

"You want him knocked out?" she answered, her voice barely audible.

Hal nodded. "If you can do it."

She paused for a second or two, then replied. "I'd like to get a little closer."

Hal made a *go ahead* gesture. "Get as close as you like," he said. He had considered sending Thorn to knock out the sentry. But it would take time for the old sea wolf to creep through the long grass and get within striking distance. Plus two men struggling, even for a few seconds, would be more likely to be spotted by the other sentries in their peripheral vision. If Lydia could do the job, it would be quicker and cleaner, he thought.

Lydia said nothing. She glanced down at her quiver and selected another blunt-headed dart. Then she dropped to her belly and, moving on her elbows and knees, started to slide forward toward the sentry.

Hal lost sight of her for twenty seconds, then she appeared once more, barely thirty meters from the sentry, rising out of the long grass, the dart held ready in her atlatl, her right arm back.

As before, she came to a fully erect stance. Her arm whipped forward and she released the dart. In the dim light, Hal couldn't see its flight. But he saw the sentry suddenly throw his arms wide, letting his spear drop. Then he went facedown in the grass. Lydia, moving smoothly and without excess haste, dropped back into cover.

Hal counted to ten, waiting to see if there was any reaction from the other sentries in the cordon. When there was no sound from either side, he gestured to his companions.

"Let's go."

They moved in a crouch, half running as they made their way up the slight slope. Stig maintained his firm grip on the Sha'shan's collar, shoving him ahead of him through the waist-high grass, holding him to a low crouch so that he would be less visible.

They came up to Lydia, who was kneeling beside the unconscious sentry. She had tied his hands and ankles and was gagging him with his own kerchief and scarf. Hal paused beside her.

"Good work," he said.

She shrugged. "It's what I do."

He glanced along the sentry line. He could make out the two nearest sentries in the dim light of predawn. But they were both facing slightly away from the line he wished to take. He beckoned his companions.

"Let's go," he said. "Keep low."

Still in a crouch, the four raiders and their hostage moved quickly through the long grass. Hal led the way, with Stig and the Sha'shan behind him, then Thorn, then Lydia. The girl paused every so often and turned to check their back trail. But there was no sign that anyone had sighted them. After several hundred meters, Hal signaled to Thorn.

"You can break the trail for a while." The shaggy-haired warrior nodded and moved to the head of the little column, shoving through the long grass, making an easier path for those behind him. They continued in this order until they crested the next shallow rise in the terrain and started down the far slope.

"We're clear," Lydia called softly from her position in the rear. Hal glanced round. They were hidden from sight now by the low ridge. He straightened, coming to full height. His knees gave a silent sigh of relief.

"All right, everyone, let's push it up. Someone's going to find those sentries, or the Sha'shan's wife, before too long."

The most logical time for that, he thought, was when the sentries were relieved. He wondered how long that might be. They hadn't had time to watch and see their schedule. He considered asking the Sha'shan, then shook his head, dismissing the idea. The man might be behaving himself at the moment, but there was no reason why he would give them that sort of information.

He took the lead again, pushing faster through the long, clinging grass, anxious to put as much distance between them and the Temujai encampment as he could.

Thorn moved up to stand beside him. "We're leaving a pretty obvious trail," he said.

Hal turned and studied the ground behind them. With five people walking one behind the other, the grass was being heavily trodden down. It would take some time to spring back to normal.

"Can't be helped," he said.

"We could move in line abreast," Thorn suggested. "The trodden-down grass would recover much quicker that way."

Hal considered the idea. Thorn was right. With the grass being crushed flat only once, it would spring back into position much sooner. By dawn, there might be no sign of their passing. But he shook his head.

"It'll slow us up," he said. Moving the way they were, with two people changing the lead every fifteen to twenty minutes, they could make much better time. If they moved in line abreast, each of them would have to break their own trail—and that would be twice as difficult for Stig and his captive. It was a better choice to move faster, even though they would leave a more obvious trail for pursuers to follow.

They struggled on, fighting the long grass again. The going was twice as hard for Stig, burdened as he was by the Sha'shan. He suspected that the man was delaying as much as he could, moving slowly, stumbling constantly and deliberately, and holding back against the nonstop urging of Stig's fist wrapped in his collar. But Stig couldn't prove it and there was nothing he could do to make the man move faster. Threats would be useless, he knew. He could threaten retaliation for the man's actions, but unless he was willing to carry out the threats, he might as well save his breath. He glared at the back of the Sha'shan's head. In a way, he admired the portly little man.

Thorn dropped back beside him. "Want me to spell you?"

Stig nodded gratefully. Thorn might be able to get the recalcitrant Temujai moving faster, he thought. Thorn wasn't one to make meaningless threats. If he threatened retaliation, he'd carry it out—probably with that big hardwood hook he wore in place of a right hand.

He released his hold on the Sha'shan's collar and Thorn quickly gripped the back of the man's jacket with his left hand. He twisted the cloth a little and turned the Temujai leader to face him.

"I've been watching you, Your Sha-sha-ness," he said. Thorn wasn't a stickler for correct titles. "And I can see you're dragging the chain and trying to slow us down. Keep it up and this is what will happen."

He rapped the hardwood hook against the top of the man's head. The blow made a distinct *klok!* as it landed and the Sha'shan staggered slightly with the force of it. Tears sprang to his eyes. It wasn't a debilitating blow. But it was a painful one. Thorn shook him with his left hand.

"Are we clear?" he said.

The Sha'shan lowered his gaze, only to receive another painful rap on top of his skull.

"Are we clear?" Thorn repeated, more forcefully.

The Sha'shan nodded, shaking his head to clear the new tears that had sprung to his eyes. "We're clear," he muttered, his voice surly.

Thorn beamed at him. "Somehow, I thought we would be. Now let's *move!*" And, as he said the last word, he shoved the

Temujai leader roughly in the direction of travel, holding him up so as to prevent any tendency to fall.

Lek'to, the Sha'shan's wife, was no shrinking violet. You didn't get to be first lady of the Temujai nation if you were. She was a brave and resourceful woman, and she was angry and humiliated by her treatment and at being left, tied hand and foot and gagged, on her own bed.

She wriggled her way to the edge of the bed, paused and rolled off, landing with a painful thud on the hard timber floor of the wagon, bruising her right elbow, which took most of the fall.

Noise, she thought. Noise would alert the sentries and bring them running. She wriggled her way to a sitting position, leaning against the bed, and peered around the room.

The shrine against the wall had several metal and ceramic fittings. If she could knock it over, they'd make the sort of noise that might bring help. But then she realized the shrine also had three red-lensed oil lamps burning. If she knocked it over, they might well set the yurt on fire.

That would bring men running too, she thought, but they might be too late to save her. She discarded the idea. The low table in the center of the room held a brass teapot and six small cups. They'd make noise if they fell. She wriggled closer to the table and hooked her feet under it, trying to tip it over. But it was too low and wide, too stable, and all she could managed was to make it slide away from her.

There was a dagger hanging in a sheath from the row of pegs along the wall. But it was too high for her to reach, and tied as she was, she couldn't rise to her feet. Even if she could, she realized, her hands were firmly tied behind her back.

She paused to think. There seemed to be nothing inside the yurt that would help her loosen her bonds or her gag.

What about outside?

There were guards ringed around the wagon, she knew. But she realized the raiders must have overpowered them to gain entrance to the yurt. No hope of help there. Then a thought struck her.

There was a loose nail at the top of the steps leading down, in the railing, close to floor level. She had been nagging her husband to have it fixed for days now. But, typical male that he was, he'd fobbed her off and forgotten to get it done.

At least, she hoped he had. She began to writhe her way across the yurt floor now, shoving her way through the entrance flap and then sliding herself on her backside toward the railing.

She reached the top of the steps and looked around. There was the head of the nail, protruding from the timber by a centimeter or so. As ever, Pa'tong had neglected her request to have it fixed.

May the Three Horse Gods bless his procrastinating soul!

Now, she thought, if she could snag the rope around her wrists on that nail, she might be able to work it loose. Or fray it until it parted.

It would take time. But time was what she had.

Lots of it.

Wearily, Hal crested the last rise leading down to the lake where the *Heron* would be waiting for them.

He staggered slightly as he stopped. His calf and thigh muscles ached with the effort of shoving through the thick grass for kilometers, with depressions and uneven terrain waiting to make him fall headlong. Doing this trip twice in a matter of hours was hard work, he thought.

The sky to the east was growing pale, with the first streaks of light showing. The lake lay ahead of them, at the bottom of the long slope of grassland. The moon was almost down on the western side, leaving a glittering path back across the water toward them. He couldn't see the *Heron*. If the ship was in place, it would be hidden against the dark bulk of the island, he realized.

He heard the others come level with him, pausing at the top of the rise as he had done. Stig had charge of the Sha'shan once more. The tubby Temujai leader sank to his knees as they stopped. Stig, for once, allowed him to do so. They were all tired.

All except Lydia, Hal thought. She seemed immune to fatigue, moving silently and swiftly through the grass, never seeming to put a foot wrong, bringing up the rear and watching for the first signs of pursuit.

"We've made it," she said.

Hal threw a warning glance her way. It never paid to be too confident. You never knew when fate might be listening in, waiting to disappoint you. Fate tended to do that, he thought gloomily.

"Nearly," he said, taking his flint from the pouch at his belt and unsheathing his saxe.

Quickly, he struck the flint against the back edge of the knife's steel blade three times, creating three brilliant flashes of light.

A shower of sparks fell from the last stroke into the grass at his feet. The grass, after being buried by freezing snow for months, and then blown by the constant wind over the past few weeks, was sere and dry. The sparks, fanned by the morning breeze off the lake, caught in the long strands and a small flame rose up.

"Watch out for that," Thorn warned him.

Hal quickly stamped the little flames out with his boot, the grass crackling underfoot. He looked back at the island, in time to see three answering flashes, brilliant against the dark background.

"They've seen us," he said. "Let's go." And he led the way down the long, gradual slope, heading for the lakeshore. They hadn't gone more than fifty meters when the low, dark shape of the *Heron* appeared, moving out of the shadow of the island and sliding through the water under oars, heading to meet them.

Nervously, he cast a look back over his shoulder. But they were alone on the vast grass plain.

Nevertheless, there was no time for delay. "Push it up," he ordered his companions, and they doubled their pace, running down the slope, slipping and sliding on the uneven, uncertain surface.

The *Heron* was halfway to the shore now. The oars moved at double time, heaving the narrow hull through the dark water, creating flashes of silver phosphorescence where they touched the surface and leaving a white wake behind her.

"Hal?" There was a warning note in Lydia's voice. She was a few meters behind the rest of them, continuing to check for any sign of pursuit. He stopped and looked back, in time to see six horsemen appear over the ridge they had just left.

He sensed that Thorn and Stig had stopped to look as well, and he waved them forward.

"Keep moving!" he ordered, his voice cracking with the strain. "Thorn, give Stig a hand. Lydia and I will slow them down!"

Thorn nodded his understanding and moved in beside the Sha'shan. Together, he and Stig gripped an arm each, raising the Temujai leader onto his toes and frog-marching him at a shambling half run toward the safety of the lakeshore. Hal watched them for a few seconds, his heart leaping to his mouth as Stig stumbled and fell, dragging the other two down with him. But he was up in an instant, urging and shoving the Sha'shan through the grass. Thorn cursed quietly and repeatedly as they blundered on.

Hal turned back to check their pursuers. The six riders he had first seen had stopped along the crest. But now they were joined by another three, then six more. Then another six. They fanned out along the horizon in an extended line, and as he watched, their numbers grew alarmingly.

"There must be a full *Ulan* there," he said. He looked once more to where Stig and Thorn were dragging the Sha'shan between them. They were only a few meters from the shore, and *Heron* was nosing in to meet them, the rowers bringing in the oars as she slid into the soft mud at the bank. Stig and Thorn floundered out through the reeds and mud, hoisting the Sha'shan high, to where willing hands were reaching over the gunwale to lift him aboard.

Ingvar seized hold and lifted the Sha'shan bodily out of their grip, depositing him in a heap on the deck. Then he reached over and hauled Thorn aboard as well. As he did so, Stig gripped the rail and heaved himself up and over with one convulsive movement. Then he glanced back to where Hal and Lydia were waiting, watching the pursuing horsemen. He measured the distance they had to cover to reach the ship, and the distance between them and the riders.

"They're not going to make it," he said.

Farther back up the slope, Hal had come to the same conclusion. The horsemen were starting forward now, moving at a walk in their long, extended line. The grass tops brushed the bellies and shoulders of their horses and the jingle of harness carried clearly to where Hal and Lydia waited. Hal unslung his crossbow and placed a bolt in the loading groove.

"Run," he said quietly to Lydia. "I'll keep them off you."

But she shook her head. "I'm not going without you," she said, readying a dart on her atlatl. "I can shoot three times as fast as you can."

The Temujai riders moved to a trot now. They weren't using their bows, Hal noticed. But each man had a long, slender lance held upright. He felt the cool air of the breeze on the back of his neck, and an idea struck him.

He dropped the crossbow and grabbed his flint and saxe once more, frantically striking the flint against the steel blade and sending showers of sparks cascading into the long, dry grass. Lydia caught on to the idea and took out her own flint and her dagger, copying his actions. She dropped to her knees, blowing on a small, smoldering section of grass. In a few seconds, a tiny tendril of flame licked up. Then it grew until there was a rapidly spreading pool of fire at her feet, fanned by the breeze.

Hal looked up at the riders. They were much closer now and beginning to move faster. It was going to be a race against time—to see if the small wall of flame that they were building would spread faster than the Temujai could ride. He scattered more sparks into the grass, watching as the breeze fanned them into flame, letting it spread until it was ten meters wide and moving toward the approaching horsemen.

As is the way with fire, the stronger the flames grew, the more they created their own draft of air, spreading the flames and driving them toward the approaching Temujai. All of a sudden, the fire front was fifteen meters wide and rapidly growing wider. The flames themselves were licking as high as a man's head and smoke curled over the grassy slope. Hal judged that they had done enough.

"Run!" he shouted. He looked for his crossbow, but it was concealed somewhere in the long grass. Abandoning it, he turned and ran, blundering down the slope, slipping and falling but simply rolling to his feet once more. Behind him, he could hear the growing crackle of the fire, the pounding of hooves and the shouting Temujai. Then another sound emerged, the panicked scream of horses as the fire surged toward them. Lydia was running beside him, perhaps half a meter ahead of him. He chanced a look over his shoulder, nearly losing his footing as he did so, but somehow managing to stay on his feet.

Behind them, the wall of red fire and black smoke hid most of the horsemen from view. He could see several vague shapes as the riders tried to force their mounts through the flames. But the horses were having none of it. They reared and plunged, and their panic was infectious.

Now he could hear the shouts of his crew as they urged the two runners to greater efforts. He glanced back again, lost his balance and fell, rolling over several times before coming to his feet and blundering on. Some of the riders had realized that they couldn't force their horses through the flames and were riding to flank them—to go around the fiery barrier and then set off after the two fleeing Skandians again.

Two of them made it around the wall of flames now and urged their horses into a gallop, thundering through the long grass as if it weren't there. A third rider emerged around the end of the barrier of smoke and flame.

Hal raced on. His breath was coming in short, ragged gasps, and there was a violent stitch in his side. Behind him, he could hear the pounding hooves getting closer, and his shoulder blades instinctively cringed, awaiting the impact of the steel lance head that he knew was coming.

*SLAM!*

The familiar sound impinged itself on his consciousness. Someone, he realized, had shot the Mangler from the bow of the ship.

Although he knew it was a mistake to do so, he turned to watch the rider pursuing him. As he did, a giant hand seemed to pluck the man from his saddle, hurling him backward, sending him crashing into the rider following beside him and bringing down both horse and man in a tangle of arms and legs.

The third rider swerved his horse wildly to avoid his two comrades, then hauled its head back, sending it pounding toward Hal. Exhausted, defeated, knowing he couldn't escape, Hal stood, awaiting his fate.

Vaguely, he heard Lydia's defiant shout behind him. Then something whipped through the air, hissing like a snake, as it missed him by less than a meter. The rider suddenly jerked back in his saddle as the heavy atlatl dart slammed into his chest. He threw both arms out wide, letting the lance drop to the grass, then somersaulted backward over his horse's rump, crashing to the ground behind it.

"Come *on*, Hal!"

Lydia's voice was close behind him. He shook off the inertia that had overcome him and turned to run the remaining forty meters to the ship. Lydia was ahead of him. Ingvar reached down, seized both her arms and heaved her up and over the railing in one smooth movement. Hal staggered after her, coming up against the dark green timbers of the hull and stopping, exhausted and drained.

"Give me your hands!"

It was Stig's voice, coming from above him. He looked up and saw his friend's face over the railing, both his hands stretched down for him. He put his hands up and let himself be whisked up and over the rail. He landed awkwardly on the deck and his knees gave way, so that he went facedown. He lay there for some time, his face against the smooth deck planks, surrounded by the sights and sounds and smells of his own familiar world.

Stig was yelling commands now, and he felt the ship moving, sliding back from the soft embrace of the mud at the lake's shore. Wearily, Hal rose to his feet and lurched to the center of the deck, leaning heavily against the stumpy mast. Ingvar, Ulf, Wulf and Stefan were on the oars, heaving the ship back from the bank, then pivoting her and sending her flying out into deep water. A hand dropped on his shoulder, and he turned to see Thorn beside him, a grin on the old warrior's bearded face. A little beyond him, the Sha'shan was sitting on the deck, cross-legged and disconsolate.

Then Stig was calling more orders, and the oars slid in and the sail handlers took their positions. Hal and Thorn moved aft to be out of the way. Lydia was already there, standing close to the steering platform where Stig had the tiller. Hal met her eyes and smiled.

"Thanks," he said. "That last one had me for sure."

She nodded gravely, glancing back to the shore, where the roiling bank of fire and smoke rose above the undulating grasslands.

"Couldn't let that happen," she said, then smiled in her turn. "We need someone on board who can steer a straight course."

Stig sniffed indignantly. Hal moved beside him and the tall first mate offered him the tiller.

"Do you want to take her?" Stig said. But Hal waved the offer away. For the moment, he was content just to be here, running his hand along the smooth, familiar timber of the starboard rail.

"It's good to be home," he said softly.

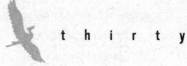

They spent the rest of the morning moored beside the island, while Hal made several preparations for their journey past the Temujai at the lake's mouth.

The crew cut down and trimmed three long saplings, then used them to raise the height of the port railing, nailing them in place and then arranging the shields above them. There was now a substantial shelter on the port side of the ship. Hal was gambling that the Temujai hadn't crossed to the western side of the river, so that no extra protection would be needed there. But with the addition of the saplings and the shields, the crew could now stand erect in the rowing wells and still remain undercover.

It was an untidy solution, but an effective one.

While the crew were busy doing that, Hal took several planks from the *Heron*'s small store of spare timbers and built a shelter around the tiller, so that he could steer the ship and be protected from Temujai arrows.

Not that there'd be too many of them, if his plan worked. But the Temujai *Ulans* usually had at least one designated sharpshooter among their numbers, and there was always the chance that while their comrades would be reluctant to loose an arrow storm at the ship, for fear of hitting their Sha'shan, the sharpshooters might try for the helmsman.

He surveyed the results of their work, satisfying himself that they had done everything possible to protect themselves. Then he ordered Edvin to prepare them a substantial meal, having no idea when they would have the chance to eat again. During the night, the inventive healer-cum-cook had caught several lake fish, and these made a welcome addition to the dried and preserved rations they had been eating. Finally, when the sun was well and truly past noon, they cast off from the island, ready to set sail for the south end of the lake.

He made one diversion, however. Before he set course south, he steered the ship back to the eastern bank and went ashore, trudging uphill and hunting through the long grass below the point where he had started the fire until he found his crossbow. At least now, he thought, he could shoot back if someone targeted him.

Unfortunately, the breeze had shifted late in the morning and was blowing steadily out of the south. They'd have to go down the river under oars, as it was too narrow for long tacks into the wind. But for now, they could relax, and let the sail take them swooping over the small waves on the lake, heading for the south shore and the river mouth.

They were still several kilometers away from the south end of the lake when Kloof raised her head and sniffed the air, emitting a low, grumbling growl. The Sha'shan, who was sitting on the deck, still tied hands and feet, glanced nervously at her and shifted away a meter or so.

"Relax," Hal told him. "She's not growling at you. She can smell something."

"Smoke," Lydia said, noticing the scent a few minutes after the dog had. "Campfires. The wind is blowing it toward us."

As she said it, Hal realized he could make out several thin columns of smoke from the shore ahead of them. For a moment, he wondered if they were part of the grass fire he had started that morning, then realized that it was well behind them, to the north and east of their current position. Then the familiar acrid smell became apparent as they drew closer.

"It's the Temujai," he said. "They got here before us."

That was no surprise. They had expected as much. And now he could make out movement on the lakeshore where the river ran out. Thankfully, all the movement was on the east bank. Apparently, the Temujai hadn't managed to cross to the west side of the river yet. That was a blessing, he thought.

"Sail down," he said quietly. When the sail handlers brought the yardarm down and gathered the sail in, he ordered Stefan, Jesper, Ulf and Wulf to man their oars. "We'll go in under oars," he told them. "We've got more control that way. Stig, Thorn, stand ready to man extra oars if we need them. Lydia, stay undercover but keep an eye out for those sharpshooters."

They moved smoothly on, slipping through the water under the steady stroking of the four oars. As they grew closer, Hal could make out more detail. He could see a cluster of yurts on the shore, and riders moving among them. There must be nearly two hundred Temujai here already, he estimated. As he watched, a group of sixty formed up on the lake's shore, next to where the river ran out of the mass of water. They were on horseback and in formation—two lines, facing the oncoming ship.

Hal glanced at Thorn, then indicated the Sha'shan. "Let's have His Nibs up and tied to the bow post where they can see him."

Thorn nodded and grabbed the Sha'shan by the elbow, lifting him from the deck and shoving him for'ard. Hal considered telling Thorn to untie the man's ankles, then thought better of it. The strong probability was that he wasn't a swimmer—swimming was not a common skill among the Temujai, after all. But if he *could* swim and his feet were untied, he might just take the chance of throwing himself overboard and swimming ashore. With his feet fastened, such a course would hardly appeal to him. Odds were, he'd sink like a stone with his legs bound together.

Quickly, Thorn tied the portly little man to the bow post, placing the Sha'shan's hands high so that he stood on tiptoe, fully visible to those ashore. The red-brocaded jacket that Hal had selected back in the wagon-yurt stood out clearly. Hal had seen the man wearing it when he and Lydia had first scouted the camp. He hoped it was a familiar sight to his men—one that would help them recognize him.

Onshore, he saw the front rank of twenty-five riders dismount and step forward several paces. In a concerted movement, their hands went to the quivers at their backs, selected arrows and nocked them to their bowstrings, eyes fastened on the rapidly approaching ship. As yet, they didn't raise their bows, holding them down and ready.

"Ease the pace," Hal called to the rowers. Ulf called a slower count for the oarsmen, and the *Heron* slowed in her headlong rush toward the shore. "Let's give them plenty of time to see him," he added.

One man at the right-hand end of the line raised his bow, sighted briefly, then released. They heard the slithering clatter of the arrow as it passed over the bow, and Hal could watch its flight as it arced up and then plunged down on a forty-five-degree angle—maximum range, he thought.

The ranging shot, for such it was, raised a brief waterspout fifteen meters ahead of the *Heron*.

"Heave to," Hal ordered and the four rowers backed water, bringing the ship to a halt before it reached the point where the arrow had cleaved its way into the water. "Hold her there," he added, and Ulf and Wulf worked their oars to stop the slow drift forward and sideways, keeping the ship in its place.

"They still haven't seen him," Hal muttered. Or maybe, he thought, they have seen him and they don't care if they hit him as well as the Skandian crew.

The man who had already shot selected another arrow, nocked it, raised his bow and shot again. It was a smooth, unhurried action that bespoke his skill and experience with the weapon. This arrow flirted into the water barely five meters from the *Heron*'s bows.

"Do you want me to take care of him?" Lydia asked quietly. "I'm pretty sure I outrange him."

Hal shook his head. "Not now. But hold on to that thought."

If she shot back and hit him, he thought, that could lead to the other archers on the shore joining in a general exchange of shots. And that could get the Sha'shan killed, which was not an outcome that would help the Herons escape. "Thorn," he called, "let them know who's tied to the bow post, will you? But be careful. Don't expose yourself too much."

Thorn nodded. He was crouched behind the bulk of the Mangler in the bows. He sidled forward, staying low, and stood behind the Sha'shan. He put his hook and his left hand under the man's armpits and hoisted him up so that his feet were on the railing and he was fully exposed to the men ashore.

"Oi! You lot!" he bellowed. "Look who we've got here!"

The line of bows came up and Hal could distinctly hear the creaking sound they made as they were drawn to their fullest extent. Then the Sha'shan yelled something at the top of his voice. He spoke in Temujai and Hal didn't understand him. But he caught the word *Pa'tong* repeated several times and it was obvious that he was identifying himself. A second later, a panicked voice from the shore yelled an order and the line of bows came down again. Hal breathed a sigh of relief. It had been a close thing. Their prize hostage had been on the brink of being turned into a pincushion before his men realized who he was.

Hal glanced around and caught Stig's eye, gesturing to the tiller.

"Take over," he said. "I'm going for'ard. Keep her edging in slowly."

Stig nodded and took his place behind the timber shield they had constructed earlier that morning. Hal dropped into the starboard-side rowing well, which was facing slightly away from the Temujai onshore, and scrambled for'ard, clambering up onto the deck in the bows.

"I've got him," he told Thorn. "You get undercover."

Thorn nodded and scrambled into shelter behind the Mangler. Hal heaved back, moving Pa'tong's feet from the gunwale and letting him sink back to the deck.

"I want to talk to someone who speaks the common tongue," he said in the Sha'shan's ear. "Call out and tell them."

Pa'tong began to call out in Temujai but Hal jerked him by the neck, cutting off the flow of words.

"In the common tongue," he said roughly. "I want to know what you're saying."

"I'm not sure if anyone there speaks the common tongue," Pa'tong prevaricated.

But Hal shook him roughly by the scruff of the neck. "Oh yes, you are," he said. "Now call him."

The Sha'shan wriggled around in Hal's grip to look at him. Hal's eyes were hard and uncompromising, and Pa'tong realized it would be dangerous to try to trick this young man. He sighed and called in the common tongue.

"Ho'mat! Are you there? Show yourself."

A rider in the center of the second line raised his arm and walked his horse forward to stand beside the dismounted archers. He called something in Temujai, and Hal shook the Sha'shan once more.

"Tell him to stick to the common tongue!" he warned.

"Speak the common tongue!" Pa'tong shouted. "The barbarian wants to know what we're saying."

"Very well, lord," the rider replied, speaking with a thick Temujai accent. "What does the barbarian want?"

Hal snorted. "Well, for a start, I don't fancy being called a barbarian," he said. He felt Pa'tong tense to deliver the message and stopped him. "Let it go," he said. Then he raised his voice and shouted to the rider on the shore, speaking slowly so that there would be no chance of being misunderstood.

"Ho'mat! As you can see, we have your Sha'shan with us. He's our hostage."

He paused.

The Temujai, realizing some reply was expected, called out. "I see."

"My men and I are all well sheltered from your arrows. If you shoot at our ship, the only person you risk hitting is your Sha'shan. Is that what you want?"

There was a slight pause. Then the *Ulan* commander replied briefly. "No."

"Then tell your men to lay down their bows and let us pass," Hal demanded. "We're going downriver and that's the only way you'll get your Sha'shan back in one piece."

There was a brief consultation on the shore as Ho'mat passed on Hal's demand to those who didn't understand the common tongue. Hal saw several of the men objecting, pointing their bows threateningly at the little ship, which was slowly edging closer to the river mouth. One of them even stepped forward, nocked an arrow, drew and shot. The missile thudded into the timber shield where Stig was sheltering.

"Lydia!" Hal called sharply. The girl rose to her feet, a dart already in place in her atlatl. Her arm went back and she cast in a smooth, powerful action. The dart flew in a lazy parabola, then slammed with surprising force into the man who had shot, dropping him instantly to the ground.

"Don't try that again!" Hal warned, hearing several surprised exclamations from the men on the bank. Then Ho'mat erupted angrily, shouting orders at his men. Reluctantly, those who had raised their bows lowered them and lapsed into a sulky acquiescence.

"Very well," Ho'mat called. "Come ahead. We'll give you free passage down the river."

"I'll just bet you will," Hal said softly, then called to Stig. "Take her downriver, Stig. Keep her as far from the east bank as you can."

Out oars," Hal said quietly. Ulf, Wulf, Jesper and Stefan slid their oars out through the rowlocks. "Give way—easily now," Hal ordered, once he saw they were ready.

The rowers bent to their oars and the *Heron* nosed smoothly into the river, the current getting behind her and adding to her speed. Ho'mat, the Temujai commander, and half a dozen of his men wheeled their horses and trotted along the riverbank, keeping pace with the ship as she moved past them. Some of the dismounted Temujai moved to follow the ship as well. One even went so far as to raise his bow, an arrow on the string. But a sharp order from Ho'mat caused him to lower the weapon at once.

"Seems to be working," Thorn said, crouched below the barrier on the port gunwale and peering out at the Temujai keeping pace with them along the riverbank.

"So far so good," Hal replied. "Pace it up a little, Ulf."

Ulf called a change in rate. The oars moved more swiftly and *Heron* accelerated, moving faster downriver and leaving the Temujai riders behind. Hal turned to watch them as the ship pulled away. Ho'mat gave a hand signal and the riders reined in, watching the ship. Eventually, the *Heron* rounded a bend and the Temujai were lost to sight.

Thorn rose from his crouched position and moved to stand with Hal. "Think we've got rid of them?"

Hal shook his head. "Not by a long shot."

"Commander!" Pa'tong called from his position in the bows. "I need to talk to you!"

He obviously was unaware of the correct title for a ship's captain, even in the common tongue, Hal thought. Not surprising really. The Temujai had little to do with ships. He nodded to Thorn.

"Untie him and bring him aft," he said.

Thorn nodded and moved quickly for'ard. He untied the bindings that held the Temujai leader to the bow post, but left his hands tied. Grabbing hold of one arm, he led him aft to where Hal waited, eyes on the river ahead of them. There was a ring bolt in the deck close by the steering platform. Hal nodded to it.

"Tie him to that," he said. As before, he didn't want to risk having the Sha'shan hurl himself overboard. When this was done, he looked at the man briefly. "What do you want?"

"I assume you are going back downriver to the lowlands?"

"That's right," Hal said, although he wasn't sure how he might manage that. The Temujai were sure to follow them, and they'd be vulnerable to attack if they tried to take the ship down the portage trails.

"What do you plan to do with me?" Pa'tong asked.

Hal paused a second or two before answering. "Take you back to Hallasholm and hold you as a hostage to make sure your people behave themselves."

Pa'tong considered this, then said, "That will work, of course. But only for a short time."

"Why so? Why not indefinitely?"

Pa'tong shrugged. "My people believe that the Sha'shan is a demigod, chosen by the Horse Spirit."

"The horse spirit?" Hal asked.

"Our most important god. We worship Mori, the Great Horse Spirit, one of the three horse gods, and obey his commands. I am his chosen one, and my people will not allow harm to come to me. As you have just seen."

"Well, that suits me just fine," Hal replied, wondering where this was leading.

"However, that only continues so long as they know I'm alive. I assume you are planning on taking me back to your city . . ." He paused, uncertain of the pronunciation. "Hallasholm, and keeping me there?"

"That's what I had in mind, yes," Hal said.

The Sha'shan shrugged. "Then once I am out of sight, there are men within my army who will work to replace me. They will begin to claim that the Skandian leader has killed me and they will agitate to be elected in my place. Unless the people see that I am alive, they will eventually agree."

"These men would do this in spite of the fact that you were chosen by your horse god?" Hal asked.

Pa'tong allowed a cynical smile to touch his normally impassive face.

"That is religion," he said. "This would be politics. The men who want to replace me would find a way to justify their actions. It would probably involve extensive sacrifices to Mori."

Hal took a few seconds to consider this. It sounded reasonable, he thought. "So what's your solution?"

"Take me to Hallasholm. I will negotiate a treaty with your Oberjarl. Then return me to my people before my rivals can begin their campaign to undermine me."

"Let you go?" Thorn interrupted incredulously. "Just let you go? How could we trust you?"

"Thorn—" Hal began.

But the Sha'shan held up a hand to still him. "It's a reasonable question." He faced the shaggy-haired warrior squarely. "I would swear a triple oath on the spirit of Mori. No Temujai would dare to break such an oath."

"Not even your friends who are planning to replace you?" Hal asked.

Pa'tong shook his head. "Not even they would dare. No Temujai would break such an oath. It would mean eternal suffering."

Hal rubbed his chin thoughtfully. "A treaty, you say?" he said at length.

Pa'tong nodded. "A non-aggression treaty, where I agree to keep the Temujai away from Skandia. To stop attacking. To stop infring-ing on your borders."

"Forever?" Hal asked.

"For a period of, say, three years." The Sha'shan studied Hal's face carefully. "You know my men will follow you down the river valley, don't you?" he said, and Hal nodded. "How do you expect to stop them when they reach the lowlands?"

"There's a point where the valley narrows. Ten of us could hold off your men there."

"For how long? A week? A month? Two months? Eventually, they would break through."

"But you'd leave a lot of your men behind if you did," Hal said stubbornly.

The Sha'shan smiled—a humorless smile. "We have a lot of men. We'd still have enough to overwhelm your forces. Trust me. This is your best option."

There was a long silence. Hal knew he was right, but was reluctant to admit it immediately.

"I'll think on it," he said.

"Do that," Pa'tong told him. "You'll need—"

Hal rounded on him angrily. "I said I'll think on it!" he snapped. "Now leave me in peace to do that."

Pa'tong shrugged, making a submissive gesture with his bound hands.

Hal caught Thorn's eye. "Take him for'ard and tie him to the mast."

They continued downriver, and Hal tossed the Sha'shan's suggestion over in his mind. The more he did, the more he realized that the man was right: This was his best option. But he had other problems to solve. The most pressing was how to get down the river—how to negotiate the portages with the Temujai on his heels. He glanced astern for what seemed like the fiftieth time. There was no sign of them but they were there, he knew. The first portage was short and relatively easy. They had gained enough of a lead over their pursuers to get the boat ashore and down the steep trail without having the Temujai catch up. But their lead would be reduced and the second and third portages would be close-run things.

There was another problem to solve. The three long timber saplings nailed in place along the port railing had ruined the ship's balance, so that she listed heavily to port. That made her steering less precise. She was constantly trying to crab to the left, fighting the tiller. He waited till he saw a clear space on the bank and turned *Heron* toward it.

"In oars," he ordered, and ran the prow at an angle onto the soft mud of the bank. The crew looked at him curiously and he gestured at the temporary barricade they had built.

"Get rid of those saplings," he ordered. "She's steering like an overweight sow."

The Herons went to work, levering the nails loose, untying the lashings that held the saplings in place and heaving the long poles over the side into the river. The current caught them and spun them away, taking them rapidly downstream.

The third one had just been pitched into the swift-flowing river when they heard a commotion behind them. As they turned to see what was happening, a horse swam into view, thrashing the water and surging toward the bank. It came ashore a few meters from their beached ship, stood for a moment, then shook itself, sending cascades of water high into the air. It was saddled and had a bridle in place. It stood in the shallows for a minute or two, regaining its strength, then tossed its head and cantered off into the trees.

Stig looked at Hal, puzzled. "What do you make of that?"

"Look!" cried Lydia, pointing into the middle of the river.

The sodden form of a man was drifting rapidly downstream with the current. His arms and legs were outstretched. His fur and leather jacket was saturated, although they could see by the way it was swollen that there was air trapped inside the garment, keeping its wearer afloat—at least for the time being. Facedown, the figure drifted past them and was lost around the bend.

"I'd say that was the horse's rider," Hal said.

Lydia frowned. "But why would he be in the water?"

"Because the Temujai are trying to cross the river farther upstream. Swimming their horses across," Hal said. "He was one who got unlucky. There'll probably be more."

They all looked at one another. They knew the implications of having the Temujai cross to the western bank. The ground was more open there so they would move more quickly in pursuit of the *Heron*. Plus there was another danger. That was where the portage tracks lay.

"A lot of them won't make it across," Stig said.

"But a lot more will," Hal replied. "And we know the Temujai don't mind taking casualties if they achieve their purpose."

"Look!" called Lydia, pointing back upstream. They followed the direction she indicated and could see movement on the opposite bank, near the last bend in the river. Then three horsemen rode into view, their horses held back to a trot. More followed them.

"Looks like they made it," Hal said. "Let's get underway!"

S tig and Ingvar joined the oarsmen on the rowing benches. With six rowing, and the powerful current behind them, the *Heron* quickly outpaced the Temujai horsemen, who had to thread their way through the thick trees on the western bank.

They were soon lost to sight as *Heron* sped downstream. But a worried frown creased Hal's forehead.

Lydia, who had taken up a position close beside him, noticed it. "What's the problem?" she asked. "We're leaving them behind."

"They'll make up a lot of ground when we reach the first portage. We should get down that one all right. But it's going to make things very tight for the second and third."

"Will they chance an attack? After all, we still have the Sha'shan as a hostage."

"According to His Nibs, there are people among his army who wouldn't be too brokenhearted if he was hit by a stray arrow. They wouldn't dare try it while we were on the river. It'd be too obvious. But if they attack us once we go ashore, it would be all too easy for a mistake to happen in the general confusion."

Lydia nodded slowly. "I see what you mean," she said. "So, what do you plan to do about it?"

Hal didn't answer immediately. He felt that if he voiced his idea, he would be committing to it. Finally, he shrugged. "We may have to run the rapids," he said.

Lydia's face paled visibly. "You mean like when we were chasing Zavac?"

When they had pursued the pirate who stole the Andomal, the river ahead of them had been blocked. They had been forced to take a side route down a steep, rushing section of water. As someone new to ships and sailing, Lydia had found the experience terrifying.

"Like that. But probably worse. That was wider and not as steep." He grinned at her, but it wasn't a very convincing grin. "If we make it, it'll put us way ahead of those horsemen behind us."

"*If* we make it?" she queried.

Hal shrugged, saying nothing.

They reached the site of the first portage and Hal nosed the little ship into the bank.

"Hurry!" he urged the crew as they tumbled over the side and began dragging the *Heron* toward the downhill track.

"Do we need to lighten her?" Stig asked.

Hal shook his head. "Not when we're going downhill. The extra weight will help us. And we'll save a lot of time."

Fortunately, they didn't have far to go and the track wasn't as steep as the other two portages. They manhandled the ship down the sloping path, with Lydia hanging back to keep an eye out for their pursuers. They reached the bottom of the portage and relaunched the ship. Lydia came running down the track behind them and clambered aboard.

"No sign of them so far," she said.

Hal nodded grimly. Already, the rowers were driving the ship out into the current at the center of the river. Hal continued to check the banks behind them as they went. There was no further sign of the pursuing riders. But soon he would have to make a decision—whether to take the ship down the second portage or risk the rapids.

As they neared the point where they would have to pull over to the western bank, beach the ship and drag it overland, Thorn came to stand beside his young friend.

"You're going to run the rapids, aren't you?" he said quietly. He hadn't been privy to Hal's earlier conversation with Lydia, but he'd known the skirl since he was a young boy; he had seen the concerned look growing on Hal's face the closer they came to the portage point.

"We may have to," Hal said, with yet another anxious glance at the riverbank behind them. "If we're caught halfway down the portage, it'll all be over for us."

"We've put some good distance between us and the Temujai," Thorn said reflectively. "It might be enough."

"And if it isn't?" Hal said.

His old friend and mentor shrugged fatalistically. "Then we put up as good a fight as we can. And if it looks like we're losing, we kill the Sha'shan."

"There are people among the Temujai who wouldn't be unhappy if we did that," Hal said. "Not so long as it looks like they didn't force the issue."

Thorn pursed his lips in a thoughtful moue. "Oh, so that's the way the land lies, is it?"

"That's the way the land lies," Hal told him, and there was a long silence between them.

"Well, whatever you decide, you're going to have to do it soon. We'll reach the next portage in a few minutes," Thorn said. He cocked an ear sideways. "Listen."

As he said it, Hal could hear the sound of the rapids ahead, rising above the normal river sounds. It was a deep-throated, rumbling roar, growing louder by the minute. He opened and closed his hands on the tiller, then glanced at the wind telltale behind him. It was an automatic reaction, and really it had no bearing on the current situation. But it was a long-ingrained habit of his when it was time to make a difficult choice.

Abruptly, he decided, and straightened his shoulders.

"All right!" he said crisply. "We'll put her ashore and take her down the track." He looked astern once more. There was no sign of the Temujai. Then he called to Stig.

"Stig! Stand by to beach the ship. We're taking her down the portage!"

Stig nodded. Several of the crew followed suit. Although Hal hadn't discussed it with them, they weren't stupid. They all realized that the portage would be a risk, and that there was a good chance their skirl would elect to run down through the rapids. They had accepted that fact with a certain equanimity. Hal was an expert helmsman and a naturally skilled sailor. Whatever his decision when it came to ship handling, they trusted him.

By the same token, they had all seen the wild downhill run of the river and they were more than a little relieved that they were not going to have to risk it.

They rounded one last bend and there was the open space on the bank where they would put ashore and drag the ship to the downhill track.

"Ulf and Wulf, stay on the oars. The rest of you, over the side as soon as we beach. Grab a hold and get shoving. Lydia, Edvin, be ready with the rollers."

There was a muttered chorus of understanding from the crew. Stefan and Jesper withdrew their oars and stowed them. Ulf and Wulf kept pulling while Hal slewed the little ship across the river, heading diagonally for the cleared section of bank. This time, they would need the rollers, but only for the first forty meters, as they dragged the ship across level ground to the beginning of the down-hill slope. Edvin busied himself getting the lengths of rounded timber ready. Lydia crouched beside him.

The ship slowed suddenly as Hal ran her up onto the bank. She skidded across the mud, coming to rest with two-thirds of her length clear of the water.

"Now!" yelled Stig, vaulting over the rail and finding a purchase point on the hull where he could push. The other crew members followed suit, splashing down in the mud and shoving at the heavy hull. It moved slowly at first, then, as Ingvar leapt down and got his massive frame behind the sternpost, she began to slide faster toward the path down through the trees. Edvin and Lydia began placing the rollers under her keel, and once they were in place, the ship moved even faster than before.

The Sha'shan remained where he was, tied to the mast.

"Hold up!" Hal yelled as they reached the top of the downhill track. The Herons staggered back away from the hull, their breath coming in mighty gasps. Several of them rested their hands on their knees, bending over to recover their breath.

Hal beckoned to Lydia. "Stow the rollers. Then get back to the bank and keep watch. Let us know if you see them coming."

She nodded. She was nowhere near as breathless as the rest of the crew. She and Edvin had had the easiest task so far. She tossed three of the rollers up over the gunwale, hearing them clatter as they rolled around inside the hull. Edvin could look after the others. They'd need them for the final portage, she realized. Then she climbed aboard, slung her quiver of darts over her shoulder, leapt nimbly down again and ran, light-footed, back to the river-bank behind them.

Stig had spent the time rigging drag ropes to the hull. They'd start the ship sliding down the dirt slope, then slow her down by heaving back on the drag ropes.

"Grab hold!" he ordered. Then he turned to Ingvar. "Ingvar, get us going."

The massive warrior put his shoulder against the sternpost, set his feet in the loose dirt and heaved. For a moment, nothing happened. Then the *Heron* began to move: slowly at first, then faster as Ingvar overcame the initial inertia that held her fast. The bow tipped down to the sloping path and the stern came up. From on board, the Sha'shan gave a shrill, panicked cry.

"Grab hold!" yelled Hal. "Don't let her get away from us!"

He had a momentary vision of the ship, out of control, careering faster and faster down the slope, smashing into trees and boulders as she went. The crew grabbed their drag ropes, digging their heels in, leaning back almost horizontal to the slope, preventing the *Heron* from gathering too much speed.

After the first initial plunge, they had her under control.

Stig glanced at his friend. "Get your crossbow and get back to Lydia," he said. "We can hold the ship. You help her keep the Temujai off our backs."

Hal looked ahead. They were more than halfway down the portage. Unless the Temujai arrived in the next few minutes, they were in the clear. He scrambled back aboard the sliding hull and seized his crossbow. He slung it and his quiver of bolts over his shoulder, leapt down again, ignoring the Sha'shan's terrified gaze, and pounded back up the trail, Kloof bounding along beside him.

Lydia was sheltering behind a tree a few meters from the riverbank. She heard them coming and beckoned for them to join her. Hal knelt beside her, unslinging the crossbow.

"Down, Kloof," he ordered, and the big dog sank to her belly, paws outstretched in front of her. She sensed the tension in the two young people, and her hackles rose. She rumbled a growl deep in her chest.

"Settle down," Hal told her. "Any sign of them so far?" he asked Lydia.

She shook her head. "Not so far. Maybe we—"

They both ducked as an arrow whimpered through the air between them. Forty meters away, a sole rider had appeared among the trees. As they watched, he nocked another arrow and shot again. This one thudded, quivering, into the trunk of the tree behind which they were crouched.

Hal put his foot into the stirrup at the front of the crossbow and heaved back on the heavy string with both hands until it clicked into place over the locking catch. He took a heavy, short bolt from his quiver and loaded it into the bow.

"I'll take care of this," he said. If Lydia were to try to launch a dart, she would have to expose herself fully from behind the tree. The crossbow would allow Hal to remain partially in cover, at least.

From farther up the bank, they heard a voice shouting in Temujai.

"Calling his friends, no doubt," Hal said. He leaned around the bole of the tree, bringing the crossbow up to his shoulder. The sights were set for one hundred meters, a distance over which the bolt would suffer minimal drop. The rider must have seen his movement because he loosed another arrow. This one glanced off the side of the tree just above Hal's head and cartwheeled off into the forest. Knowing it would be several seconds before the man could shoot again, Hal centered his sights on the Tem'uj's chest and squeezed the trigger lever.

The crossbow had a much slower rate of shooting than a

longbow or the short recurve bows that the Temujai used. But it was far easier to aim and shoot, not needing the months and years of practice spent developing an instinctive feel for the weapon. And Hal's specially designed sights made it an extremely accurate piece.

The rider had just nocked an arrow to his bow when the crossbow bolt slammed into his left shoulder, spinning him sideways in the saddle. He let out a cry of pain as he lost his balance and fell to the ground. His horse, startled, skipped a few paces away, with a frightened whinny. At that moment, three more Temujai emerged from the trees behind him. Seeing their comrade hurled to the ground and crying out in agony, they hastily retreated back into the cover of the trees.

Grunting slightly with the effort, Hal recocked the crossbow and loaded another bolt. Lydia stepped out from behind the tree. When the Temujai came into view again, she wanted to be ready to shoot. Having to move out of cover gave the enemy several precious seconds' advantage. This way, as soon as she saw them, she could launch a dart. Hal could shoot from cover, so he stayed behind the tree trunk, the crossbow ready. Dimly, he heard the shouts of his crew as they worked the ship down the portage slope and the sound of the hull sliding over the ground.

"What now?" Lydia asked.

"We wait for them to make a move," he replied. "Then we stop them."

## chapter thirty-three

Without warning, the three riders burst from cover once more, riding at a gallop.

But this time, they had separated, with three or four meters between each man. They shot as they came and their arrows hissed and whipped through the air around the two Herons. Fortunately, the heavy foliage affected the accuracy of their shooting, as the arrows struck branches and saplings and ricocheted off at wild angles.

Hal and Lydia shot at the same time. But unfortunately, they both aimed at the same target and the rider in the center went down, transfixed by a dart. As he reeled in his saddle, Hal's bolt hit him in the leg as well. The other two came on, swerving wildly among the trees.

"I'll take right!" Lydia yelled, to prevent them both targeting the same man again. She whipped a dart away and plucked the right-hand rider from his saddle, sending him crashing to the soft ground. His horse reared, spun on its heels and cantered back the way it had come.

Hal, meanwhile, was struggling to recock the crossbow. But in his haste, he missed the latch as he drew the string back. Lydia was reaching for another dart, but the horseman was almost upon them. He had discarded his bow, seeing the arrows deflected by the undergrowth, and was wielding a long, slightly curved saber. He was drawing back the razor-sharp blade when a black-brown-and-white shape erupted from the ground by his horse's feet. Kloof, with a snarling roar, sprang high at the rider, startling his horse and sending it shying to one side. The saber slashed harmlessly through thin air, half a meter away from Hal as he continued to struggle with the crossbow.

Kloof hit the ground behind the swerving horse, rolling over twice. Recovering her feet, she dropped into a crouch, her hackles huge, her eyes slitted and a series of rumbling snarls sounding from her chest. The Tem'uj, an expert rider like all his tribe, recovered his seat in the saddle and, rearing his horse onto its hind legs, spun it in place to face the immediate threat—the huge, snarling dog. He spurred the horse forward, his arm going up and back again with the sword. Steering the horse with his knees, he swerved it at the dog, trying to ride her down. But Kloof was ready for the move. She darted to the right, then back to the left, moving faster than the rider and horse could counter her actions.

The rider, unbalanced as his horse swerved wildly trying to

follow Kloof's movements, grabbed at the reins with his sword hand, letting the sword fall to hang from the lanyard around his wrist. As he did so, Kloof leapt again, her massive jaws clamping shut like a bear trap on the Tem'uj's hand, locking his wrist in a viselike grip. Then she dropped back to earth again, her entire fifty kilograms of weight dragging on the rider's arm, hauling him out of the saddle and sending him crashing to the packed leaf mold of the forest floor.

The Tem'uj yelled in pain as Kloof continued to worry at him. Instinct told her that she had to keep him off balance and stop his recovering. With her hindquarters bunched, she kept her deathlike grip on his arm and dragged him across the ground, her rear paws scrabbling at the loose dirt, jerking and heaving at him to prevent him rising to his feet again. The growling and snarling continued unabated. Her eyes were closed with the effort.

Struggling desperately against the dog's powerful drag, the Tem'uj managed to reach with his left hand and draw the long dagger that was hanging at his belt. He brought the razor-sharp blade up and was about to plunge it deep into Kloof's side. He knew exactly where to stab to kill a dog, and now he planned to put that knowledge to use.

His blade was mere centimeters from Kloof when Hal shot him.

The Tem'uj fell back, his eyes wide with shock. The knife dropped from his fingers. Instantly, Kloof released her grip on his wrist and backed away, her hackles slowly subsiding, although she continued to growl softly. Hal knelt to study the wounded Tem'uj more closely.

Behind him, Lydia maintained a watch on the trees. "How is he?" she asked.

"He'll live," Hal said briefly. The bolt had hit the man high on the right shoulder. It would be a painful wound, but not a fatal one. "But he won't be using that bow of his for a while."

From far below them, they heard Thorn calling. The old sea wolf was used to issuing orders that could be heard above raging storms, high winds and thundering surf. His shout carried easily up from the bank below them.

"Hal! Lydia! Come on!"

They exchanged a quick glance. Hal checked the trees behind them once more. As yet, no more riders had appeared. He rose to his feet.

"Let's go!" he said, and they ran for the downhill path farther inland. The marks in the soft earth were clearly visible, where *Heron's* keel had dug a deep groove through the loose dirt and leaf mold that covered the ground. The earth either side was churned up by the boots of the Herons where they had held her in check on the way downhill. Ever fearful that more Temujai would arrive, Hal and Lydia pounded down the path, slipping and sliding, moving faster and faster as gravity took hold and their strides lengthened. Kloof, her tail waving wildly to keep her balance, leapt and bounded ahead of them, barking excitedly. By the time they reached the bottom of the track, Hal and Lydia were both staggering, half falling.

They blundered to a stop, chests heaving, recovering their breath for a few seconds. Kloof danced around them, tail wagging, barking encouragement. *Let's do that again!* she seemed to be saying.

"It's all right for you," Hal said dourly. "You've got four feet."

"That was faster than going up," Lydia said, ruffling Kloof's shaggy head.

Hal gestured toward the riverbank, some fifty meters away. "Let's go," he said.

They set off at a run. They were halfway there when they heard shouts behind them and the sound of hooves thudding on the soft earth. They redoubled their efforts, and he glanced over his shoulder. As yet there was no sign of any pursuit. But the sounds were getting closer.

They burst out of the trees by the riverbank. *Heron* was already refloated, lying close to the bank with the crew on board and four oars manned. Stig and Thorn stood by the stern rail, waiting to help the two late arrivals on board. Hal felt himself plucked bodily off the bank by Stig's powerful arms. He was whirled up and over the railing and deposited on the deck. A few seconds behind him, Thorn heaved Lydia on board. Their feet had barely touched the deck planks when Stig was bellowing orders.

"Shove off! Oars out and stroke as hard as you can!"

Edvin was at the tiller. Ingvar, armed with a long pole, shoved the ship away from the bank and the oars bit into the water. Edvin sent *Heron* curving away across the river, heading for the far side where they would be a more difficult target for their pursuers.

They heard shouts behind them and Hal turned to see a party of five Temujai riders arriving at the bank, already falling far behind. Two of them raised their bows and released.

"Down!" Hal shouted.

Those crew members who weren't manning oars crouched

below the bulwarks. Only the Sha'shan remained exposed. The two arrows whipped past the spot where Hal crouched. One continued over the deck and disappeared into the river beyond. The other buried itself into the tightly rolled port sail, a few meters from the Sha'shan. Pa'tong shouted a sequence of what were obviously obscenities at his men. Abruptly, they ceased shooting.

The *Heron* flew on downriver, driven once again by the current. Hal, watching the banks flying by, realized they were traveling faster and faster as the river narrowed. Ahead of them, he could hear the roar of the rapids growing louder. He looked back upstream and saw vague flashes of movement among the trees. The Temujai had closed the distance between them while they dragged the ship downhill.

"We won't get away with that again. They're too close," he said to Thorn.

"Looks like it's the rapids for us," Thorn agreed. Then a savage grin spread over his face. "Be just like old times."

"Orlog's beard, I hope not," Hal said, remembering the adrenaline rush and the moments of sheer terror they had all felt plunging down Wildwater Rift as they went in pursuit of the pirate Zavac. But at least that experience had taught them all what to expect and how to counter the dangers involved—to a point.

Realizing that the boiling downhill rapids would be on them in minutes, he issued his orders.

"Ulf and Wulf, stay on the oars." The twins nodded their understanding. "Stig, you and Stefan in the bows, please, with spars to fend us off any rocks that get in the way. Thorn, go with them and keep watch."

Thorn, with his huge strength and reflexes, would have been the logical choice to assist Stig in fending off. But his hook meant that he couldn't handle a long, heavy pole as efficiently as Stefan could.

"Ingvar," Hal continued, "get me an oar to steer with and lash it to the sternpost."

Ingvar nodded and took an oar from the rack that ran the length of the ship. In the boiling, heaving waters of the rapids, the tiller would be all but useless. An oar fixed at the stern would give Hal the extra leverage he would need to heave the ship around.

Ingvar lashed the long oar to the sternpost, winding the lashing around the two in a figure-eight shape, so it projected out behind the ship. He glanced up at Hal.

"Ready, Hal," he said.

The skirl stepped quickly to the stern and took hold of the butt of the oar, lowering the blade into the water and heaving experimentally, sending the bows from one side to the other.

"That's fine," Hal told him. "Unship the tiller now and stand by to help me if I need to shove the ship around."

He let his gaze travel around the ship, looking to see if he needed to deploy anyone else for special duty. He decided he didn't and called to the remainder of the crew.

"Edvin, Jesper, Lydia, back into the stern, please. We need to keep the bow as high as possible. Grab hold of a couple of oars in case we need help fending her off the rocks."

"What about His Nibs?" Thorn called, gesturing to the Sha'shan, a huddled figure at the base of the mast. The man looked pale. He had no real comprehension of what was coming, but he knew it was going to be extremely unpleasant.

And dangerous.

"He can stay where he is," Hal said. He didn't want the Sha'shan in the stern with the rest of the crew. If they needed to move, he'd be in the way. "Check his bindings," he added as an afterthought.

Thorn ran nimbly aft and leaned down to check the thongs that tied the Sha'shan's wrists to the mast. He signaled to Hal that they were firmly tied, then retraced his steps to the bows.

The ship was moving faster now as the current grew stronger. She began to yaw to one side and Hal had to heave on the steering oar to straighten her up again.

"Ulf! Wulf!" he called. "Faster! We need to keep steerage way!"

It seemed madness to row even faster than they were traveling. But the *Heron* had to be moving faster than the water flowing around her, or she would become like a twig on the water, carried along by the current and impossible to steer accurately.

The twins bent their backs to their oars and heaved, grunting with the effort. *Heron* accelerated until she seemed to be moving at breakneck speed.

Then they rounded the final bend, and the rapids lay ahead of them.

## thirty-four

The center of the downhill race was smooth and glossy, like a piece of curved, polished metal. On either bank, the water smashed and boiled around the rocks, sending a constant curtain of spray high into the air over the river. Waves bounced back from the shore toward the middle of the river, where the sheer speed of the current smoothed them out once more.

Trusting that there were no rocks in the center of the stream, Hal headed the ship toward it. He was off center, to the left of the smooth-looking passage. As the bow tipped down over the edge, the ship was still not aligned properly.

She shot downward, her bow hanging over the drop for a few heart-stopping seconds, then slamming into the racing water, fanning huge sheets of spray on either side. Hal felt the current taking control of her. The water was moving past them, faster than the ship was traveling, and he lost steerage way.

"Ulf! Wulf! Pull harder!" he yelled.

The twins increased their efforts on the oars, but the stern continued to yaw to the left. Hal might not have steerage way, but he could still use the leverage of the steering oar to drag the ship back onto a straight course. He heaved, but the force of the current was too great and he felt her swinging further, threatening to broach.

If that happened, she would be lying crosswise to the current and they wouldn't last five seconds. The racing water would roll her over and she would become another piece of flotsam being hurled downriver, spilling her crew out into the water, with no control over her actions.

"Ingvar! Help!" Hal yelled.

Ingvar scrambled to seize the steering oar with him. Together they heaved, hauling the ship's stern bodily to the right. The oar bent alarmingly under Ingvar's enormous strength, and Hal felt a moment of panic. If that oar broke, they were finished.

"Ease up a little!" he shouted.

Ingvar reduced the pressure on the oar. The frightening bend in the shaft disappeared and, strangely, their reduced efforts seemed to have a greater effect. Slowly, the stern began to swing back to the right, to starboard, until the ship was centered in the wild current.

But then Stig, in the bow on the port side, sighted a rock a few centimeters below the surface, bearing down on the *Heron*'s vulnerable planking. He braced his feet, shoved his pole out and set it against the rock, at the same time heaving with all his might to take the bow to the right.

Which caused the opposite reaction in the stern, swinging it back to the left, undoing all the work that Hal and Ingvar had done, placing the ship diagonally across the current once more.

"Heave!" yelled Hal, and their combined effort slowly brought the stern back until she was almost centered in the current. Then Thorn yelled a warning to Stefan and pointed to another fanglike piece of rock, this time just below the surface, on the starboard side. Stefan lunged with the long spar in his hands, got a solid purchase on the rock and heaved. The bow swung, this time to the left, causing a corresponding swing to the right at the stern.

When it happened, Hal and Ingvar were still heaving on the steering oar, trying to bring the stern back to the right. The sudden additional force took them by surprise as the stern swung wildly in the direction they were seeking. Ingvar, caught off balance, stumbled and fell to the deck, leaving Hal struggling with the oar, trying to stop this new and unexpected swing to the right.

Ingvar was up again in a second, back beside Hal, adding his strength to the skirl's.

But they were behind the rhythm of the river, constantly having to react to the wild swings and swoops the *Heron* was making. They would correct the movement, but then find they had overcorrected and have to work once more to bring the ship under control. Hal felt a grating impact under his feet and his blood ran cold as *Heron* just managed to scrape over an underwater rock shelf, which had been invisible in the racing water.

The drag threw the ship to the right. It couldn't have happened at a worse time.

"There's another drop!" Thorn yelled the warning a second or two before *Heron* plunged over another shelf in the river, which created a downhill drop of several meters. *Heron* shot out over the drop, with half her length clear of the water. Then her nose dropped with an alarming crash into the river, and water flooded over her decks.

Amidships, the Sha'shan lost his grip on the mast, although he was still tied securely to it. He was tumbled about by the raging water as it swept over the decks, waist deep. He yelled out in panic, but then the water drained away and he was left lying on the deck at the foot of the mast.

In the stern, Hal and Ingvar clung to the steering oar, wedged against the bulwarks to receive the force of the water smashing over the ship. Hal felt himself sliding away as the water tugged at him. Then Ingvar had a firm grip on the collar of his jerkin and heaved him back to his position once more.

"Thanks," Hal spluttered. He'd swallowed a mouthful of river water and coughed it up now.

Ingvar nodded. "We're off center," he said. "She's still trying to broach."

Hal nodded, heaving on the oar and almost getting the ship straight with the current again. For'ard, he could hear Stig, Thorn and Stefan yelling to one another, warning of new hazards flying toward them. The ship heaved and tossed as they shoved her away from the rocks. But Ingvar was right, she was still slightly side on, with her stern trying to sag away to the left.

"We're nearly through it," Hal said, peering ahead, blinking the spray out of his eyes and seeing the river leveling out some seventy meters ahead. "Just keep her straight for a few minutes longer."

At the oars, Ulf and Wulf were still heaving valiantly, trying to gain Hal the steerage way he needed. But the current was too fast for them, and *Heron* was swept downstream, on the very edge of being out of control. Only Ingvar's mighty strength was keeping her more or less straight, but with the constant counterswings caused by Stig and Stefan in the bow, even he couldn't bring her completely under control.

They started to sag off again to the left, heading for a boiling maelstrom where the river's main current ran through a tumble of rocks, sending spray and white water into the air in a constant mist. Sensing the ship sliding sideways, Ulf and Wulf rowed even harder, and the bow began to swing back.

The river ran down another meter-high step here. There was a narrow path through the rocks, just wide enough to let the *Heron* pass through. Hal pointed to it and shouted above the roar of the wild water.

"Head for the center of the gap! Ulf! Wulf! Pull for your lives!"

With the twins rowing frantically and Hal and Ingvar heaving on the steering oar, they managed to line the ship up with the narrow gap between the rocks. She shot into it, bows high as the remaining crew members huddled as far aft as they could get. Then, as the bows started to come down, Hal saw the rock that had been hidden by the drop in the river.

There was nothing he could do to avoid it. They were

committed to their course, and there was no way they could check or turn the ship.

*Heron* smashed down onto the rock with a horrible cracking sound and an impact that Hal could feel through the deck under his feet. His heart wept. He could tell his beautiful ship was badly hurt.

Fortunately, the rock was flat, with no projecting spurs to bite into the hull's planks. But the terrible impact had done massive damage. The current plucked her clear and swept her away downriver, sagging sideways, but slowly recovering as they reached calmer water.

"Is she all right?" Ingvar asked. He'd heard the cracking noise and felt the stunning impact under his feet as well.

Hal shook his head. "I don't know. I don't think so." But there was no time now to think about it. He yelled at the crew members huddled in the stern.

"Back on the oars! We need to get to where the river narrows."

Jesper scrambled to the rowing benches. Stefan came from the bows to join him. Then Ingvar and Stig, realizing the need for speed, joined the rowing team as well.

Hal had no time to remount the tiller. He remained on the steering oar as the ship picked up speed again. But she felt strange, responding awkwardly to his movements of the steering oar, seeming to fishtail when he tried to turn her.

"Edvin!" he snapped. "See if she's taking on water."

He'd be surprised if she weren't, he thought. That impact could have sprung loose half a dozen planks, if it didn't cause any more serious damage.

Edvin hurried forward to the hatch that led down into the hull where they could check water intake and, if necessary, pump it overside. He was back in a few minutes.

"She looks all right, Hal," he said. "There's a bit of water. Maybe a seam or two has opened. But nothing we can't handle."

Hal grunted, twitching the steering oar again and feeling the sluggish, *broken* response from the ship. There was something wrong, he knew. Something more serious than a few strained seams in the hull.

Edvin noticed the movement. "How's she steering?"

Hal hesitated before he answered. "Badly. She's sagging and twisting when I try to turn her." He paused, then added, "Maybe it's the steering oar."

Edvin nodded hopefully. "Maybe. She's bound to feel different without the tiller."

Hal said nothing. In his heart, he knew the problem didn't lie with the steering oar. But he had no more time to think about it. They were coming to the spot he'd mentally chosen to stop the Temujai's attack. The river ran through a canyon and the banks narrowed. The eastern bank had barely two meters of flat ground before the rocks soared away above it. On the western side, the side where the Temujai would appear, it was a little wider. But still defensible, with only twelve meters of clear space between the water and the surrounding cliffs.

"We're going in!" he called. "Stig, Jesper, get ready to moor up. The rest of you, easy on the oars now."

Gingerly, under the reduced thrust of the oars, he felt his way to the bank, letting the bow slide onto the mud as gently as he could manage. *Heron* came to rest, heeling over to the right as she nosed into the muddy shore. Stig and Jesper rigged mooring ropes. Hal stood in the bows with Thorn, pointing to the narrowest part of the bank.

"I need you to hold them here," he said. "I'm heading for Hallasholm with the Sha'shan. I'll send help back, but you need to stop them. We can't let a couple of thousand Temujai break out onto the coastal plain. We'd never hold them."

Thorn nodded. "We'll build a rampart and a shield wall here," he said. "So far, there are only a couple of hundred of them and they can only come at us on a narrow front. As I've said before, they're not the best close-in fighters in the world. We are." He clapped his young friend on the shoulder. "Don't worry. They won't get past us here. Just don't be too long about coming back."

Stig climbed back aboard and joined them. "How's the ship?"

Hal bit his lip. There was no point in hiding the truth, he realized. "She's in a bad way," he said. "I think the keel is cracked."

Stig's face went a paler shade. "Broken?"

Hal shook his head. "If it were broken, she wouldn't stay afloat. It's cracked. I can feel her twisting and flexing when the current hits her or when I try to turn her."

"So how will you get to Hallasholm?" Thorn asked.

"I'll take Edvin with me and we'll sail. Two of us can handle her in a pinch. She should hold up. It's only a half day's sailing and I'll treat her gently. Just as long as the weather stays clear."

They all glanced at the sky. There were the usual errant clouds drifting across the blue. The wind was offshore.

Thorn sniffed the air experimentally. "Doesn't feel like a change," he said. Then he turned and yelled at the crew.

"Let's get the ship unloaded. Ulf, Wulf, Stefan, start digging a ditch between that split tree and the riverbank. The rest of you get busy unloading weapons and supplies. We're going to hold off the entire Temujai nation here, so make that ditch as deep as you can."

When the defensive position was finished to Thorn's satisfaction, Edvin prepared a meal for the crew. So far there was no sign of the pursuing Temujai. It was one good thing about their wild ride down the rapids, Hal thought gloomily. They had moved so quickly that they far outstripped the riders making their way through the thick trees.

Thorn finished his meal, wiped his plate with a piece of flatbread and licked his fingers. He nodded his thanks to Edvin.

"You make a good meal, even when you're working with dried or salted food," he said. Then he turned a mock scowl on Hal. "And you're taking him with you—leaving us to Jesper's tender mercies." Jesper was the second-choice cook when Edvin wasn't available. His skills were limited, to put it kindly.

"Oh, thank you very much," Jesper said now. "There's no need for you to eat what I serve up."

"I'll have whatever he doesn't eat," Stig offered cheerfully.

Jesper sniffed disdainfully. "That's hardly a compliment to my cooking. You'd eat a warmed-over dead badger."

Stig beamed at him. "Dead badger? Is that what we're having for supper? Oh, yum."

There was a general chuckle of amusement from the rest of the crew, and Hal looked around them warmly. These were the people who, several years ago, had been deemed not fit to be picked for any of the other brotherbands—the rejects. Yet here they were, cheerfully preparing to hold off hundreds of Temujai warriors in defense of their homeland.

"I wish I could stay with you," he said softly to Thorn, who shrugged the sentiment aside.

"Better for you to get back to Hallasholm and raise the alarm as soon as possible," he said. Then, after a pause, he added, "How're you going to handle the ship, with just two of you?"

Hal had been thinking of this. Now he replied without hesitation. "I'll set the port sail before we leave. Once we're at sea, the wind will be from our starboard side so we can sail on a long reach back to Hallasholm."

"Once you're at sea," Thorn repeated. "But what about going downriver?"

"I'll use the port sail and yardarm when we're on a starboard tack," Hal answered. "When we tack to port, I'll keep her on a foul tack."

A foul tack was when the wind came from the same side as the hoisted sail, flattening a third of it against the mast. It reduced the sail's power by more than fifty percent. But it would keep them moving.

Stig frowned as he heard this. "That'll slow you down."

Hal nodded. "True. But we'll have the river current with us and that's still flowing pretty quickly down here." He glanced around, looking up at the sun to gauge the time, studying the clouds to make sure the wind hadn't shifted. "Well," he said, "we'd better be going. Edvin? Let's get aboard." He grinned. "Jesper can look after the washing up."

"Oh, thank you as well," Jesper said, with a put-upon expression on his face. Edvin grinned. He'd been collecting the dirty plates and spoons from the rest of the crew. With a flourish, he handed them to Jesper.

"Be my guest," he said, and followed Hal to the bank, where *Heron* stirred restlessly against her bow and stern lines, as if anxious to be on her way. The Sha'shan was already on board, tied once more to the mast.

Stig clambered lithely aboard with them, reached down to haul Kloof on board, then hoisted the port-side yardarm and sail. The sail flapped loosely in the breeze, without the sheets being tightened to hold it in place. Edvin moved to take hold of the sheets, ready to harness the wind's power into the large triangular sail. Hal cast off the stern line, and Stig did the same at the bow. Then he ran lightly back and shook Hal's hand.

"Don't worry," he said, "We'll stop those pony-people here."

"I know you will," Hal replied.

"Just don't be too long coming back with some help," Stig said cheerfully. Then he dropped lightly over the rail and shoved the ship out into the current. Several of the other Herons joined him, pushing the ship out at an angle. There was a chorus of goodbyes and good wishes from those remaining behind as Edvin hauled in the sheet and tightened the sail into its usual smooth curve. Hal had refitted the normal tiller, and now he felt it bite as the ship started to glide through the water, angling out into the river.

Driven by the fast-running current and the sail, *Heron* sped downriver, angling across the wind. In a few minutes, she had rounded a bend in the river and was lost to sight.

"Right," said Thorn briskly. "Let's get ready to receive our guests."

The eastern bank was drawing closer as they ran on a long tack downriver. Hal decided not to get too close before he brought the ship about. Better to do so while he still had plenty of speed in hand.

"Ready to tack!" he warned Edvin. "Going about . . . now!"

He heaved the tiller over and Edvin released the sheet, letting the sail fly loose. With the keel fin lowered and giving them extra purchase on the water, *Heron* came around smoothly. The sail flapped and lost power, flattening against the mast, but the little ship had enough speed to cross the eye of the wind. Once she had done so, Edvin hauled on the sheet again, tightening the sail.

They both felt the reduced speed as the sail, impeded by the mast for a third of its length, came taut again. The ship crabbed awkwardly, and Hal felt that looseness once more, the sense that the hull was twisting against the forces of wind and water. But she kept moving and just maintained steerage way, while the current pushed her downriver.

Hal waited until he felt he had enough room for a long tack to port, then brought her around again so that the wind filled the sail completely, blowing it out from the mast.

It filled with a *WHOOMP!* as the wind took it. The ship lurched under the increased thrust, and again he felt the hull flexing and twisting.

"How's she feel?" Edvin called.

Hal shrugged. "She's okay," he said noncommittally. She wasn't, he thought. But there was no use saying so. She'd either hold out for the run down to Hallasholm or she wouldn't. There was nothing he could do about it. At least this way there was only extra pressure on the keel when they tacked. Later, when they reached the open sea, it would be a different matter. He grinned at Edvin's worried expression.

"She'll be fine," he said reassuringly. "I should know. I built her."

And that was the problem. He had built her and he knew her so well. And she wasn't fine. Not by a long way.

At the barricade, Thorn and Stig paced up and down. As before, they had used the spoil from the ditch to raise a rampart behind it. The ditch itself was lined with sharpened stakes driven into the earth. Stefan and Ingvar had felled some small trees and they used these to raise the barrier behind the ditch so that it was shoulder height. Above that, the big round shields of the defenders formed a further rampart.

They walked a few meters upriver and turned to look back at the fortifications. Spearheads bristled above the earth wall. Each of the crew had two spears, which gave the impression of more defenders than there really were. Several meters behind the barrier, they had built a mound for Lydia, hedged with saplings driven lengthwise into the earth and nailed together with cross bracing. They formed a shield for the young huntress to shelter behind, while still allowing her a clear field to cast her darts over the heads of the defenders and into the attacking Temujai force. Ingvar had suggested that he should stand by her with a full-length shield to protect her from arrows, but Thorn had rejected the idea.

"We need you in the front line," he told the huge warrior.

Ingvar, who tended to be overprotective when it came to Lydia, began to demur. But she laid a hand on his forearm, stopping his protest.

"He's right, Ing," she said calmly. "You'll be more useful at the barricade."

Ingvar, in his heart, knew that she was right. The defense of the barricade was centered around Thorn, Stig and Ingvar, the crew's most fearsome fighters. Ingvar, with his massive strength and the long reach of his voulge, was an integral part of the shield wall.

"Have we forgotten anything?" Thorn asked, studying the defensive line.

Stig shrugged. "Maybe we could have taken the Mangler out of *Heron* and set it up where Lydia is."

But Thorn shook his head. "It'd take one or two men to handle it and shoot it. And we can't weaken the shield wall that way."

"True," Stig agreed. "So, what's the drill when they turn up?"

"Same as at the lake," Thorn told him. "They'll probably start off with an arrow storm. But on level ground like this, they'll have to stop once their men begin to advance. The ditch and the stakes will stop their horses, so they'll have to dismount and fight on foot."

He paused, his eyes scanning the scene of the coming battle, visualizing how it would progress. "As long as they're shooting, we stay down behind the shields, locking them together to create a solid wall. They can shoot as much as they like. They'll only be wasting arrows. But sooner or later, they'll have to attack. They may ride in initially, although there isn't a lot of room for a mounted attack—maybe only four or five horses abreast. When they see the ditch, they'll stop and probably turn back. Or they might dismount and come forward on foot. If they do, the ones behind them will have to stop shooting."

Thorn walked to a point three meters from the ditch and scuffed a line in the sand with his boot. "If they attack on horse-back," he continued, "we'll let them get to here and then hit them with a volley of spears. We'll throw one each and keep the other one for close fighting. Even our boys should be able to hit their targets from this range," he said, ruing the fact that he hadn't drilled them further in spear throwing, as he had intended. "But if we can bring down three or four of them, that'll make matters a lot more crowded and awkward for the attackers who follow them."

"Maybe we should limit the spear throwing to you and me and Jesper?" Stig suggested. Thorn and Stig were both skilled spear throwers—even though Thorn was using his left hand. And Jesper was the best of the rest of the crew. "We'll throw two each in rapid succession. That should stop a few of them."

Thorn nodded agreement. "Good idea," he said. "And I'll get Lydia to join in as well. She's worth her weight in gold with that atlatl."

They paused and looked around, checking one more time to see if there was anything they had forgotten, any weak point they should protect. But they could find nothing. Thorn knew his business when it came to setting a shield wall. He'd been doing it since he was a young man. And Stig was now a seasoned veteran as well. Between them, they didn't miss much.

Then Stig grinned to himself. There's always something you don't think of, he thought. Then, when the fight starts, you're scrambling to take care of it. He looked up as there was a whistle from the earth rampart.

Jesper was waving to them and pointing upriver. "Looks like our guests have arrived," he called.

Thorn and Stig made their way back to the rampart, picking their way carefully through the sharpened stakes in the ditch, then scrambling up the earth wall. Jesper leaned out, offering a hand to help them up the loose, slippery slope.

As he dropped over the wall onto the earthen step behind it, Stig reflected on how difficult that short climb might have been if Jesper had welcomed them with a spear point, instead of a helping hand. That was something the Temujai would discover in a short while, he thought.

Thorn turned to study the ground behind them. There were six horsemen visible. They had reined in about eighty meters away, waiting for the rest of their force. As the Skandians watched, another dozen riders appeared, shouldering their way out of the trees and forming up on the narrow bank behind the first half dozen.

"Stay undercover, everyone," Thorn cautioned. There was no guarantee that a rider in the rear ranks, concealed from their view, mightn't start shooting while they were unprepared.

But his warning was unnecessary. The Herons stayed crouched behind the barrier of the earth wall and their locked-together shields. For several minutes, there was an impasse. The Temujai sat their horses, watching the small group of Skandians blocking their way. The Herons remained hidden behind their wall, only their eyes visible as they waited for the Temujai to make their first move.

It came without any warning. The initial six horsemen moved off as one. Thorn had heard no verbal command nor had he seen a visual signal. One moment, the horsemen were sitting motionless. The next, they were trotting forward in line abreast.

"They're well drilled, I'll give them that," he said, reluctantly admiring the discipline that typified Temujai operations. Skandians didn't have that same rigid discipline, he thought. They were more inclined to act as individuals in battle, as witness the wide variation in their weapons—his massive club, Ingvar's voulge, Stig's battleax and Hal's darting sword. They all fought differently, although he had trained the Heron brotherband to work as a team, each member supporting his companions.

That lack of rigid discipline was a blessing and a curse, he reflected. Skandians might not be able to mount a machinelike, implacable attack on a position. But they were unpredictable and an enemy never quite knew what to expect—particularly an enemy like the Temujai. They relied on an unbending adherence to set patterns of fighting: the initial arrow storm, followed by a close-quarters attack either on horseback or on foot. As he had the thought, he heard the first clatter of arrows striking against the shield wall as the second rank of horsemen released a volley that traveled in a giant parabola, sailing over the heads of their first rank and whipping down into the shields set on top of the wall.

"Stay down!" Thorn repeated, again unnecessarily. The crew had seen the effect of Temujai arrow volleys when they had faced them at Fort Ragnak. Above the rain of arrows, he heard the hoof-beats speed up, coming closer. He risked a look through a narrow gap between his shield and the next in line. The six horsemen were bearing down on them now, bunching up as the space on the bank narrowed. They were almost knee to knee and only twenty meters out when they saw the ditch ahead of them.

Up to that point, they may well have been planning to urge their horses up the earth wall and send them smashing into the shields above it. Now, at a shouted warning from their leader, they hauled back on the reins, causing their horses to rear back and slide, stiff kneed, in the soft earth.

At the same time, the rattle of arrows on shields lessened, then stopped, as the riders blocked the sightline of their comrades behind them. There was a moment of indecision, of most un-Temujai-like uncertainty. Thorn took advantage of it.

"Stig! Jesper! Now!" he bellowed. Seizing one of the spears planted butt-first in the dirt beside him, he stood up, head and shoulders above the shield wall, and cast the spear at the milling group of riders. On either side of him, he saw Stig and Jesper doing the same. Without waiting to see the result of his first cast, he seized his second spear, weighed it in his hand, checking its balance, then sighted and cast.

He heard a whistling hiss as one of Lydia's darts flashed overhead and slammed into a rider.

Three of the Temujai and one horse went down under the barrage. The riderless horses added to the confusion, stamping and whinnying, trying to turn away and flee past the other horses, whose riders desperately fought to bring them under control. Thorn was tempted to order another volley of spears. But their numbers were limited and they'd be needed as the fight went on, he realized.

For the moment, the result was a good one. The cramped area in front of the barrier was further constricted now by the bodies of the riders and the dead horse. The next wave would have to pick their way past them.

This time, he heard a shouted command, and the surviving horsemen wheeled their mounts and galloped away. Almost immediately, the rattle of arrows on shields started again.

After several minutes, the shooting slackened, then stopped as the Temujai archers realized they were wasting arrows to no effect. Again, the two sides eyed each other over the eighty-meter gap between them.

"That was easy," Stig called cheerfully.

Thorn shook his head in a warning. "Next time won't be. They learn quickly," he said. He was peering through the narrow gap in the shields again. There was still danger from occasional arrows loosed at the shield wall. They struck at irregular intervals, thudding into the wood-and-cowhide shields or whimpering over the top of the wall. He turned and looked back at the raised mound where Lydia sheltered behind the wall of saplings. There were at least a dozen arrows in the wall. The Temujai had seen her and quickly realized the danger from her darts.

"Are you all right back there, Lydia?" he called.

She answered immediately. "I'm fine, Thorn. Do you want me to take a few long-range shots? I could reach them easily from here."

He considered the idea, then rejected it. Lydia's supply of darts was limited and they would be better used in a general attack than in a few random shots now.

"Wait till they attack. There'll be less chance of them shooting back at you and you can plug any gaps that might open up."

"Whatever you say," came the unconcerned reply.

"They're on the move again!" Stefan called.

Thorn turned quickly back to scan the riverbank. This time, the horsemen had dismounted, realizing that their horses placed them at a disadvantage in the confined space between the river-bank, the valley wall and the ditch. They advanced on foot, some twenty of them. Most had swords drawn—the long, curved sabers that they favored—and had small round shields of wood and hard-ened cowhide. Half a dozen carried the long, slender lances that they occasionally used from horseback.

They knew that the Skandians had no bows or slings so they could advance safely. Lydia was the only one of the defenders who had a projectile weapon available. It was a safe bet that at least a dozen of the bowmen who remained behind were targeted on her shelter, waiting for her to show herself.

"Stay undercover, Lydia!" Thorn shouted. "They'll be watching for you!"

The twenty men advanced, moving in two loose ranks. As before, the closer they came, the more they were compressed by the narrowing terrain. Once again, the rattle of arrows hitting the shield wall commenced. There was a grunt of pain from Stefan. Thorn turned and saw him clutching his calf, where an arrow had found its way through a small gap in the shield wall and hit him. Ulf moved to help him, grabbing up a medical pack that was standing ready. Edvin had prepared half a dozen of these before he had left and distributed them among the crew. Ulf snapped off the barbed head where it had passed clean through the muscle, then pulled out the shaft. Stefan grunted in pain again, then Ulf smeared a painkilling paste on the wound and rapidly wound a linen bandage around it.

"Are you all right?" Thorn called. They couldn't afford any gaps in their line. There were too few of them as it was.

"I'll be fine," Stefan replied. His voice was strained. Obviously, he was gritting his teeth against the pain. Once the painkilling paste, derived from the drug warmweed, took effect, Thorn thought, that wouldn't be a problem—at least for an hour or two.

Ulf finished binding up the wound and helped Stefan to his feet. Stefan tested his weight on the wounded leg and grimaced. Then he hobbled a few steps, his movements becoming easier as the paste took effect, numbing the leg.

"That's fine," he said. "Thanks, Ulf."

"Heads up!" Jesper shouted. "They're at the ditch!"

Almost immediately, the arrow barrage died away, as the

attackers masked the sightlines of the archers behind them. The Herons stood up behind the shield wall, spears ready to thrust at the attackers. As they did so, three of the Temujai carrying lances thrust their long, slender weapons through the shield wall, into the narrow gaps where the circular shields didn't quite meet.

"Watch out for those lances!" Stig shouted, swaying to avoid a lance thrust blindly toward him. He shoved his shield sideways, trapping the lance between it and Wulf's shield, which was next in line to his. As the Temujai tried to pull it free, he smashed the head off it with a sideways swipe of his ax.

Elsewhere along the line, the defenders copied his action, leaving the lances harmless without their metal points. Seeing that tactic had failed, the lancers drew their sabers and began to clamber up the earthen bank with their comrades.

"Let's get 'em!" Thorn yelled, thrusting at a climbing warrior with his spear, sending the man hurtling back into the ditch, taking another attacker with him.

A group of three Temujai warriors, scrambling on hands and knees to climb the slope, appeared over the parapet, yelling battle cries and quickly rising to their feet, swords drawn and shields ready. Their cries died away as they found themselves facing Stig, standing ready with his shield and his battleax. He slammed his shield into the nearest of the Temujai, sending the man sailing bodily through the air to crash back into the ditch. Fortunately for the attacker, the pointed stakes were angled outward, away from him, and he flattened three of them under his body weight. He lay there, winded, as his comrades struggled past him, some of them actually stepping on him in their haste to gain the earth wall.

The second of the three Temujai lunged at Stig with his saber. The tall Skandian flicked the blade aside with his ax, then used his shield as a weapon once more, bringing the iron-rimmed edge up and driving it into the Tem'uj's rib cage. The attacker gasped in pain, then, seeing the ax beginning to swing in a horizontal arc toward him, let himself fall backward down the earth slope, after his comrade.

The third man swung at Stig's head but the big shield was already in place to block the swing. The sword's edge caught in the rim of the shield and its owner foolishly tried to free it, leaving himself open to a counterattack from the big, long-handled ax. He too went sliding back down the slope. Unlike his two companions, he didn't move when he hit the bottom.

Along the rampart, individual battles were being waged. Ulf and Wulf, fighting as a team, hurled four Temujai back down the slope. A fifth was slow in rising to his feet after scrabbling his way through the loose earth. Wulf's sword took him in the center of his body as he stood. The man cried out in pain but managed to retaliate, with a horizontal stroke aimed at Wulf's hip. But he was already falling and the sword caught Wulf lower down, just above the knee. The sail trimmer staggered back from the parapet. The leg gave way underneath him and he fell awkwardly, dropping his sword and clutching at the wounded leg to stem the blood flow.

Near the middle of the rampart, Ingvar stood like a colossus. His voulge darted in and out, trapping defenders with the hook, dragging them forward off balance and then dispatching them with the spear point or the ax head on his terrifying weapon. The Temujai seemed to have no counter for his attacks. They had never before faced a weapon like this, wielded by such a powerful warrior. A growing pile of bodies sprawled on the ground around him.

But then disaster struck. One of the Temujai scrambled up the slope toward the gap in the line that had been left when Wulf staggered back and fell. He was approaching Ingvar from an oblique angle, and the giant warrior's peripheral vision was his weakest point. He didn't see the attack coming until it was almost too late. The Tem'uj's saber slashed at Ingvar's head and the big Skandian reacted just in time, bringing up the shaft of his weapon to deflect the sword.

The hardwood shaft stopped the blade at the last moment. But the impact of the sword caused the shaft to slam backward into the side of Ingvar's head. The force of the blow wasn't serious, but the result was. The shaft smashed into the support frame of Ingvar's spectacles, shattering the frame and sending the dark lenses spinning away, leaving him almost blinded. Ingvar groped wildly at the blurred figure before him. He got a hold on the Tem'uj's untanned leather jerkin and heaved him up and out. The Temujai warrior screamed as he hurtled through space and landed heavily in the ditch, taking down two more attackers who were picking their way through the sharpened stakes to join the attack.

Left semi-blinded on the parapet, Ingvar staggered, hands outstretched for balance. Another Tem'uj, seeing him helpless, drew back his saber to lunge at him.

Ulf saw what was happening just in time. He leapt across the space to where Ingvar stood, swaying uncertainly, and hit him with his shoulder, sending him crashing back inside the wall, just as the saber stabbed through empty space. The Tem'uj was off balance as his thrust met no resistance, and Ulf quickly dispatched him with an overhead cut from his own sword.

But now the defensive line was weakened, with Stefan injured and limping and Wulf and Ingvar out of the fight. A Temujai squad commander saw the gaps in the line and shouted to his men to follow him. He led four others along the top of the earth bank in a renewed attack. Ulf, caught off guard, retreated before them, desperately parrying their blows and thrusts. More of the Temujai below saw their comrades driving him back and began scrambling up the earth wall to join the attack.

Then a massive voice boomed out over the cries and shouts and the clash of swords on shields.

"Stig! With me!" Thorn yelled, and hurled himself at the group of attackers forcing Ulf back. He smashed into them, sending one reeling. Then his massive club began its deadly work: thrusting, swinging, smashing, hammering. The Temujai had no answer to his power and his blinding speed. They began to fall back, shoving at one another to avoid the huge, shaggy-haired figure as he drove into them. Then Stig joined him from a different angle, the long-handled ax whirling in terrifying arcs as he cut and smashed at the enemy. The two Herons wreaked total havoc on the Temujai. Those who had been rushing to join the attack suddenly turned back, scrambling over one another in their haste to get back down the rampart and across the ditch to safety.

Stig and Thorn kept up their onslaught, scattering the attackers, breaking their will and sending more than half of them sliding back down the earth wall with terrible wounds.

It was too much for the survivors. Faced by the two seemingly invincible Skandian warriors, they turned and ran, scrambling and sliding down the rampart and across the ditch.

Three remaining Temujai, who hadn't noticed the sudden panic that had overcome their comrades, were engaging Jesper and Stefan. Stefan's leg wound had opened up again and he hobbled on one leg as he tried to support Jesper in the uneven fight. Jesper cut at one of the attackers, hitting him on the lower arm and causing him to drop his sword. But he didn't have time to follow up on the advantage as a second Tem'uj struck at him, forcing him to defend desperately. Jesper parried his stroke, then leapt back as the third attacker lunged. Stefan's sword blade deflected the saber just in time, with a rasping clang of metal on metal.

Then there was a mighty roar behind the three attackers as Thorn and Stig raced down the rampart and hit them from behind. The Temujai had no chance. Jesper stepped back to let his two terrifying shipmates have fighting room. Within seconds, the three Temujai were sprawled facedown on the top of the rampart.

Thorn stepped back, breathing heavily, and watched the attacking force fleeing back to their lines. He looked around the thin line of defenders. Ingvar was helpless. Stefan's wound was bleeding again and his leg had stiffened. Wulf was wounded in the thigh. There was muscle damage and his leg could hardly bear his weight. Thorn shook his head wearily. With three of their number out of the fight, things were looking grim.

"Next time's not going to be so easy," he said.

## chapter thirty-seven

The sea was ahead of them and Hal kept the *Heron* on a starboard tack as she raced out past the river mouth, skimmed over the sandbar and rode up the face of the first roller.

Luckily, the waves were small, barely more than a meter high. But even so, as *Heron*'s bow sliced into the first one and rode up and over it, Hal felt that same frightening flex in her hull. This time, he even heard the timbers groaning deep inside the ship below the waterline. He swung the bow to port. If he kept her butting head-first into the seas like that, she wouldn't last long, he knew. But by taking the waves at an angle, he lessened the impact. The hull still twisted and flexed as *Heron* went up and over each wave. But there was less direct impact, less sense that the ship was battering herself to pieces.

The wind stayed steady from the south, and Edvin was able to cleat off the sheet, keeping the sail locked in position. After ten minutes or so, Hal could feel the ship growing heavier, more sluggish and less responsive. Whereas she normally soared up and over the waves like a seabird, now she was heavy, wallowing in the troughs, rising reluctantly to each successive wave. They'd bailed her out back at the riverbank, but she had undoubtedly sprung a few planks, he thought, and she was filling with water with every minute that passed.

"Edvin!" he yelled. "Rig the pump and start pumping her out!"

His sole crewman waved assent. He delved into the lockers beside the rowing benches and brought out the portable stirrup pump—another of Hal's innovations. Most wolfships were bailed out by hand. But *Heron* had a smaller crew than a full-sized wolfship and Hal was always looking for ways to lessen the physical labor demanded of them. Edvin scrambled onto the central deck, raised the hatch that led to the bilges, and lowered the pump's intake hose into the void. He began furiously working the handle up and down and, a minute later, the first gush of water poured out of the pump. Quickly, he arranged the exhaust hose over the gunwale, then started pumping again. A steady stream of water poured out over the side, and after several minutes Hal felt the ship becoming lighter, more responsive.

"Keep it up!" he called.

Edvin nodded, too busy to reply. *Clonk, clonk, clonk* went the pump handle, and the water poured back into the sea in a constant stream. But Hal knew Edvin couldn't keep on pumping indefinitely. It was exhausting work. Sooner or later, Hal would have to spell him, leaving him to steer the ship.

He was less than comfortable with that idea. The ship was badly wounded and he felt he needed to nurse it along, avoiding putting too much strain on the damaged keel. Edvin was a good helmsman, but Hal was a better one. He had an instinctive feel for his ship and he didn't want to hand her over to anyone else in her current state. He realized that the Sha'shan was sitting on the deck by the mast, taking in everything that was going on and watching Kloof nervously as the huge dog watched his every move. He had complained about the dog earlier to Hal, worried that she was likely to bite him—and a bite from Kloof was no minor matter.

"She'll only bite you if I tell her to," Hal informed him. "And if you don't behave yourself, I will tell her."

Now, as he watched the Sha'shan, Hal saw a solution to the pumping problem.

"Put Pa'tong to work on the pump!" he called, seeing Edvin's rhythm becoming more ragged. "Tell him he'll drown along with us if the ship goes down. I'm not going to untie him from the mast."

Edvin leaned back with a sigh of relief. He gestured to the Sha'shan to take a turn on the pump. Pa'tong shook his head haughtily. Apparently, he didn't do manual labor. Edvin shouted at him angrily, making hand gestures to reinforce what he was saying. He mimed the ship sinking beneath the waves, then pointed at the Temujai leader and then overside into the sea. The meaning was clear. If she sinks, you'll sink with her.

Kloof amplified the warning with a deep, rumbling growl, rising to her haunches. She could see Edvin was angry with the stranger, and Edvin was one of her favorites. He was, after all, the ship's cook.

With a surly glance at Hal, Pa'tong took hold of the pump

handle and began to work it—jerkily at first, then more smoothly as he found his rhythm. Once more, water streamed overside. Kloof sank back to her position on the deck. Then she bounded to her feet and ran to the rail, barking excitedly.

Edvin leapt to his feet, shading his eyes as he stared out to sea, yelling excitedly and pointing.

"Hal! It's a ship!"

Pa'tong ceased pumping, scrambling to his knees and looking in the direction Edvin indicated. The slightly built crewman cuffed him over the side of the head and gestured for him to keep pumping. Pa'tong complied, but with extremely bad grace.

Hal was looking in the direction Edvin had indicated as well. He made out the large triangular sail of a full-sized wolfship, one of many in the fleet that he'd converted to the fore and aft sail rig that *Heron* carried. She was about a kilometer farther out to sea, moving west under full sail. As he watched, her hull seemed to foreshorten and her starboard sail disappeared, to be replaced instantly by the port sail and yardarm. The new sail filled and the ship came round neatly, with the wind behind her.

"She's turning toward us!" Edvin yelled as the ship bore down on them, a white bow wave foaming before her. Hal could make out the insignia on her sail now—a wolf running at top speed.

"It's *Wolfrunner!*" he shouted. "Rollond's ship!"

Rollond was an old friend. He had been one of the other two brotherband leaders who had competed with the Herons when they first began their training. He was a highly capable skirl, an excellent seaman and a much admired warrior, second only to Stig among their contemporaries.

The bigger ship rounded to neatly and ran alongside *Heron* as the crew released the sheets and gathered in the sail. Edvin scuttled across the deck and uncleated their own mainsheet, letting the sail fly loose and taking the way off *Heron*. The two ships rocked in the waves, side by side, separated by seven or eight meters. Rollond's tall figure left the steering oar on the starboard side of the stern and stepped to the port side. His hands cupped round his mouth as he yelled a greeting to Hal.

"Hal! Where are Thorn and the others?" He peered curiously at *Heron's* empty decks and rowing benches. "Do you need help?"

Hal nodded vigorously. "Lend us a man to help with the pump," he shouted back. "We're taking on water. Thorn and the crew are back at Ice River holding off a Temujai attack. We've got to get the Sha'shan"—he indicated the huddled figure by the mast—"to Hallasholm to make a treaty."

While they had been talking, Rollond's first mate had directed one of the crew to throw a grapnel and a line across. Now, with the grapnel's hooks set firmly in the *Heron's* rail, several of the crew tailed onto the line and hauled the ships closer. The two hulls bumped gently together and one of *Wolfrunner's* crew stepped lightly across to the *Heron's* deck, moving quickly to take over the pump from the Sha'shan, who had neglected the work as he watched the other ship draw close. Rollond stepped aboard a moment after his crew member and moved aft to talk with Hal. Kloof welcomed him with a slow-wagging tail. Rollond watched the steady stream of clear water gushing over the side.

"What happened?" he asked.

"We hit a rock and cracked the keel," Hal told him. Rollond

grimaced in sympathy. Hal's expression told him that the damage was serious. "I'm certainly glad to see you," Hal continued.

"It's no accident we're here," Rollond told him. "Erak's had us patrolling this section of the coast for the past four days, in case you needed help. Did you say that's the Sha'shan?" he asked curiously, changing the subject and indicating the bedraggled figure sitting on the deck.

"That's right. I've got to get him to Hallasholm to sign a treaty with Erak. It'll stop the Temujai trying to invade us."

Rollond whistled in surprise. This was big news. "And you say Thorn and Stig and the boys are holding off a Temujai attack?"

Hal nodded. "They've set up a defensive position on the bank of the Ice River, where the valley narrows. It's about two kilometers inland."

"How many Temujai?" Rollond asked.

Hal pursed his lips as he considered the question. "At the moment, about a hundred and fifty. But there are more on the way. Luckily, they can only come at Thorn and Stig ten or twelve at a time. I need to get the Sha'shan to Hallasholm, get the terms of the treaty agreed, then get him back to Ice River to call off his men."

Rollond gestured to *Wolfrunner*, bobbing gently up and down on the small waves alongside. *Heron* was rising and falling more sluggishly, although with a fresh hand on the pump, she was becoming noticeably lighter.

"Better get him on board *Wolfrunner*. We'll take you back to Hallasholm and get this treaty sorted out."

Hal hesitated. His hand opened and closed on the tiller. *Heron* was badly damaged. She might not make it back to Hallasholm.

On the other hand, Stig and Thorn and the crew were badly out-numbered, and Rollond had thirty or more fully armed, well-trained fighting men on board. Thirty warriors manning the earth rampart could hold off the Temujai easily.

"Well, what do you say?" Rollond urged.

"Here they come again!"

The warning was followed almost immediately by the inevitable hail of arrows against the shield wall. Stig, Thorn, Ulf and Jesper crouched below the rampart, ready to scramble up and repel the Temujai once the arrow storm ceased. Stefan, Wulf and Lydia were behind them. Lydia had forsaken her shooting position behind the wooden shield. The Temujai had her well targeted there and she could achieve little in the event of an attack. Now she stood ready with a spear to support the four fighting men in the depleted defensive line. Stefan and Wulf, injured as they were, could still form a secondary line of defense, and both of them were armed with spears.

Ingvar, to his absolute fury, could take no part in the coming fight. He was virtually sightless without the special spectacles Hal had made for him some years previously.

"Don't you have a spare pair?" Jesper had asked him.

Ingvar turned a bleak look in his general direction. "Of course I do. They're with my kit on the ship."

And for once, Jesper knew better than to comment further.

The arrows ceased slamming into the shields. They had left all ten shields erect on the wall, to prevent the Temujai knowing that there were three fewer defenders. Thorn peered through a small gap and saw a line of dismounted Temujai scrambling across the ditch.

"Let's get 'em!" he roared, and Stig, Jesper and Ulf joined him as he clambered to the top of the wall and presented a defiant face to the attackers.

Three of the Temujai, seeing the shortened line of defenders, veered to the left, climbing the wall where there appeared to be nobody to stop them. Thorn waved his left hand toward them.

"Lydia!" he yelled. "They're coming up on the left."

The girl hefted her long spear and ran to the left-hand end of the wall, just as the first two Temujai appeared over the top, angling in to attack the defenders from the side.

She set her feet and thrust savagely up with the spear. The Temujai had eyes only for the line of four warriors confronting them and they never saw the attack coming from below. She hit the first man in the hip. The spearhead sliced into him and she twisted and shoved. The Temujai sank to his knees on top of the wall, then toppled over. His companion now saw the girl in the trench below. He slid down the inner earth wall, deflecting her spear thrust with his small round shield, and drew back his saber.

From a few meters away, Wulf hurled his spear, taking the man in the center of his body and hurling him back against the wall. The third man, seeing his companions' fate, slipped back over the wall and slid down to the ditch. He'd try again in a safer place, he thought.

Meanwhile, Thorn and Stig stood shoulder to shoulder, with Jesper and Ulf a little behind them, guarding their flanks. The club and the ax wreaked terrible damage on the attackers, smashing, hacking, tearing at them, sending them reeling or flying bodily off the wall into the ditch.

But there were simply too many attackers. As the Herons beat back two or three of them, four or five more took their place and the defenders were becoming hard pressed. Stig had been wounded twice—minor injuries, but ones that would eventually sap his strength as the fight went on. A saber point had opened a long, shallow gash in Thorn's forehead. It too was a minor wound, but like all scalp wounds, it bled profusely and blood poured down into his eyes, half blinding him. He smashed and slammed with the club, seeing the enemy warriors vaguely through a red mist. His left hand held his saxe and he used it to cut down any who got inside the reach of the club.

But for every man he smashed down, there were two more to take his place. The Temujai had seen how the line was weakened and rushed forward to deal with these stubborn Skandians. Their commander realized that there were only a few warriors left to defy him. In typical Temujai fashion, he poured more and more of his men into the attack, disregarding the losses inflicted on them.

And the ruthless tactic was working. Thorn slammed yet another scrambling Temujai swordsman with his club, snapping his slender blade at the hilt and crunching into the man's shoulder. As the Temujai went down, Thorn stepped back to gain a few seconds' respite. But a few seconds was all he got. More of the eastern riders were scrambling up the slope to confront him. Wearily, he raised the massive club once more, just managing to deflect a sword that was thrust at him.

But before he could counterattack, a spear thrust past him from behind and to his right, slamming into the small shield of the suddenly terrified attacker. The Tem'uj reeled back under the impact, taking two of his companions with him. Along the wall, there were sudden cries of alarm from the Temujai troops as more and more Skandian warriors appeared—as if from nowhere—dozens of fresh warriors who went at the Temujai with swords, axes and spears, driving them back in confusion.

Thorn looked round to see Rollond's grinning face a few meters away.

"Hal said you might need a little help," Rollond said.

## chapter thirty-eight

With Rollond's crewman, Torval, helping Edvin on the pump, the flow of water over the side was constant. And they cleared it at a much faster rate. But Hal could feel the ship wasn't responding as he thought she should. The only answer was that, as the hull flexed and twisted, more planks worked their way loose and the influx of water increased to a point where the two men pumping the water out couldn't match the volume coming in. The ship grew heavier and more reluctant to rise to the waves. And the extra weight she carried was obviously having an adverse effect on the damaged keel.

Nervously, Hal edged her in, closer to the shore.

"If she looks like sinking," he muttered to himself, "I'll run her ashore and we'll make it back to Hallasholm on foot."

The prospect of her sinking was becoming more and more likely with each passing minute. He realized it was going to be a race against time.

As an added complication, the extra weight of water in the bilges meant that from time to time she didn't rise soon enough as a new wave swept in. Instead, she would wallow heavily and the wave would break over her, flooding the decks and the bilges with seawater, replacing most of what they had laboriously pumped out of her.

Pa'tong was a nervous onlooker as the two Skandians worked at the pump. Hal had considered keeping him working too, but Edvin and Torval were more adept at the job. Pa'tong was clumsy and nowhere near as efficient as either of the others.

Kloof remained stretched on her belly on the central deck, her chin on her paws, keeping her unblinking gaze fastened on Pa'tong. He was still uncomfortable around the giant dog, but seemed to have accepted that he was probably safe from her—so long as he didn't annoy Hal.

So, the *Heron* wallowed on, rising and falling sluggishly as the waves swept under her. Now Hal was sure he could see the deck twisting as she crested the larger waves and floundered down the reverse side. Gaps were starting to form between the deck planks. He could only imagine what was happening to the hull planks below the waterline. In some places, the rope-and-tar mixture that sealed irregularities in the decking could be seen working loose.

Torval, who had just finished a ten-minute spell on the pump, came back to the steering platform, casting a critical eye over

*Heron's* staggering progress. He had been on board her before and knew that this was nothing like her normal light, soaring action.

"Is she going to make it?" he asked Hal.

Hal set his jaw stubbornly. "She'll make it. We're only a couple of kilometers from Hallasholm now."

Torval pursed his lips skeptically. Wishful thinking wouldn't keep her afloat, he thought.

A few seconds later, Hal relented. "Better get a few small kegs ready to use as floats," he said. "Just in case."

Torval nodded and went for'ard. There were several kegs lashed in place in the bow, holding ready supplies of drinking water. He tapped the bungs in and emptied the water over the side. A coil of light rope was hanging close by. He cut several two-meter lengths to use as lashings for the kegs in case they were needed. He placed them on the deck next to the Sha'shan.

Edvin looked at him curiously.

"Hal's idea," Torval said. "In case we sink."

Edvin nodded. He could swim, like all the *Heron's* crew. But he wasn't a strong swimmer, and he was sure Torval couldn't swim at all—few Skandian sailors could. Neither could Pa'tong. Hal, he knew, could swim like a fish. At a gesture from Torval, he relinquished the pump handle and the *Wolfrunner* crewman took over the work. Water continued to gush overside, but they both sensed the *Heron* was settling deeper into the water.

Kloof rose, shook herself and ran to the bow, standing on her hind legs, with her forepaws on the gunwale. She began barking furiously.

Edvin turned his weary gaze forward. His heart leapt with

hope as he realized he could see Hallasholm—a cluster of low timber buildings, with smoke curling from a dozen chimneys. They were barely half a kilometer away from safety and he could see the gap in the harbor wall, and a glimpse of the little beach behind it.

He turned to call the news to Hal, but the skirl gave him a tired wave.

"I see it," Hal said.

With safety so close, Edvin grabbed the pump handle from Torval and put on a burst of high-energy pumping. Water gushed and foamed out of the pump. Torval, after a few minutes, took the handle back and maintained the high speed that Edvin had set. Then Edvin took a turn again.

It seemed their sudden burst of energy was having an effect as they passed the pump back and forth between them. Pa'tong watched them anxiously. Even he had been able to feel the sluggish response of the ship over the past fifteen minutes. Now he could see that the *Heron* was riding lighter, responding more easily to the helm and the pressure of the sail.

"I'll turn toward the harbor mouth shortly," Hal called to them. "When I do, let the sail out completely. We'll run in with the wind directly behind us."

Edvin signaled that he understood. They would have to turn left once more when they passed through the harbor mouth, but they should have enough residual speed to reach the beach. Torval slumped back from the pump with a groan of exhaustion, and Edvin grabbed the handle and started pumping again. Up for'ard, Kloof began barking excitedly.

Judging the moment, Hal shoved the tiller right over. *Heron* swung to port, heading at an angle for the harbor mouth.

"Now!" he yelled. "Let the sail right out!"

Edvin scrambled to release the sheet and the sail swung out to port, driven by the wind. As soon as it was at right angles to the hull, he hauled the sheet tight and she accelerated for the gap.

But at the very moment that the sail took effect and sent her lurching forward, a rogue wave hit her starboard quarter, throwing her off line and heading for the stone mole itself. Hal hauled desperately on the tiller to swing her back. As the conflicting forces of wind, wave and tiller hit her, the damaged keel finally let go. They flashed past the mole, into the harbor itself, and the ship sagged horribly, just for'ard of the mast. Only her speed was keeping her afloat now, and Hal headed her for the beach, feeling her sinking beneath him as the finally shattered keel ripped open more planks and seawater poured into her ravaged hull.

Her prow hit the sand just as she lost the last of her buoyancy and settled beneath the water. As she grounded, she twisted one final time. There was a loud *CRACK!* from below and she was left lying on her side—with the forepart of the ship tilting to port and the aft section to starboard.

With tears streaming down his face, Hal stroked the smooth timber of the tiller.

"Good girl," he said softly. "You got us home after all."

"And you say you'll be able to call off the current attack?" Borsa asked, eyeing the Sha'shan shrewdly. Borsa was Erak's hilfmann, or chief administrator. His hair and beard were white and he had spent a lifetime judging people, assessing whether or not they were telling the truth. He sensed that the Temujai leader was.

"Only if you return me to Ice River within the next day or so," Pa'tong replied evenly. "Any longer and those who would seek to replace me will be able to convince my people that you've killed me. Then there will be no treaty."

"And what's to say that I can rely on your word?" Erak said aggressively. It seemed to him they would be taking an awful lot on trust if they simply returned the Sha'shan to his people.

Pa'tong switched his gaze to the burly Oberjarl. He took no offense at the question. He would have asked the same in Erak's place.

"I will swear an oath on the skull of the Great Horse Spirit Mori," he said simply.

Erak raised an eyebrow. He often swore to minor Skandian gods. He often swore *at* them as well. He knew such oaths were not binding. They were usually only conversational gambits.

But Borsa had made it his business over the years to study the Temujai and their beliefs, as well as those of other potential enemies.

"No Temujai would break that vow," he told his Oberjarl. "It's their equivalent of our Vallasvow."

Erak sat back a little. A Vallasvow was something different from his everyday oaths. It was definitely not something that was lightly taken. If a Vallasvow oath-taker broke his word, he would die within seven days. It was such a powerful oath that Erak didn't even like talking about it. As far as possible, he even avoided using the word itself. He looked at his hilfmann.

"You're sure about that?"

Borsa nodded emphatically. "Definitely."

Hal sat silently by, watching the discussion unfold. It was out of his hands now. In the hours since he had beached the wreck of the *Heron*, things had moved quickly. The little ship had been dragged up above the high-water mark. Erak and Svengal had appeared on the beach, where Hal had explained Pa'tong's willingness to sign a peace treaty with the Oberjarl. He had also explained the urgency involved, and the situation at Ice River, where the Herons and *Wolfrunner's* crew were holding off the attacking Temujai. Erak had dispatched another wolfship to reinforce them, and Pa'tong and Hal had been conducted to Erak's Great Hall, where they were now sitting at a large pine table, settling the details of the treaty.

"So, you will guarantee not to take any offensive action against Skandia, either at Ice River Valley or at Fort Ragnak?" Erak said now.

The Sha'shan nodded. "You will have my solemn vow."

"For a period of five years?" Erak continued.

Pa'tong raised an eyebrow in his turn. "Three years," Pa'tong corrected him, pointing to the draft of the treaty on the table between them. "As your hilfmann has noted."

"Right. Three years," Erak said, shrugging slightly. It had been worth a try. He looked down at the parchment where Borsa had written out the terms of the treaty. They were simple enough—no hostilities between the two nations, no encroachment on each other's territory for the agreed period. Simple was best when it came to treaties, Erak believed. That way there could be no prevarication, no pettifogging legal interpretations that would allow one side or the other to break the terms. He cleared his throat and jerked his head at Borsa and Hal, indicating that he wanted to talk to them privately. He rose from the table.

"If you'll excuse us, Sha'shan," Borsa said as he rose to follow his Oberjarl. Pa'tong shrugged and made an assenting gesture with both hands. Hal rose as well and followed his two countrymen to a spot a few meters away, where they could talk without the Sha'shan overhearing them.

"What do you think?" Erak asked in a hoarse whisper. Speaking in lowered tones didn't come naturally to him. He was looking at Hal as he asked the question.

The young skirl shrugged. "I think it's the best we can get. We'll have three years without having to worry about a Temujai attack."

Erak sniffed. "But it will give him three years to gather his forces and get ready to attack us."

"His forces are already assembled. What more can he do?" Hal pointed out. "And by the same token, we'll have three years to fortify our position in Ice River Valley."

"He's right, Erak," Borsa pointed out. "If Hal's description of the situation there is accurate . . ." He paused and glanced at Hal, a question in his expression.

Hal nodded affirmatively. "It is."

Borsa continued. "In three years, we can make that position well-nigh impregnable."

Erak pursed his lips and thought over what they had said. Then, typical of the man, he came to a decision.

"You're right," he said. He turned to Pa'tong and raised his voice. "All right, Sha'shan. Let's sign that treaty. Then I'll have *Wolfwind* take you back to your people."

The Sha'shan bowed his head in agreement.

As Borsa sat at the table again and began to make a few final amendments to the document, Erak took Hal's arm and drew him aside. He had seen the wreckage of the *Heron* where she had landed at the beach. A team of men had dragged the shattered hull up above the tidemark. Like all Skandians, Erak understood the deep bond that a skirl formed with his ship and the terrible sadness and despair that came when a ship was lost.

"Well done, Hal," he said simply. "I know what this has cost you."

The two forces faced each other along the narrow bank of the Ice River. Since the arrival of *Wolfrunner* and Rollond's thirty crewmen, the defensive rampart was fully manned. And the second wolfship dispatched by Erak gave them ample reserves in case of an attack. The Temujai realized this and had held off any further attempts to overrun the wall.

From time to time, archers working individually or in pairs would snipe at the earth rampart and the row of shields—now augmented by those belonging to the *Wolfrunner* crew. The defenders had learned to remain undercover and had constructed covered walkways behind the wall so they could move about without risking being shot.

The Temujai had also taken to lobbing arrows over the wall so that they fell into the space behind it. But the Skandians had quickly countered this by building shelters with thick timber roofs, under which they could relax in safety.

So a stalemate existed.

Thorn and Rollond were crouched behind the shield wall, peering at the enemy riders eighty meters away. Each day had brought new reinforcements to the Temujai. There were now several hundred bivouacked among the trees on the bank. But no matter how many of them there were, they could still only attack over a front of eight to ten men. Which meant the Skandian defenders could hurl them back easily.

As the two Skandian leaders watched, they saw three archers step forward from the Temujai line and raise their bows.

"Arrows!" Thorn called, and any Skandians moving in the open space behind the wall hastily sought shelter. A minute or so later, a hail of half a dozen arrows plunged into the little compound they had built. But by then, the defenders were all safely undercover, and the arrows rattled harmlessly off the timber roofs and walls.

"Wish we had a few of those Araluens with us," Rollond commented. "It'd be nice to give those Temujai some of their own medicine back."

Thorn nodded. "They know we've got no projectile weapons," he said. "They can stroll about in the open without risk."

"Ship coming!"

The hail came from one of the lookouts by the riverbank. The two Skandians turned to see another wolfship coming upriver, its oars rising and falling in a rapid rhythm, looking for all the world like the wings of a bird.

Thorn looked quickly around, measuring angles with his eye. As yet, the new arrival was concealed from the Temujai forces. And if she beached behind *Wolfrunner*, as she appeared to be about to do, she would remain so.

"It's *Wolfwind*," he said. "Erak's ship."

*Wolfwind* nosed into the bank behind the spot where Rollond's ship was moored. As Thorn had observed, the curve of the river concealed her from the Temujai eighty meters away. As she began to disembark her passengers, he felt an unholy sense of joy. The first ten men to come ashore were a squad of Araluen archers, their longbows slung across their backs, and fully laden quivers at their belts.

"Stig!" Thorn bellowed.

*Heron*'s first mate had gone to the riverbank to welcome the new arrivals. Stig turned now as he heard his name called.

Thorn waved to get his attention, then beckoned to him. "Bring those Araluens up to the shield wall!" he called.

Stig nodded and called to the ten archers, leading them toward the wall, staying under the cover of a roofed walkway as they came. They filed into the space below the rampart, looking about them curiously. Thorn beckoned to their leader.

"I'm Thorn," he said. "Are you in charge of this lot?"

The man nodded. "I'm Dean," he said. "I've heard about you."

"Nothing good, I'll be bound," said Stig, and earned a scowl from the old sea wolf.

Thorn beckoned Dean forward to a small gap in the shield wall. "Take a look," he said.

The archer commander craned up and peered through the

gap. After several seconds, he turned to Thorn. "They seem very confident," he said. "Walking around without a care in the world."

"That's because they don't know there are archers here," Thorn told him.

Dean's face split in a grin. "Do you think we should let them know?"

"I think that would be a very good idea," Thorn said.

Quickly, Dean deployed his men along the line of the rampart. They stepped up onto the packed earthen step behind the wall, bringing them level with the shields mounted on top. They crouched to remain hidden while Dean issued instructions.

"Take a look. Pick a target, then stand up and start shooting when I give the word. Five arrows each should do it." He waited while his men studied the situation, and the Temujai who were wandering carelessly among the trees. "Everyone ready?" he asked, and a chorus of answering growls came to him. "Then shoot!"

The nine archers stood erect, their upper bodies now exposed above the shield wall. As one, they drew back their bows, sighted and released. The first flight of arrows was still in the air when they released their second shots. As they flew, the first volley struck home, and panic reigned in the Temujai lines as men fell, crying out in pain or lying still. Then the second volley arrived and more men fell. The Temujai scattered, running for the cover of the trees. A few reached for their own bows and tried to shoot back. But more Araluen arrows arrived and struck them down.

Thorn, watching through a narrow gap, nodded grimly.

"Been wanting to do that all week," he said. "Good work, archers."

"All right, men, stand down," Dean ordered. He knew that before long, the Temujai would recover from their initial panic and begin shooting back.

"That'll keep their furry heads down," Rollond said. "They've been having it all their own way for too long." He gestured to Dean. "Take your men back and get them settled. We may need them later."

"Leave that," said a new voice. "We'll need them now."

Unnoticed by the others, Svengal, skirl of *Wolfwind*, had made his way to the wall. Beside him was a familiar figure, clad in his red-brocaded jacket—which by now was looking a little the worse for wear.

"Well, what do you know?" Thorn cried. "His Nibs is back. And what do you have in mind, Your Sha-sha-ness?"

"The Sha'shan has signed a treaty with Erak," Svengal told them. "He's here to call off his men and lead them back to the high country."

Thorn looked impressed. "By Orlog's dirty socks!" he said. "Hal pulled it off after all?"

The Sha'shan spoke in the common tongue. "Your commander is a very capable young man," he said. He looked at Svengal. "We'll need a green tree branch for a flag of truce," he said "And perhaps two of you would escort me back to my men?"

"Stig and I will do that," Thorn said immediately, and Stig nodded agreement.

"I want to see their faces when they're told to back off," he said as Svengal beckoned to one of the Skandians nearby and dispatched him to find a tree branch.

• • • • •

Ten minutes later, they were ready. Stig waved the young sapling above the parapet for several seconds, making sure that the Temujai had seen it. Then Pa'tong rose from behind the shield wall and called to his troops. There were a few moments of confusion among the Temujai, then a voice answered him.

He looked at Stig and Thorn. "They've recognized me," he said. "We can go forward."

They scrambled over the wall and down the earth rampart, picking their way carefully through the ditch before regaining level ground on the other side. Both Skandians carried shields and both were armed—Stig with his ax and Thorn with a sword in his left hand. They walked half a pace behind the Sha'shan, their eyes alert and moving constantly, searching for any sign of treachery. On the wall behind them, Dean and his men stood ready, bows raised and arrows nocked. Twenty spearmen stood beside them.

There was no sound from the Temujai camp as the small party approached. Then one Temujai warrior ran forward to meet them and dropped to his knees before the Sha'shan.

"Lord!" he cried. "Welcome back!"

Pa'tong smiled at him and gestured for him to stand. "Ga'tan," he said. "It's good to see you. But speak in the common tongue." He turned to his two escorts. "Ga'tan is one of my senior *Ulan* commanders."

Stig and Thorn nodded at the Tem'uj as he rose. They towered over the slightly built man.

Ga'tan looked at Pa'tong, a puzzled expression on his face. "But

General Ho'mat said you were dead—that the barbarians had killed you," he said.

Pa'tong's smile became somewhat thinner. "I'm sure he did. I must have words with him." He nodded to Stig and Thorn. "Thank you for your help. We'll be leaving for the high country in a few minutes. You can return to your friends now. Ga'tan will see that I'm safe."

He gestured for the *Ulan* commander to lead the way and followed him toward the Temujai lines. As they left the two Skandians behind, more and more of the Temujai began streaming out to greet their Sha'shan, cheering and waving their hats in the air, mobbing him and calling greetings.

Thorn turned to Stig. "I suspect Ho'mat might have a little explaining to do."

Stig grinned. "I expect he might have a lot of explaining to do," he corrected. Then he gestured to the Skandian shield wall. "Let's go home."

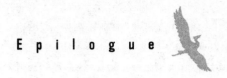

# Epilogue

Hal was sitting disconsolately on the beach, close to the wreckage of his ship, as *Wolfwind* ran easily through the harbor mouth and tied up alongside the mole, in her usual position. She had left the previous afternoon, ferrying the Sha'shan back to Ice River. Now she was back, and as he watched, he saw his crew beginning to disembark. He rose to his feet and hurried down the beach to the mole, greeting them as they came ashore. Stig and Thorn moved ahead of the others and embraced him.

"Good to see you made it," Thorn said. He looked along the beach, and his face twisted in grief as he saw the wrecked ship lying there. "She's ruined?"

"She got us home before she gave up," Hal said.

"She was a good ship," Stig said. His face too showed his grief.

Hal simply nodded. He didn't have words to express his feelings. Then he looked along the mole, and his face clouded with concern as he saw Stefan, Wulf and Ingvar being helped across the gangplank to shore. Ulf was supporting his brother. Jesper had charge of Stefan, and Lydia, of course, was leading Ingvar. Hal started toward them but Thorn stopped him.

"They're all right," he said. "Stefan took an arrow in the calf. Wulf has a sword cut on the thigh. But they're fine."

Edvin, who had heard news of *Wolfwind*'s imminent arrival, hurried past them to look after his wounded shipmates.

"They'll be even better now that Edvin has taken charge," said Stig, grinning. Edvin was regarded as the finest healer in Hallasholm.

"What happened to Ingvar? Is he all right?" said Hal, the worry in his voice obvious. The thought that his giant friend might have come to serious harm was too much for him to bear. He had been feeling guilty over the fact that he had deserted—in his mind—his friends in the face of danger.

Stig patted his arm. "He's fine. His spectacles were smashed, that's all. He's angry more than anything because he couldn't take part in the final battle."

"And what about you two?" Hal asked. Stig was bandaged in several places and a bloodstained cloth was wound about Thorn's forehead.

The old sea wolf shrugged. "Nothing serious. They hit me in the head, which is my least vulnerable point."

Hal shook his head miserably. "I should never have left you," he said. "I'm so sorry."

But Thorn embraced him roughly. "It's as well you did. You

found Rollond and sent him to help. He and his men came as a great surprise to the Temujai, let me tell you. Then you took your life in your hands sailing a wrecked ship back here with the Sha'shan. If you hadn't done that, we'd still be fighting at Ice River. Believe me, you have nothing to apologize for."

"I take it the Sha'shan convinced his men to withdraw?" Hal asked.

Stig nodded. "The fighting's over. They've headed back up to the high country. Thorn and I escorted him back to his people under a flag of truce. On the whole, they were pretty glad to see him." He paused and smiled. "Although a couple of his senior officers seemed less than delighted to find out that he was alive."

The crew were filing past now, on their way to their homes ashore. They gathered around their skirl, calling cheerful greetings to him. When he had sailed away from Ice River on the badly damaged *Heron*, they had half expected never to see him again. Stefan and Wulf grinned at him when he inquired as to their well-being.

"Nothing serious," Wulf told him. "I'll be fine in a week or so." Stefan echoed the sentiment.

Then Jesper pointed sadly at the wrecked ship on the beach. "I take it she's finished?"

Silence settled over the crew as they regarded the twisted hull.

Hal nodded sadly. "She won't sail again," he said. "I've been salvaging what I can reuse."

Coils of rope, the yardarms and sails, the tiller and other fittings were stacked neatly on the sand, along with a row of kit bags. The Mangler, still under its tarpaulin cover, was set to one side.

"I've unloaded your personal gear," he told them. "You can collect it later. For now, go and get a hot drink and something to eat. Your families will be wanting to see you're all right."

One by one the Herons straggled off, calling their goodbyes and promising to meet up again later. Hal was left with Thorn and Stig, and the three of them made their way back down the beach to where the *Heron*'s shattered hull lay.

"You said you were salvaging what you can reuse?" Stig said. There was a note of hope in his voice.

Hal nodded. "I plan to build a new ship," he said. "There are a few improvements I'd like to make."

Thorn smiled, relieved to hear the determination and positive tone behind the words. "Don't change her too much," he said. "She was a good ship."

"Maybe I'll give her a longer waterline," Hal said. "That'll make her faster."

Stig wandered over to the wrecked hull and busied himself removing something from the bow post. He walked back to where his two friends stood.

"So, when do we start?"

Hal looked curiously at him. "We?"

Stig nodded. "The brotherband. After all, we helped you build the last one. Did you think we'd leave the new one to you? You might get it all wrong."

A wide smile spread across Hal's face. Suddenly, his spirits lifted. He may have lost this beloved ship. But his friends were still standing by him, ready to help him face the future.

"I hoped you'd feel that way," he said.

Thorn was taking a last look at their old ship. "What do you plan on calling the new one?"

Hal formed a small, uncertain moue with his lips. "I hadn't really decided," he said.

Stig chuckled and handed him the item he'd just taken from the bow post. It was the beautifully carved, hand-polished figurehead of a seabird, its long, sharp beak open in a defiant challenge.

"How about *Heron*?" he said.

# RANGER'S APPRENTICE

THE RUINS OF GORLAN — INTERNATIONAL BESTSELLING AUTHOR — JOHN FLANAGAN

THE BURNING BRIDGE — INTERNATIONAL BESTSELLING AUTHOR — JOHN FLANAGAN

THE ICEBOUND LAND — INTERNATIONAL BESTSELLING AUTHOR — JOHN FLANAGAN

THE BATTLE FOR SKANDIA — INTERNATIONAL BESTSELLING AUTHOR — JOHN FLANAGAN

THE SORCERER OF THE NORTH — INTERNATIONAL BESTSELLING AUTHOR — JOHN FLANAGAN

THE SIEGE OF MACINDAW — INTERNATIONAL BESTSELLING AUTHOR — JOHN FLANAGAN

ERAK'S RANSOM — INTERNATIONAL BESTSELLING AUTHOR — JOHN FLANAGAN

THE KINGS OF CLONMEL — INTERNATIONAL BESTSELLING AUTHOR — JOHN FLANAGAN

HALT'S PERIL — INTERNATIONAL BESTSELLING AUTHOR — JOHN FLANAGAN

THE EMPEROR OF NIHON-JA — INTERNATIONAL BESTSELLING AUTHOR — JOHN FLANAGAN

THE LOST STORIES — INTERNATIONAL BESTSELLING AUTHOR — JOHN FLANAGAN

THE EARLY YEARS — THE TOURNAMENT AT GORLAN — JOHN FLANAGAN

THE EARLY YEARS — THE BATTLE OF HACKHAM HEATH — INTERNATIONAL BESTSELLING AUTHOR — JOHN FLANAGAN

# THE ROYAL RANGER

# BROTHERBAND
## Chronicles